THE WHISPER OF SILENCED VOICES

AFTER THE RIFT, BOOK 3

C.J. ARCHER

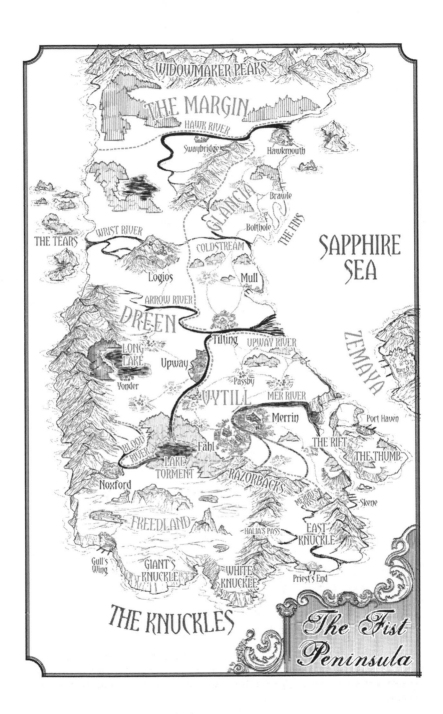

CHAPTER 1

*T*hree days was long enough for Doctor Ashmole to settle in to Mull. It was time I visited him to pass on the medical records of our patients, as well as to inform him that I was available for midwifery cases.

The problem was, I didn't want to. Giving him the records would be like handing over the last piece of my father's legacy. A legacy he'd built over decades and nurtured as tenderly as he'd nurtured me. I couldn't face drawing a line under his career, his life, and the role he'd played in the Mull community. Handing over the records felt like giving away part of myself.

Yet I had to do it, for the sakes of the patients. Although some wanted me to continue to tend to their aches and pains, they knew I could not. They would have to be satisfied with merely buying medicines from me and put their trust in the new doctor.

According to gossip at the market, Doctor Ashmole had moved into a run-down cottage on the edge of the village with his wife. He was a recent graduate of the medical college at Logios, which didn't inspire confidence in the villagers exchanging the gossip. I did my best to reassure them, reminding them that my father had been a fresh graduate once too.

I had gathered up the patient records and was stacking them in a small handcart when Doctor and Mistress Ashmole arrived on my doorstep.

1

"This is fortuitous," I said after introductions. "I was on my way to see you." I indicated the cart. "These are the patient records."

Doctor Ashmole's dark, serious eyes didn't spare a glance at the cart but scoured the hall, taking in the kitchen entrance behind me, and the closed door that led to my father's workshop. He was a slender man with a shiny pink scalp showing through thinning blonde hair. His face was pink too, contrasting starkly with his black clothing.

I smiled. "Do come in. Would you like tea?"

Doctor Ashmole took a step across the threshold, but his wife grabbed his arm and jerked him back in line with her. "We cannot stay," she said. "There's much to be done."

"I'm sure there is." I tried to maintain my smile, but it was almost impossible when faced with two unfriendly expressions. Mistress Ashmole resembled her husband in many ways. She was also slender with dark eyes that hardly spared a glance for me or the cart, preferring to inspect her surroundings, including the street. Her hair was drawn back with such severity that her eyes pinched at the outer corners. Her broad-brimmed hat protected her face from the summer sun and probably accounted for her lack of freckles. Her sharp cheekbones bore the small circular scars of a childhood pox. There'd been an outbreak in Tilting twenty years ago but only sporadic cases since.

"We ought to go through the records together," I said to Doctor Ashmole.

He looked down his thin nose at me. "That won't be necessary, Mistress Cully. I'm capable of reading them."

So that was how he wanted to play. Or, rather, not play. I would have gladly shut the door in his dour face, but the only ones to suffer from such pettiness would be the patients. "There are some things you should be aware of. For instance, Owen Fish came here four days ago with chest pains. Has he been to see you yet?"

"I cannot divulge confidential patient information." Doctor Ashmole reached for the cart handle, but I stepped in his way. Both he and Mistress Ashmole bristled.

"Then you should seek him out," I went on. "Without asking him questions, I couldn't diagnose the severity of his pains, but I sent him away with a bottle of catspaw tonic."

"You can't do that!" Doctor Ashmole snapped.

"I can. I'm an apothecary."

"Qualified medical advice is required before dispensing medicines."

I pushed down my rising anger. It would serve no purpose. "It's not against the law to dispense medicine when there is no doctor available to give a diagnosis. Owen Fish came to me four days ago. You arrived in Mull three days ago."

Doctor Ashmole's nostrils flared. His wife's eyes narrowed to slits. "There is a doctor at the palace, is there not?" he asked.

"Doctor Clegg, an employee of the finance minister," I said. "He doesn't like to come to the village or tend to anyone who is lower than a knight."

His lips flattened. "Don't let it happen again."

"It won't, now that Mull has a doctor." I was pleased that my voice didn't give away the frustration plucking my nerves. Years of dealing with difficult patients had trained me well. "May I say how happy we all are that you've finally arrived. I was beginning to despair that my letters to the college had been thrown away. I'm thrilled they've sent a new graduate to replace my father. I'm sure you'll find much variety to cut your medical teeth on here in Mull. You might find us a little too provincial after Logios and Tilting, although that's changing." I bit my tongue to stop myself blabbing. It wasn't the best time for my nervousness to reveal itself.

"How do you know we're from Tilting?" Mistress Ashmole asked.

"Your—" I cut myself off from pointing out her pox scars, and grasped at the first alternative that came to mind. "Your dress is the latest fashion. I imagine the capital is a very, er, fashionable place."

"Nonsense," Mistress Ashmole said, her spine stiffening even more. "Fashion is for the weak-minded and ungodly. I have more important things to do than concern myself with vacuous endeavors."

If I hadn't been so rattled, I would have taken more care in my choice of words. She was quite clearly *not* a lover of fine and fashionable things. Her dress was black and plain, the collar as white as snow but lacking lace or other embellishment. It sat high at her throat, and the sleeves reached her wrists. Most young women wore shorter sleeves in the summer. It also didn't fit her very well, being loose at the chest and through the waist.

"What I meant to say was, it's very well made."

She scowled. "The records, Mistress Cully," she said with a nod at the cart. "We'll be on our way."

"Of course." I didn't move aside. This was too important a moment for such a brief discussion. "I'll be continuing my duties as midwife," I added.

"You are within your rights to do so," Doctor Ashmole said.

I hadn't been asking for his permission but smiled anyway.

Mistress Ashmole looked me up and down as if seeing me for the first time. "I expect it must unnerve the expectant mothers to have a midwife who hasn't gone through childbirth herself. Unless I'm mistaken."

"You aren't."

"You're unmarried." Once again Mistress Ashmole cast a meticulous eye up and down my length. Her thoughts were written in the upturn of her nose, the lift of her top lip. With my blue dress, complete with short sleeves, she must think me quite weak-minded and ungodly. "I believe you are all alone."

"Your source of information is mistaken," I said. "I have many friends in Mull. Who is it, by the way?"

"Who is what?"

"Your source of information?"

It must be someone who disliked me to call me friendless. Ivor Morgrain sprang to mind, with his jealousy surfacing after his failed attempt to court me. Aside from Ivor, there were no villagers who'd say such a cruel thing about me. Unless it was the Deerhorns. Lady Deerhorn in particular would say that and more to anyone who listened. I'd first come to her notice when I attended a party at the palace that I should not have. Her sights had focused even more tightly on me after I refused to help her son spy on the Duke of Gladstow.

A breeze swept through the street, whipping up dust and rattling the sign of Hailia's cupped hands hanging above the front door. Doctor and Mistress Ashmole both looked at it then shared a glance.

"Good day, Mistress Cully," Doctor Ashmole said with a nod for me. They turned to go.

"Wait," I said. "The patient records. Don't you want them?"

"Of course."

I tugged the cart to the front door and he took it from me. "There's one other thing," I ventured. "My father and I created a potion that eases pain. It's very effective. I'll sell it to you at a discounted price."

"That won't be necessary," Mistress Ashmole said.

I ignored her and addressed her husband. "Surgeries are much easier when the patient is pain-free and calm. It's expensive to make and the ingredients are rare—"

"It's the work of the devil," Mistress Ashmole cut in.

I blinked at her. "Pardon?"

"If Hailia and Merdu wanted us to live without pain, they would have made it so."

"You cannot be serious."

Her lips thinned. "Your concoction is for the weak, those who do not allow the god and goddess into their heart." She spun around and marched off.

Doctor Ashmole pulled on the cart handle and followed her.

I glanced up at the sign of Hailia's hands above the door. "You wouldn't be so cruel," I told the goddess.

I was about to return inside when Meg emerged from her cottage and signaled for me to join her.

"Who were they?" she asked, staring along the street in the direction in which the Ashmoles had gone.

"The new doctor and his wife."

"He looks more like an undertaker and she the chief mourner. What are they like?"

"He could be the finest doctor to come out of the college in recent years, but I suspect his bedside manner will be on the curt side. And Hailia help anyone in pain."

"Why?"

"Never mind."

"My family will continue to come to you anyway, Josie. My mother is suspicious of anyone new to the village."

"Everyone is," I said on a sigh. "But you can't keep coming to me." Like many of Mull's locals, Meg's family had continued to ask me for medical advice after my father's death. I had to turn them away or risk being fined for practicing medicine when I wasn't qualified to do so.

"We can if we don't pay you for your services. That reminds me. There's a bowl of stew for you. It's a little watery and flavorless but it's fine with bread."

Mistress Diver had taken to getting around the law by paying me with food. She argued she was simply providing for a neighbor in need. I doubted her reasoning would hold up under close scrutiny, but it was unlikely to come to that. Sheriff Neerim was too busy keeping the peace, and stopping Mullians like Ivor Morgrain from rioting, than worrying about me practicing medicine.

"Thank you for the offer, but your family hasn't needed me for several weeks. You don't have to keep feeding me."

She dismissed me with a wave of her hand. "Are you free to go to the market with me?"

"Again? You went yesterday."

"I forgot onions."

"No, you didn't. I saw one in your basket."

"I need another."

I pressed my lips together to suppress my smile before Meg saw it. If she suspected me of teasing her, she'd change her mind and not go. I didn't want that. Not when I knew she was lying about the onion so she could see Max.

The sergeant of the palace guards had been leading a small cohort through the village as a show of strength ever since a riot had almost broken out three weeks ago. Ivor Morgrain and his friends had followed their leader, Ned Perkin, in causing dissention in the village. Upset over the newcomers to Mull taking their jobs and driving up the prices of rent and food, they'd demanded something be done about it. The problem was, very little *could* be done. Only the king or village council could create more employment by funding capital works in the area. So far, the village had funded the new custom's building and the dredging of the harbor to deepen it. Private enterprise was building more warehouses and offices at the dock. The king had washed his hands of further funding, including providing charity to the poorest residents, despite Dane, Theodore and Balthazar attempting to reason with him. His Majesty was far more interested in finding himself a wife while he kept his mistress busy by throwing parties for the nobles who had been there the entire summer.

I collected my purse and basket from the kitchen and rejoined Meg. We walked arm in arm to the village green, our hats angled so they protected our faces from the sun. At least in my case, that was why my hat was at an angle. In Meg's, I suspected she was preparing to meet Max by hiding the wine colored birthmark on her neck and jaw as best she could.

"Lyle is angry with me," she said when we rounded the corner. "I defended Sheriff Neerim's employment of the Vytillians, and he got cross."

I hadn't thought Meg's brother would be against employing outsiders. When I had explained to him that Vytillians needed work just as much as Glancians, he'd seemed to understand my point. He'd also nodded agreement when I told him a Vytill presence in our law enforcement ranks might dissuade the disreputable Vytillians from causing trouble. It seemed he said one thing to me and another to his sister.

"Will you speak to him, Josie? Make him see that not all foreigners are bad? You're good at that."

"I think you're mistaken," I said on a sigh. "I'm not nearly convincing enough."

We passed a pair of guards on horseback. I greeted them by name and they smiled back, but Meg didn't notice, with her arm obscuring her view and her birthmark as she held onto her hat brim. In their crimson palace uniforms, the men looked very dashing. The two young women walking on the other side of the road, giggling into their hands and tossing coquettish looks at the guards, seemed to agree.

"The sheriff's new recruits will be ready to start soon," I said to Meg. "And the guards can return to their regular duties at the palace. The captain will be pleased to have a full roster at his disposal again."

She nudged my arm. "It's a shame he won't be in the village as much. I know you like coming to the market more often in the hope he'll be on duty."

"I hardly see him at all anyway." I nudged her back. "Max is the one who'll be here less."

"Ouch. Stop elbowing my ribs."

I spotted Erik sitting on his horse beneath the shade of a tree and waved at him. He rode out to join us, moving his mount deftly through the crowd at the edge of the market.

The big Marginer guard grinned as he hailed us. "Josie! It is good to see you." He leaned down and drew Meg's hand away from her hat. "Greetings, Meg. I tell you last time, do not hide. I wish to see you." He leaned down even further and lowered his voice to a seductive level. "*All* of you. You are pretty."

Meg blushed fiercely and stared down at the ground, but at least she didn't try to cover her face again.

"Oh look, there's Max," I said, waving at the sergeant. "No more flirting, Erik. Max won't like it."

"He knows I cannot help if women find me handsome." He puffed out his chest.

I rolled my eyes and was about to tell him that wasn't what I meant when Max joined us.

"Good morning, Josie, Meg. Fine day for it," he said.

"For what?" Erik asked.

"For, er, going to the market." Max shifted in the saddle. "Weren't you two here just yesterday?"

I waited for Meg to say something, but she continued to stare down at the ground. It was the same every time we came to the village and saw Max, which was indeed every day, lately. She wanted to see him yet she didn't speak to him. The birthmark made her insidiously shy. Her shyness didn't seem to bother Max too much, though. He simply spoke to her as if she'd spoken to him first and often held a one-way conversation for several minutes without so much as a pause.

"If you're after apples, don't go to that stall," he said, pointing to Selwyn Grigg's cart. "The freshest produce is gone. Try further into the market."

"Thank you," I said and nudged Meg again.

"Thank you," she repeated. "I'm after onions."

"In that case, you'll want the grocer at the back." Max then went into a long explanation as to why those onions were superior to any others he'd seen in the market.

"I think you've been here too long," I said, laughing.

"The relief duty will be here soon," he said.

"Will one of them be the captain?"

"No, but if you want to see him, just come to the palace. He'll have some time off later in the day, before the king's early evening walk."

I thanked him but declined the invitation. For one thing, I wouldn't impose on Dane when he hadn't invited me. For another, I'd vowed to keep my distance. He'd made it clear there couldn't be anything between us. For all he knew, he had a wife or lover somewhere, and his honor forbade him from being with me when he could have made a commitment to another. Until his memory returned, we could not explore the feelings blooming between us. I admired him and his convictions too much to make it harder for him.

"You are welcome at the palace any time, Josie," Erik said. "Hammer would like to see you, but he lies and says he does not."

"Erik," Max warned.

"I do not understand him. Josie is pretty, yes? She is nice, yes? He likes her, yes?"

"Shut up," Max growled. "You talk too much."

Erik rested a hand on his hip. "And you are idiot too. Meg is—"

"You have work to do," Max barked. "I suggest you get back to patrolling."

Erik laughed. "Aye, sir." He wheeled his horse around only to wheel it back to face us again. "I almost forget, Josie. The lump on my little friend is gone. The maids are rejoicing all over the palace. Thank you for the medicine."

"Little friend?" Meg asked.

"Don't!" both Max and I cried.

Erik tossed the matted blond coils of his hair over his shoulder and laughed as he rode off.

Meg blushed again and a pink tinge colored Max's cheeks.

"If he's anything to go by, the Margin folk are mad," he said. "He's right, though, Josie. Come to the palace any time, and not because of Hammer. Quentin misses you. He doesn't stop talking about you and your medical skills."

"Tell him to come to my cottage for tea and cake if he has the time."

"If I tell him that, he'll make the time."

"You too, Max. Join us for tea when you're free." I hoped he understood I was referring to Meg when I said 'us'. His blush didn't fade, so perhaps he did.

He thanked me and headed off in the same direction as Erik.

Meg and I finished our marketing, buying the grand total of one onion. Neither of us was in a hurry to return home, so we stopped to talk to friends. I wasn't sure if Meg was avoiding going home because she knew she'd have to help her mother with the housework or if she was hoping to see Max again.

In my case, going home meant walking into an empty house with very little to occupy my time. With so few pregnant women in the village, and the larder stocked with as much medicine as I could afford to make, I was at a loose end. There wasn't even housework to do, since I'd cleaned from top to bottom last week to keep idleness at bay.

By the time the midday sun hung high in the sky, the stall holders had packed up and shoppers drifted away. I tried tempting Meg with a dip in the shallows at Half Moon Cove, but she couldn't afford to stay away from home for the entire afternoon as well as the morning.

"My mother will call me lazy," she said as we ambled toward our street.

"You do too much, Meg."

"I'm sorry. Another time."

"Don't apologize. I'm not sure I could face the walk to the cove in this heat anyway."

We entered our street and both stopped. A gentleman on horseback waited outside my house. He sat somewhat awkwardly, as if he were afraid of falling off. It wasn't until he turned that I realized why. The gentleman held the reins in his left hand. His right arm lay across his lap, limp.

Lord Barborough.

"He looks important," Meg said in a hushed whisper. "It's his high forehead. It gives him an arrogant air."

"You are right on both counts," I said. "He's important and arrogant. I'd better see what he wants."

"You won't invite him in, will you?"

"Certainly not."

Lord Barborough was one man I didn't want to be alone with. I wasn't yet sure if he was a danger, but he certainly could be. As the representative of King Philip of Vytill, Barborough was powerful. A mere village woman with no family had very little protection against men like him.

Meg and I parted outside her door but she did not go in. She remained on the stoop and watched, her gaze unwavering as it settled on Barborough. She might be shy about her birthmark, but she was fierce when it came to looking after loved ones.

"I've been waiting an age," Barborough snapped as I approached. "Where have you been?"

"I don't believe I have to account for my movements to you," I said.

"We have an agreement."

"And I have fulfilled my part of the agreement as best as I can. You, my lord, have not."

I had gone to him to learn more about magic, but he had only given me a little information so far. In return, he had asked me to question the servants and find out where they came from in the hope it would help him piece together the puzzle of the palace's origins. Dane, Balthazar, Theodore and I had fed him false answers and gained a little knowledge from him about the sorcerer, but it wasn't enough. He knew more.

The problem was, I couldn't tell him the truth about the servants' memory loss, and I couldn't keep feeding him lies. If he discovered I was lying, he would follow through on his threat and tell the king that I'd been asking about his involvement in the palace's mysterious creation. Speculating about the king using magic brought up the question of his right to sit on the throne, and that was treason.

"You haven't fulfilled your part of the bargain to my satisfaction," he said. "I told you last time, I need more. What have you done lately? I've hardly seen you at the palace."

"That's because I have no reason to be there."

"Not even to see your captain?"

"He's not my captain."

He barked a brittle laugh. "Come now, Mistress Cully. You're sleeping with him."

"If that's what your spies told you, you need better spies."

He bristled. Clearly he didn't want anyone to know he had spies at court. In truth, Dane wasn't positive, but he suspected a man like Barborough wouldn't venture into the palace without a spy or two. The servants could be discounted, since they believed their fates and memory loss were tied to King Leon's fate, so that left the nobles. With most wanting Leon to marry the Vytill princess, it was possible they'd spy for Vytill's representative.

The two dukes, however, wouldn't. Buxton and Gladstow didn't want Leon marrying Vytill's princess; they wanted the throne to be vacated altogether so one of them could take it.

"Don't test me, Mistress Cully," he snarled. "You have already crossed the line once by informing your friends about me. Cross it again and that pretty nose will get sliced off."

My breath caught in my throat. "I don't know what you're referring to. What friends?"

I tried to sound innocent, but it rang false to my ears. I *had* told Ivor Morgrain that the gentleman he thought was a Glancian advisor, keen to hear about Mull's problems, was in fact a Vytill lord who wanted to stir up trouble. Ivor had passed the information onto Ned Perkin, the self-appointed leader of Mull's troublemakers. I wondered if Ned had confronted Lord Barborough, or whether he simply shut the door in his face when Barborough tried to attend their meetings again.

Barborough bared his teeth. "Don't pretend. That captain might believe your act, but I know women like you. Your kind are cunning, slippery. Your sweet tongue and big eyes won't work on me. I'm immune to your charms."

I kept my mouth shut. Talking would only rile him more and my trembling voice would betray my fear.

He wheeled his horse around and I had to quickly step out of the way. "You owe me, Mistress Cully, and I expect to see the fruits of your labor. If you don't present me with information soon, you'll need more than a disfigured neighbor and the captain of the guards to help you. You'll need the intervention of the sorcerer itself."

I watched him ride off down the street. Once he was out of sight, I let out a shuddery breath.

Meg joined me, her brow creased in concern. "What did he want?"

"Nothing," I said before adding, "He needed medicine."

"But he left without any."

"I have to make some up."

"So he's coming back?" She screwed up her nose. "There's something about him I don't like but I can't put my finger on it."

Meg was an excellent judge of character. I wished I had been more discerning when I'd decided to ask Barborough for answers about magic. He might be the Fist Peninsula's foremost expert on the topic, but no answers were worth being in his debt. Not when he held the threat of treason over my head, and one small misstep could see him tell the king.

CHAPTER 2

*T*he arrival of a message from Dane was the highlight of my day. Indeed, of the last several days. I had become pathetic and dull since Father died, with far too much time on my hands. The only thing that could save me from becoming even more pathetic would be a spate of village pregnancies, but with the men outnumbering the women by a substantial margin, the situation was unlikely to change soon.

The message was brought by Quentin, leading a horse named Sky. Sky and I were acquainted, having accompanied Dane and his horse on a short ride into an unused part of the palace gardens. One ride did not make me an able horsewoman, and I wished Dane had sent a carriage instead.

"Come on, up you get, Josie." Quentin cupped his hands and waited. When I didn't step into them, he looked up. "Put your foot here, grab the pommel, and I'll hoist you up. The pommel is that bit that sticks up at the front of the saddle."

"Thank you, I know what the pommel is. I'm just concerned that I'll break your fingers."

"I'm stronger than I look."

I doubted that. As the youngest member of the palace guards, the scrawny lad was out of place among the strong men. He didn't excel at any of the guards' tasks like fighting, swordsmanship, riding and looking fierce. He needed protection from the likes of

14

Sergeant Brant. In ordinary circumstances, he wouldn't be a guard. He would be tucked away in a Logios college, studying, or assisting in a shop. But his situation wasn't ordinary. Each servant remembered only three things—their name, the names of the other servants, and their role at the palace. Without knowing why they'd lost the rest of their memories, it would be foolish to change anything. Dane believed they'd been assigned guard duty for a reason.

I wasn't so sure it had been that well thought-out. For one thing, Quentin made a terrible guard. For another, Sergeant Brant shouldn't have been given so much power. He and Max had only the captain above them in the chain of command. Max was a good man, but Brant was a thug. The question was, *who* had made the decision?

"Wait here," I said and disappeared back inside. I returned with a stool and positioned it beside Sky.

Quentin pouted. "I could have done it. You don't look heavy."

I felt a little sorry for him. The other guards teased him mercilessly, and he usually took it in his stride, but perhaps the teasing was finally getting to him.

I put out my hand. "You may assist me, sir," I said, affecting an accent similar to Kitty's, the duchess of Gladstow.

Quentin's pout disappeared. He took my hand and I stepped onto the stool then into the stirrup. I settled on the saddle and clutched the pommel tightly when Sky shifted her weight.

Quentin chuckled as he handed me the reins then strapped my pack to the saddle. "She's a good old nag, nice and calm." He mounted his own horse and urged it forward. Sky followed meekly. "I learned to ride on her," he said.

"You couldn't ride at all in the beginning? Not even a little?" I asked.

"Couldn't ride, couldn't hold a sword right, couldn't fight to save myself. Not like the others. I could read and write, though, which some of them can't. But it doesn't do me much good in the garrison or the practice yard. Brant only respects hard hitters, not writers of poetry. Do you want to read some of mine? It ain't bad, if I say so myself."

"I'd love to." I gave Sky a little squeeze with my thighs and she picked up her pace and fell into step alongside Quentin's horse. "I wonder what you were before you came here."

"I try not to think about it. Theodore says it'll only make us melancholy, and he's right. I only think about the future."

"Very well," I said cheerfully. "Then tell me why I've been summoned to the palace this time. Is one of the maids with child?"

"It's Laylana. Captain wants you to check on her. She's sick."

Ordinarily I would refuse, but no one outside of the servants knew of Laylana's existence. She had lost her memory too, but unlike the others, she lost it over and over again, beginning afresh with no knowledge of what had gone before. Dane worried it was slowly driving her mad. She'd once run off, desperately asking if anyone in the village knew her. When Dane's men had taken her back, and explained what happened, she locked herself away in a room in the palace depths.

I didn't like it. She needed sunlight and fresh air. But she refused, and instead cowered in her bed. It was no wonder she was sick.

Quentin and I talked all the way to the palace. He asked me a lot of questions about medicines, diseases and conditions. I'd given him a book on the human body to read some weeks ago and he couldn't stop talking about what he'd read. He would make a fine doctor, if he only ventured away from the safety of the palace. Perhaps one day he would. Perhaps one day, he and the other servants would get their memories back and resume their old lives.

The palace stood at the end of the long avenue like a glittering jewel topping a scepter. The sight of it never ceased to dazzle me. It was unearthly in its magnificence, and unparalleled in all of the Fist Peninsula. The kings of Vytill and Dreen were said to be jealous, while Freedland's anti-monarchist ministers were scornful of the cost. Only the Zemayans openly spoke of magic, but the word was whispered behind closed doors here in Glancia.

Sky followed Quentin's horse past the stables, across the gravel yard to the palace's main gate, the gold glinting in the sunshine. The two guards on duty opened it and we entered the outer forecourt. A footman assisted me to the paved ground and retrieved my pack from the saddle. He greeted me by name, but I couldn't recall his. There were too many servants for me to remember them all.

Quentin asked the footman to find the captain before escorting me past the right-hand pavilion where visiting dignitaries, their servants and some entertainers were housed. We walked in the shadows cast by the palace's northern wing to the garrison. The door stood open, perhaps to allow air to circulate.

Inside, however, it was still warm and stuffy. A guard sat on a chair, his bare feet propped up on the table, his head tipped back. A soft snore filled the room. Another guard looked up and smiled drowsily at me.

Quentin knocked the sleeping guard's feet off the table. He awoke with a start and a swear word on his lips. "Feet off," Quentin said. "They're filthy. And don't swear. You're in the presence of a lady."

"She's the doctor, not a lady," the guard said. "And she don't care if I'm asleep when I'm off duty."

"The captain will. He'll be here soon."

The guard grunted, which I assumed was gratitude for the warning, and picked up the sword cloth that had been next to his feet on the table. He busied himself with cleaning the weapon. When Dane strode in a moment later, he was none the wiser.

The captain had the annoying habit of looking unruffled and not at all hot, even on a sweltering day. I, however, was sweating just from the walk from the gate.

Dane's gaze swiftly took me in before looking away. "Nice to see you again, Josie."

"And you, Captain." I refused to call him Hammer since it was neither his name nor a very good moniker for him. Nor could I call him Dane in front of the others since he hadn't told them his real name.

"Have you been well?" he asked. The muscles in his face twitched in what I suspected was a wince.

I smiled. "Yes. You?"

"I'm fine."

"Good. Now that the obligatory pleasantries are over, do you want to escort me to Laylana's room?"

His lips curved into a smile that would make even the coldest female heart flip. Mine didn't stand a chance and fluttered madly. He must have guessed the effect he had on me because his smile grew warmer and those clear blue eyes softened as they met my gaze. Perhaps I had a similar effect on him. I hoped so.

"I'll take her," Quentin piped up.

"You've got work to do," Dane said.

"I'm off duty now."

Dane ignored him and pushed open the internal door that led to the corridor. "I hope he didn't talk you to death on the way here," he said, taking my pack from me as I passed.

"Not at all. We talked about medicine."

"Sorry."

I laughed. "I liked it. Since my father's death, I don't get to talk about medical matters often. As much as I adore Meg and my other friends, our conversations are usually of the gossipy variety. They don't like to talk about diseases."

"Strange people," he quipped.

We walked along one of the palace's many narrow and winding corridors, lit only by flickering torchlight. When we passed other servants, we had to draw closer together, our arms touching. It would be easy to grasp his hand and entwine his fingers in mine. We could even do it without anyone noticing.

But I didn't dare. Being alone with Dane was awkward. I didn't know where to look, how to act, or what to say. After we'd kissed, everything had changed between us. On the one hand, my regard for him had deepened, but on the other, he'd made it very clear we couldn't kiss again.

"How have you been?" he asked as we turned down another corridor.

"You've already asked me that," I said.

He hesitated. "I thought perhaps you might answer me truthfully away from the others."

There were no other servants in this corridor. The only sound came from our footsteps on the flagstones and our voices echoing off the stone walls. "I did speak the truth. I'm fine."

"Morgrain hasn't bothered you? Or anyone else from the village?"

"No."

"Have you been into The Row?"

"Only to see Marnie and her baby. She thanks you for the food, by the way, and the employment."

"I didn't employ her husband, the sheriff did."

"But it was on your suggestion, wasn't it?" When he said nothing, I added, "Marnie and I both know it."

We were approaching Laylana's room but I didn't want to go in yet. I didn't want this conversation to end. On a whim, I grasped Dane's hand, forcing him to stop.

"Because of you, Marnie's family will soon move out of The Row and into better lodgings. She asked me to thank you when I saw you, so I'm thanking you now." I squeezed his hand in an attempt to show gratitude, but it wasn't enough. Kissing him would have been better.

"I wish I could do more for the people of The Row," he said. "That boy, Remy, shouldn't have to grow up there. It's dangerous, and it will become more so as he gets older."

The Row was the sort of place where boys didn't remain boys for long. I'd seen children only a little older than Remy fighting in the gutters. I'd seen them take money from men before those men visited the boys' mothers or sisters behind a dirty curtain. It was no place for a child. No place for anyone.

Marnie lived there too with her husband and three children, including a newborn. With no prospect of work and no money, their situation had been dire. They'd given up everything to move to Glancia from The Thumb, the outcrop of land in Vytill that had become an island after the series of quakes known as the Rift sliced it off from the mainland. Their situation wasn't unique. Indeed, it was a common story among newcomers to Mull, looking for work at the dock. The problem was, Mull was ill prepared for the swelling population, and although there were more jobs due to the increased activity at the harbor, there weren't enough for every man. Marnie was lucky. With her husband now employed by the sheriff, she'd soon get her family out of The Row. Without a husband, Remy's mother, Dora, had little chance of ever leaving.

"I have had a visit from someone, as it happens," I said, letting go of his hand. "But I'll tell you more after we've seen Laylana. What ails her?"

"She feels tired all the time and has aching limbs," he said. "She also has a cough she can't shake."

I knew what was wrong with her without even seeing her, but I asked him to unlock the door anyway. "When did she last lose her memory?"

"Three days ago."

"It must be so frightening for her," I said, more to myself than Dane.

"Not as much as it used to be. Come in and she'll show you."

Laylana sat up in bed, reading a book. Her pale skin looked even more ghoulish with her lank, dark hair framing her face. She was a Freedlander with a naturally stocky build, but even so, she was too thin.

Dane introduced us, for Laylana's benefit, but she gently admonished him. "I know who she is."

"You remember me?" I asked, hopeful.

"The captain told me to expect you. And I have this." She plucked a piece of paper from the stack on the table beside the bed. It was a sketch of me, done in charcoal, with my name clearly written at the top.

"The likeness is remarkable," I said. "Did you do this?"

"One of the footmen. He's an excellent artist."

She gathered up more of the papers. Some were sketches of people I recognized—Dane, Max, Theodore, Quentin—and others contained words written in a neat hand.

"He draws the faces of those who come in here regularly so I recognize them again after my memory disappears. I've written down who they are, and anything else I need to know when I start again. When I wake up with no memory, I at least recognize my own handwriting."

Beside my name, she'd written a short paragraph describing me as the village doctor's daughter and midwife, as well as the words kind, trustworthy, courageous. She had even written a short description of the incident that had occurred in this very room between myself and Lord Frederick Whippler, the poisoner I'd helped capture. That must be why she thought me courageous. In truth, I'd been terrified. I'd only fought him off because I had no other choice.

Dane showed me another piece of paper titled READ THIS FIRST. The rest was written in a tightly packed scrawl in Laylana's hand, informing herself of her memory loss, where she was, the predicament of the other servants, who she could trust and other details of her life here. It was woefully limited. Like the others, she knew so little of herself.

"It helps me begin again," she said.

"She used to wake up terrified when her memory was wiped," Dane said. "But since starting these notes and with these sketches, she can quickly re-learn everything she needs to know, without fear."

"There is still some fear." Laylana coughed, a dry, brittle cough that wracked her body.

I asked her to lean forward and placed my ear to her back. Her breathing sounded a little short, but not dangerously so, and there was no rattle. "Do you know how long you've had this cough?"

Laylana glanced at Dane. "About five days," he said.

I checked inside her mouth, in her eyes and ears, and asked her to describe the aching limbs. Her answers confirmed my initial thoughts.

"You're suffering from lack of sunlight," I told her. "You need to go outside on occasion, preferably in the middle of the day when the sun is its strongest."

"But I can't," she said, sinking back into the pillows. "I can't be seen."

"Why not?"

"The lords and ladies will think I'm a maid and ask me to fetch something. I won't know where to go or what to do. I don't know my way around the palace or the gardens."

"Unlike the rest of us, Laylana doesn't know her position here on the staff, or who the rest of us are, or the layout of the palace, only her name."

No wonder she was too frightened to leave the room. It would be the only place she felt safe.

"What will they think if they see a maid going for a walk?" Laylana coughed again and Dane passed her a cup of water.

"There are parts of the gardens where few nobles go," I said.

"No," Laylana said, her voice rising. "It's too much of a risk. You must understand, Josie, it's not my safety I'm worried about. It's everyone else. If someone finds out that I've lost my memory, it will lead to questions about the rest of the staff."

And perhaps the king himself, I might have added but did not.

"One of my men will accompany you," Dane said. "I'll find a gardening uniform, and you can spend your time in the pottage garden. Nobles don't go anywhere near it."

"There," I said, taking her hand. "You won't need to worry about getting lost or answering questions. All the guards know your predicament. You'll be quite safe."

"I suppose," she hedged.

"Doctor's orders," I said, smiling. "Or it would be, if I were a doctor."

She only needed a little more convincing before agreeing. Dane promised to send a man for her today with a spare uniform worn by the garden staff. It would be her first outing for weeks, so her hesitation was understandable, but she seemed to grasp the importance of it. She added it to her notes as we left.

We didn't return to the garrison. Dane wanted to pay me for the visit and Balthazar controlled all palace expenditure. His office was located nearby. Dane opened the door without knocking, earning a scowl from the elderly master of the palace.

"Good morning, Josie," he said, returning to the ledger on the desk in front of him. He wrote something down then dipped the pen in the inkwell. "I see Hammer found an excuse."

"Pardon?" I asked.

"An excuse for you to come to the palace. What was it this time?"

"Laylana's ill," Dane told him.

"She's been cooped up in that room too long. Any fool could have told you that. You didn't need to bother Josie about it."

"It's no bother," I said. "I have nothing better to do."

He peered at me over the rim of his spectacles. "Hmmm," was all he said before lowering his gaze again.

I glanced at Dane. He folded his arms over his chest and didn't appear to notice. "Josie requires payment," he said.

"How much?"

"Five ells for a simple house call," I said.

"Ten," Dane said.

"Usually my patients try to bargain the fee down, not up."

"The palace is a long way from the village."

"I'm surprised he didn't say twenty," Balthazar muttered. He removed a key from a chain around his neck and handed it to Dane.

Dane unlocked a metal box sitting on the floor in the corner of the room and counted out ten ells. He handed them to me and returned the key to Balthazar.

I thanked them and sat down. Balthazar arched a bushy brow and set down his pen. "You have something to say, Josie?"

"Lord Barborough visited me yesterday."

"Yesterday," Dane said flatly. "Why didn't you send for me immediately?"

"It wasn't necessary."

"I disagree. Barborough is a threat to your safety. Next time, send for me straight away."

"I will, if it's necessary."

His brow plunged and he crossed his arms again. Balthazar chuckled.

"What did he want?" Dane asked.

A knock interrupted us and Theodore entered upon Balthazar's command. "Josie! So good to see you." The king's valet kissed my cheek and shook my hand, all the while beaming his friendly smile. "We've missed you."

"And I've missed you all, too." I did not look at Dane, for which I was proud of myself.

"Sit," Balthazar said, "since Hammer won't. Josie was just about to tell us something important."

"About Laylana?" Theodore turned worried brown eyes onto me as he lowered himself into the chair.

Unlike Dane, and some of the other palace staff, Theodore's heritage was easy to determine from his flat face and straight dark hair. He was from Dreen, without question, and I'd told him so when we first met. It was surprising he hadn't left the palace to go in search of his past there. Perhaps fear of the unknown kept him here. Perhaps it was the need to be with others in the same predicament that stopped him leaving. Understanding and companionship were powerful anchors.

"Laylana's fine," I told him.

"She just needed sunlight, didn't she?" he said.

Balthazar smirked at Dane.

"Josie had a visit from Barborough yesterday," Dane said. "She was about to tell us what he wanted."

"I'm sure you can guess," I said. "He wanted more information about the servants. He noticed I hadn't been to the palace much of late and reminded me that my obligation to him hadn't ended."

"Reminded you how?" Dane asked darkly.

"With his usual threat of exposing me to the king."

Dane shifted his stance. "Did he harm you?"

"No. He was too worried about falling off his horse." My attempt to lighten the somber mood that had descended over us fell flat. The look on Dane's face was as thunderous as a stormy sky.

Balthazar wiped a gnarled and wrinkled hand over his face, down his jaw. "You can't continue to avoid him. He might follow through on his threat, and we can't give the king any reason to accuse you of treason."

"The king wouldn't do anything about it, surely," I said.

They all looked away.

"But I saved the life of his favorite lady!"

"Lady Miranda Claypool is no longer his favorite," Balthazar said.

"He thinks I saved *his* life."

In truth, the king's life hadn't been in danger. Also, when he'd fallen off his horse, he'd preferred my counsel to Doctor Clegg's. In hindsight, it could have been because I was a young woman and Doctor Clegg an aged man. The king had certainly liked me touching his injuries.

"That might not be enough to keep you in his favor if you do something that displeases him," Theodore said.

"He's becoming more unpredictable," Dane added. "We used to be able to control him, but not anymore."

"Control is too strong a word," Theodore said with a shake of his head.

Balthazar grunted. "Manipulate, coerce, direct, influence...do any of those words suffice, Theo?"

Theodore sighed. "In the beginning, he could be *advised*. Now, he prefers his own counsel."

Balthazar grunted again. "You mean he only listens to that whore of a mistress."

"Bal!" Theodore glanced anxiously at the door. "Don't call her that."

"No one can hear us down here, even if Lady Morgrave or the king cared to breathe the same air as us. The walls are too thick in this part of the palace. Why do you think I chose this room as my office?"

Chose or created? Sometimes I wondered if Balthazar was the sorcerer. He knew everything about the palace, and the revels he'd organized were magical in their magnificence. He'd laughed off my suspicions, however, although he hadn't entirely dispelled my theory.

"If Lady Morgrave is influencing the king," I said, "you can be sure she's doing so at the bidding of her parents. Lady Deerhorn in particular would love to manipulate him into raising her family higher."

"No doubt," Balthazar said. "The problem is, how do we limit Lady Morgrave's influence when the king won't listen to us?"

"I still think we should put pressure on her husband," Dane said, as if this were a conversation they'd had before. "He must hate that his wife has become the king's mistress."

"Must he?" Balthazar asked idly. "Just because *you* would hate it, Hammer, doesn't mean he does. Perhaps he likes the compensation he received from the king. Perhaps he likes being connected to the most powerful woman in the realm."

"No man likes to be cuckolded."

"You are not like other men, though. Is he, Josie? He's unique."

I wasn't sure if he wanted an answer or was attempting to bait Dane or me, so I kept my mouth shut.

"Don't change the subject," Dane snapped.

"As it happens, you're right." Balthazar's eyes twinkled with mischief, making him seem much younger. "I overheard some gossip yesterday. Lord Morgrave has vowed to win back the love of his wife."

"Did he ever have it?" Dane asked.

"I don't think their marriage was a strong one," Theodore added. "He's much older than her, and I overheard two ladies talking about the wedding. Lady Morgrave's parents had to force her to marry his lordship."

I'd heard the same thing. While Lady Morgrave was young and pretty, her husband was old, foul-tempered, and a drunkard. No woman would want to marry him. Not even for his wealth and title. Lady Deerhorn must have been very persuasive to get her daughter to accept.

"Apparently several Glancian lords have begged Lord Morgrave to control his wife and ensure she whispers things in the king's ear that benefit them," Balthazar went on. "Hence his vow to win her back, although not necessarily remove her from the king's bed. He seems to like the thought of controlling the king through her."

"What sort of things do they want her to influence?" I asked.

Balthazar peered at me over his spectacles again. "The kingdom's affairs are not your concern, Josie."

"They want Lady Morgrave to urge the king to marry the Vytill princess," Dane said.

Balthazar rolled his eyes to the ceiling. "Was I not clear enough?" he muttered.

"Josie knows so much already," Theodore said. "Why hold back information now?"

"Most of the nobles see the marriage as the best alliance Glancia can make," Dane told me. "It will ensure peace between Glancia and Vytill for a generation, at least."

Since Lady Morgrave was already married, *she* couldn't become the new queen. But she could still wield the power of one, if she was clever and the Vytill princess wasn't.

"Does Lady Morgrave know what Princess Illiryia is like?" I asked.

Dane and Theodore shrugged.

"Why?" Balthazar asked.

"Because a woman like Lady Morgrave will only choose a wife

for the king if she knows she's a silly twit, easily manipulated. She won't want his wife to have any influence over him. An even worse outcome for Lady Morgrave and the Deerhorns would be for him to fall in love with his queen and discard his mistress altogether. Is Princess Illiriya plain or pretty?"

"According to Barborough, she is a beauty," Balthazar said. "The portrait he brought of her would suggest he's speaking the truth, but portraits are not a reliable source."

"Have any other Glancian nobles seen her in person?" I asked. "Can they verify Barborough's claim?"

"None. She's been tucked away in her father's castle since birth. Few Glancian lords venture across the border, and reports from diplomats don't mention the princess at all, except for the fact that she exists."

"Then Lady Morgrave is unlikely to turn the king's head toward her," I said. "It would be unwise with so little information, and I don't think Lady Morgrave is unwise. Her mother certainly isn't."

"So what will she do?" Theodore asked. "Who will she choose as Glancia's future queen?"

"The Dreen princess is as much an unknown as the Vytill one," Balthazar said. "I think Lady Morgrave will choose a Glancian noblewoman for the king. Someone young enough to be molded into any shape. Someone pleasant to look at, but not too pretty and certainly not someone with any character and wit."

They all looked at me. "Just because I'm from Glancia doesn't mean I know its ladies," I said. "Before coming to the palace, the Deerhorn family members were the only nobles I'd seen. If you want to learn the names of likely candidates, you ought to speak to Lady Miranda Claypool. She will probably help, and we know she has no interest in marrying the king herself."

They continued to look at me.

I sighed. "You want me to ask her, don't you?"

"You're friends with her," Balthazar pointed out.

"And with the duchess of Gladstow," Theodore added. "Between the two of them, you should glean some valuable information. You might even learn who Lady Morgrave's eye has fallen on."

Both Miranda and Kitty had visited me once in the village, though they had not come a second time. According to Miranda's letters, Kitty's husband forbade her to be friends with me. Miranda had found her own freedom somewhat curtailed too, since her parents learned she frequently ventured away from the palace. I didn't resent them for it. They were fearful of her safety after she was poisoned. The Duke of Gladstow, however, was just a snob.

"I'll do my best," I said. "But it's not easy for me to mix with them. If we're seen, people will gossip. The Duke of Gladstow will be angry."

"Gossip certainly rules the palace," Dane muttered. "It's the most valuable currency within these walls."

"You can only try," Balthazar said to me. "If you learn something, report it to one of us."

"What will you do with the information?" I asked.

"That will depend on what you find out. Perhaps nothing. I simply want to be one step ahead of Lady Morgrave and the Deerhorns. We need to be prepared." He made it sound like a war was brewing.

The thought made my skin prickle. If the king rejected Princess Illiriya, would Vytill attempt something as drastic as invasion? They coveted the wealth Glancia had gained after the Rift turned Mull into the richest harbor on the Fist. Their power would fade in the coming years if they didn't do something to retain it. If a political and trade alliance couldn't be made through marriage or diplomacy, then they might resort to forceful measures.

That theory had prompted King Leon to order an army be raised in Glancia. I'd been privy to the conversation he'd had with Balthazar, Theodore and Dane about it, but I didn't know if anything had been set in motion yet. Recruiters certainly hadn't appeared in the village.

"That brings us back to Barborough," Dane said to me. "If you're seen more at the palace, he'll think you're questioning the servants. That will keep him satisfied for a little longer."

"Only until he thinks I've had enough time to gather information," I said. "What shall I tell him when he asks me?"

Dane opened and shut his mouth then shook his head.

It was Balthazar who answered. "Tell him the servants you've spoken to made their own way to the palace after learning of vacancies through marketplace gossip. They all come from different villages around the Fist, and none had worked for royalty before."

"He'll want to know which villages," Dane said. "And where they learned to be maids, footmen, guards and gardeners. If she gives him a name of a village or noble house, he'll send someone to make inquiries there."

"Then what do you propose she tell him?"

"She could avoid him."

"How? He knows where she lives. He can come and go freely from the palace."

"I could make it so he can't," Dane shot back.

Theodore gasped.

A muscle bunched in Balthazar's jaw. "And how will you do that, *Hammer*?"

The room fell silent. Dane and Balthazar glared at one another, and the air grew thicker with each passing moment.

Finally Theodore cleared his throat. "We'll keep that option as a last resort."

Dane shifted his weight and rested his hand on his sword hilt. "I have to return to work. Josie?"

I rose and picked up my pack, but he took it from me. "Will you tell Lady Miranda I'm here to see her?" I asked. "Tell her I'll meet her in…"

"On the lawn at the edge of the lake past the greenhouse," he filled in. "No one will be out there in this heat. Do you remember it?"

How could I forget meeting him there? It had been one of those warm, languid days, forever etched in my memory, where time had ceased to have meaning. I could have stayed out there with him for days and not cared to return home.

I went to leave, but Balthazar called me back into his office. "Be careful, Josie. Don't underestimate Barborough. He desperately wants to know if magic is involved in the palace's creation."

"He isn't the only one," Theodore said.

"Has anyone considered the fact that he could help?" I asked.

"If we told him everything, he might shed some light on the mystery."

"I think you overestimate his magical knowledge," Dane said.

"And underestimate the importance of his role as Vytill adviser," Balthazar added. "If he thinks Leon performed magic to be on the throne, he will whisper in certain ears. Ears that can destabilize the monarchy."

He meant the dukes. If the two Glancian dukes worked together to remove the king, then fought one another over a vacant throne, the perfect environment would be created for Vytill to storm in to the country and take over.

I swallowed heavily and nodded. I was in over my head with these political machinations, but it wouldn't be of any use to let these men see it. They needed me, and I'd do what I could to help, even if my help was nothing more than exchanging gossip and feeding falsehoods to Vytill's representative.

"I'll return your pack to the garrison," Dane said as we walked back along the corridor. "Exit the palace on the forecourt side and avoid nobles. I'll send Lady Miranda to you."

"Thank you." I wanted to ask him when I'd see him again, but I didn't think my question would be welcome. He still seemed very tense and not inclined to flirt.

"If you see Barborough..." He blew out a breath. "Just be careful."

"I will."

"And Josie." He put a hand on my arm and we both stopped. Torchlight illuminated one side of his face, casting the other in deep shadow. "I meant what I said in there. If the situation becomes too precarious, I'll do something about it. I won't let him hurt you." His fingers skimmed down my bare arm, sending a wash of heat through me. He lightly brushed the edge of my hand before setting off along the service corridor at a brisk pace.

I stared at his broad back for a moment then trotted to catch up. We parted ways in the garrison. He deposited my pack on a chair and left the way we'd entered. I exited through the external door and walked in the palace's shadow toward the first pavilion bordering one side of the inner forecourt.

The water in the fountain trickled a cool, welcoming tune, but no one paddled in it. Village children would have loved to splash in the shallows, but there were no children in the palace. Two young noblewomen and two elderly ones ambled past, fans flapping furiously. One of the elderly ladies complained of the heat and asked why they had to choose the warmest part of the day to go for a walk. The other elderly lady said it was because it was sweltering inside.

Two guards walked slowly by and nodded at me. They looked hot and bored, as did the sedan chair carriers. Sweat dripped from their brows, down their necks, and dampened their hair. They wore full palace livery with a crimson waistcoat and jacket over their shirt. I hoped they were given plenty of rest and water to drink. No doubt Balthazar would make sure of it. He seemed efficient yet considerate. I wasn't sure if that was because he wanted the staff to perform with maximum effort, or because he genuinely cared about their welfare.

I was about to pass the second pavilion when one of the sedan chair carriers shouted.

"Help! Someone get help!"

I picked up my skirts and ran back to where the sedan chair sat on the red, white and black marble flagstones. The door was open and the carrier who'd shouted stood there, uncertain, staring inside. The other stood behind him and I quickly realized he had been the one to shout. The first looked to be in shock.

"What is it?" I asked, reaching them at the same time as the two guards. I could not see past them, however, as big as they were.

"Move aside!" one of the guards ordered. "Stand back, let us through."

"What is it?" I said again.

"H-he's dead," said the first carrier. "His lordship is dead."

"Let me see." I tried to push aside the two guards but my efforts were in vain. "If he's not dead, he might require medical attention. So move!"

The guards parted, and I slipped between them. But I didn't immediately check for a pulse. I didn't need to. The signs of death were clear in the gray pallor of his skin and the open, vacant eyes.

But it wasn't those signs that made my heart dive and my mind reel. It was the fact that I knew him. I'd seen him in the village, but only once. It had been his wedding day. The day he'd married Lady Violette Deerhorn, now Lady Morgrave.

"Well?" asked one of the guards. "Is he alive?"

I checked his pulse to be sure. "Send for the captain," I said. "Tell him Lord Morgrave is dead." I would wait for Dane to arrive and tell him privately that his lordship had been murdered.

CHAPTER 3

*I*t didn't take long before a small crowd of nobles and servants gathered around the sedan chair, vying for a view of the dead Lord Morgrave. By the time Dane and Sergeant Brant arrived, I'd been pushed out of the way altogether.

"Stand clear!" Brant ordered. He manhandled a footman out of the way and pushed through the people, not caring whether he jostled servant or noble. More than one gentleman protested but Brant ignored him.

Dane met my gaze before he ordered everyone to step back with less aggression yet more command than Brant. The crowd moved to allow Dane in to inspect the body.

"Out of the way! Let me through!" came a voice at the edge of the crowd. He was ignored until he shouted, "I'm a doctor! Let me through."

The gathering parted again to reveal Doctor Clegg, medical bag in hand. He took a moment to catch his breath and sweep his graying hair off his damp forehead before asking Dane to step aside.

"You're too late," Brant said. "He's dead."

"I'll be judge of that," Doctor Clegg said.

"I know what a dead body looks like."

"Mistress Cully has already checked," added one of the sedan chair carriers.

Doctor Clegg searched the crowd before his cool gaze settled on me. "Mistress Cully could have made a mistake. She isn't a doctor."

"It don't take a medic to know he's dead," Brant snapped.

Doctor Clegg set his bag down and ducked his head into the sedan chair cabin. A hush fell over the crowd. Dane caught my gaze and jerked his head toward the gate. He mouthed "Go" in case I didn't understand his meaning.

I edged away from the sedan chair along with the rest of the crowd being ordered to move on by Brant and the other guards. Neither they nor I left the vicinity, however, and I was close enough to hear the exchange between Doctor Clegg and Dane.

"What did he die of?" Dane asked.

"Heart failure," the doctor said.

Heart failure! Was he blind? How could he have missed the signs of poisoning?

"Remove the body," Dane ordered his men. "Take it to the cellar."

Doctor Clegg picked up his bag. "I'll inform Lady Morgrave. It'll be better coming from me."

I stepped toward them. "No!"

Brant drew his sword. "No further!" he barked.

I thrust my hands on my hips and glared at him. "We both know you're not going to use that on me, so put it away."

He bared his teeth in a twisted grin. "Please test me, Josie. It will be my pleasure to prove you wrong."

I swallowed and lowered my hands to my sides. "Lord Morgrave didn't die of heart failure."

That wiped the smile off his face. He opened his mouth to speak, but Dane ordered him to put his weapon away and see that the crowd dispersed.

"I asked you to leave," Dane said to me when we were alone.

"He didn't die of heart failure," I said again.

He grabbed my arm and marched me away from the others. "Don't let Clegg hear you."

"Clegg is a fool," I hissed. "Anyone with medical knowledge can see Morgrave's heart didn't give out. There are too many other signs for him to simply rule it heart failure."

He glanced over his shoulder to where Doctor Clegg stood by the sedan chair, bag in hand, watching us with a frown. "Make it seem as though you're leaving but double back when the area is clear. I'll be in the garrison."

I crossed the inner forecourt to the larger outer one and the guards at the gate let me through, but not before asking what the commotion was about. I walked slowly and only glanced back when I reached the coach house. The crowd on the inner forecourt had thinned, the sedan chair removed, and Dane was nowhere in sight.

Even so, I stayed in the coach house for some time. It was cooler anyway, and the scent of leather and blacking polish smelled pleasant. The coachman and their assistants had little to do, since so few nobles had ventured out in the heat, and were glad to join me for conversation, particularly when I had gossip to impart. I told them Doctor Clegg had ruled Lord Morgrave's death the result of heart failure, but I didn't tell them I disagreed with it. Dane was right; I had to be careful. Declaring a man had died from poisoning could be seen as giving a medical opinion. Doctor Clegg would gladly inform the authorities.

I went in search of more conversation in the stables on the opposite side of Grand Avenue. The grooms were just as eager to hear about Lord Morgrave's death, though not as surprised. He'd just returned from a ride and, according to the groom who'd taken his horse, he'd not looked well.

I borrowed a wide brimmed hat one of the ladies had left behind in a carriage and returned to the palace wearing it low over my face. If anyone cared to look closely, it was obvious I wasn't a palace maid, but no one paid me any mind. No nobles remained on the forecourts anymore, only patrolling guards.

I pushed open the door to the garrison where Dane immediately stood upon seeing me.

"You still here?" Quentin asked. "Did you know Lord Morgrave was found dead?"

"She was there, idiot," Brant said.

"You saw him? What did the body look like? I've never seen anyone after they've died of heart failure. I s'pose you've seen lots. What are the signs?"

35

"Josie hasn't got time for your questions," Dane growled. He opened the door, expecting me to walk through to the service corridor beyond.

"Balthazar's office?" I asked as I passed him.

"He's waiting."

Theodore was there too, occupying the same chair as earlier. He stood upon my entry but Balthazar remained seated on the other side of the desk. He leaned on his walking stick, both hands folded over the head. He nodded grimly and asked me to sit.

"How did Lady Morgrave take the news?" I asked.

"She put on a good show, by all accounts," Balthazar said.

"I don't think it was an act," Theodore said with an admonishing look for the master of the palace. "She looked genuinely shocked when Doctor Clegg informed her."

"You were there?"

"I was with the king, and he was with her, along with several others, playing cards."

"How did the king react?"

"That's none of your concern, Josie," Balthazar said.

"He looked shocked too," Theodore told me. "He's still with her. I think he was genuinely horrified at the notion of a nobleman dying here at the palace."

"He'd be even more horrified if he learned it was murder," I said.

"Don't say that outside these four walls," Dane said quickly.

"I think Lady Morgrave did it," I went on. "Her shock was just an act. Or if not Lady Morgrave herself, then her mother or other member of her family. Lord Morgrave's death benefits the Deerhorns. Now his widow is free to marry the king."

"Let's not jump to conclusions until a thorough investigation has been conducted," he said darkly.

"It's hardly a jump, Captain," I said, my voice rising. Why was he being so obstructive? Didn't he want to investigate? "More like a small step. A tiny one, in fact."

"Even so."

Balthazar stamped the walking stick into the floor. "Why don't you think Morgrave died of heart failure, Josie?"

"There was evidence of poisoning. Heart failure generally

doesn't have many *unique* outward signs. It's not until the heart itself is inspected that the doctor can say for certain if that was the cause of death."

Theodore wrinkled his nose. "You mean the heart is removed from the chest?"

"It's forbidden to dissect a human cadaver outside the medical college," I said. "They do it for educational purposes, but only after a priest or priestess has performed a special rite."

He turned away, his face pale.

"Granted, not everyone can identify the signs of poison," I went on. "It's not a common cause of death, and Doctor Clegg may never have seen an affected body before, but after my experiences with Miranda and the dog, I'm quite certain that's how Morgrave died."

"What signs?" Dane asked.

"His fingernails were a purplish color and he'd frothed at the mouth. But the most obvious sign was the smell. Do you remember the dog, Captain?" I swallowed. "And my father?"

Dane nodded. "But I didn't smell that same smell on Morgrave."

"That's because you didn't open his mouth. I did. If Clegg was doing a proper inspection, he would have noticed the distinctively sweet smell of the poison made from cane flower. It was what Lord Frederick Whippler used on my father, but not Lady Miranda."

Dane settled a hand on his sword hilt. "But Morgrave hadn't vomited. I saw no evidence of it in the sedan chair. All the other victims of poison threw up."

"Could he have vomited before getting into the sedan chair?" Theodore asked.

"He did," I said.

They all looked at me, brows arched.

"I asked in the stables," I added. "The grooms said he was pale and sweating upon his return. He needed assistance getting off the horse but refused any further help. He threw up in the stable yard then got into the waiting sedan chair. It was the last time he was seen alive."

"Did you gather a sample?" Dane asked.

Theodore made a gagging sound and covered his mouth.

"The grooms were too efficient," I said. "They'd already washed it away."

"So we can't know for sure if he was poisoned."

"It seems very likely that he was."

"I agree," Balthazar said. "If Josie thinks the evidence points to poisoning, I'm inclined to believe her. She has more experience than Clegg."

"Clegg's diagnosis of heart failure was too quick for my liking," Dane added. "He should have waited until he'd studied the body further."

I agreed. "Even if he didn't know what the smell or the fingernail discoloration meant, he should have been curious and performed a closer inspection."

"Or he could have asked you, knowing that you've witnessed poison cases before," Theodore said.

"He would never stoop to asking me."

None of them disagreed with that.

Balthazar sighed and leaned heavily on his walking stick. "It seems we have a problem. If we announce that Josie believes Morgrave was poisoned, we'll be throwing suspicion onto the widow and her family. The king might not care. However, if he refuses to investigate, he'll only make it seem as though he is complicit in the murder. Even worse, it will make him seem as though he is a Deerhorn pawn. We can't have that."

"No one will announce anything," Dane said. "Josie can't be seen to have given a diagnosis."

Balthazar gave a curt nod. "So we all agree. Nothing is to be done."

"No!" I cried. "You can't just let the murderer roam free. Justice should be served."

Balthazar sighed again. "That's the problem with youth. You think everything is black and white, and that justice should always be dealt. Josie, these people are ruthless. If they killed a nobleman who stood in their way, they won't hesitate to silence anyone who suspects them of his murder. I prefer the murdering stop here, don't you? I've grown used to having you around. "

His words made my scalp crawl, but he was right. If I threw cold water over Doctor Clegg's diagnosis, I would draw unwanted attention to myself. I couldn't expect the king to save me. Lady Morgrave meant more to him than I did.

Theodore swore softly. It was so unexpected that we all stared at him. "Apologies, Josie, that was uncalled for. But you all know what will happen, don't you? Lady Morgrave will marry the king. She'll be our new queen."

"Not necessarily," Balthazar said. "The king might still be persuaded to marry the Vytill princess. He knows it's in the king-dom's best interest to do so."

"And who is going to convince him of that?" Dane asked. "He doesn't always listen to us anymore, and he has never listened to his advisors."

"I haven't given up on him yet. He might be a fool in many ways, but he does take his responsibility to Glancia very seriously. I know he does. It remains to be seen if his head can overrule his..." Balthazar glanced at me. "Other parts."

"I hope you're right." Dane rested a hand on the door handle. "Josie, I'll escort you out."

"I'm not leaving the palace yet," I said, rising. "I was on my way to speak to Miranda, and I still plan to do so."

"There's no longer any need. It doesn't matter which ladies are suitable marriage candidates for the king now. He'll only have eyes for Morgrave's widow."

"True, but gossip is just as important as ever. Besides, I'd still like to see her."

He watched me as I passed him into the corridor. "Then I'll tell her you're waiting for her by the lake."

* * *

I WAITED AN AGE FOR MIRANDA. It was too hot in the sun so I moved into the shade of the trees lining the edge of the lawn. From afar, she looked as serene and cool as ever, but as she drew closer, I could see the flush to her cheeks and the shine on her forehead.

"I'm pleased to see you are real, after all, and not a doll come to life," I said, smiling.

"Pardon?"

"You look hot."

She lowered herself with the grace of a dancer onto the lawn and leaned back against the tree trunk too. "I feel like I'm melting." She eyed the lake on the other side of the lawn. "It looks so inviting."

"You wouldn't dare, not this close to the palace." We had once paddled in a pond in the forest in only our underthings, but that had been far enough away that we weren't worried about being seen. There may be few people about today, but it was too risky there.

"You're right, I wouldn't. I'm far too demure to do such a thing."

I laughed. I'd thought her very demure when I'd first met her, but further acquaintance had proved she had a mischievous side.

"The captain said you wanted to see me," she said. "Is that just an excuse to come to the palace to see him?"

"No! I did want to see you."

Her smile turned wicked.

"I had to attend to one of the female staff, and thought I could pay a call on you too while I'm here," I said. "Although visiting you is not as easy as visiting my other friends."

"It's all right, Josie. I don't mind if you use me as your ruse to see him." She grinned, but it quickly faded. "Did you hear about Lord Morgrave?"

I was about to tell her I'd seen the body when a voice interrupted me.

"Miranda! Miranda, where are you?" It was Kitty, the duchess of Gladstow. She must be on the path on the other side of the trees. "Miranda, I saw you come this way. Where are you?"

"Do you mind?" Miranda whispered to me.

"Of course not," I said. "I enjoy her company too."

"Through here, Kitty!" she called out.

A moment later, the duchess appeared. She looked even hotter than Miranda, and she was breathing heavily, her bosom billowing above the tight bodice. She flipped out her fan with a flick of her wrist and flapped it furiously at her face.

"Good day, Josie," she said with a wan smile. "Now I see why Miranda came all the way out here on such an awful day. I thought she'd gone mad. I was genuinely fearful that the heat had boiled her brain."

I laughed. "Come and sit down before you collapse, Kitty," I said, daring to use her first name rather than her title.

She didn't seem to notice. She was far too busy being horrified at my suggestion. "On the ground?"

"You've never sat on the ground before?" Miranda asked.

"Not unless a blanket has been set down first. Or a gentleman's cloak, of course."

"Do many gentlemen lay their cloaks down for you?"

Kitty sighed. "Not anymore."

Miranda patted the grass beside her. "Come and sit. It's too hot to stand."

Kitty crossed her ankles and lowered herself, thrusting out her backside, her arms raised for balance. She changed her mind half way down, straightened, and tried again, only to give up once more.

"I know there's an art to this." She put her hands behind her and leaned back, but quickly abandoned the method.

"Didn't you ever sit on the floor as a child?" Miranda asked with a laugh.

"I thought there might be a better way, but all right. I'll pretend as though I'm five again." Kitty gathered up her skirts then went down on her knees then sat on her bottom, her feet out beside her. "There." She arranged her skirts around her. "I knew I could do it."

Miranda smiled sweetly. "And if you feel something crawl up your leg, be sure to brush it off before it reaches your—"

"Miranda!" Kitty opened her fan again with a violent shake. "Honestly, you can be so rustic, sometimes."

"And you are quite the prude. It's a wonder this court hasn't cured you of that yet."

Kitty eyed Miranda over the top of her fan. "Are you referring to you know who and their you know what?"

"Do you mean the liaison between the king and Lady Morgrave? Yes, I am referring to that. But there are others, if you know where to look."

Kitty suddenly lowered the fan to her lap. "Who?"

Miranda dismissed her with a wave of her hand. "Forget them. We were just about to discuss the death of Lord Morgrave."

Kitty resumed her fan flapping. "I don't feel sorry for him." She looked around as if afraid she'd been overheard, then leaned in. "He was a disgusting man."

"In what way?" I asked.

"His manners were appalling, and his language worse. He'd gamble and throw tantrums when he lost. He borrowed money from my husband but never paid him back. He was often drunk. He visited us last year and attacked one of the maids as she prepared his room. I had to order the footmen to stand guard in the servants' wing all night."

"No wonder you're not sorry to see him dead," I said. "What about Lady Morgrave? Did she seem sorry when she found out?"

"She was certainly surprised," Kitty said, confirming Theodore's opinion. "She claims he had never complained of chest pains before."

Miranda stretched out her legs and pulled the green cotton skirt to her knees. "Once she moves past the shock, she'll be relieved. I didn't know him as well as you, Kitty, but I overheard him say nasty things to her. Things no man should say to his wife."

"It's what husbands do, Miranda. They say cruel things. Sometimes they don't mean it and are sorry afterwards. Well, husbands of our station are, if you know what I mean."

"No, I do not. No man should call his wife a whore, not even one of *our* station."

Kitty looked out to the lake. "Even if he's right?"

Miranda and I exchanged glances. "Kitty," Miranda began. "Is something wrong?"

"Has your husband said something cruel to you?" I asked.

She sniffed and turned back to face us, a smile plastered on her lips. "Violette *is* a whore, though, isn't she? Just a different sort to those you see in the village brothel."

"Perhaps they're in love," Miranda said. "The king's kind and generous, and he can be charming sometimes. Compared to Lord Morgrave, he's quite appealing."

I didn't entirely agree with her. I'd seen the king in a different light to both these women. I'd seen him throw a tantrum, be selfish and immature. He certainly wasn't someone I could fall in love with, but I hadn't been married to an ogre like Morgrave or had a mother like Lady Deerhorn.

"Do you think he'll marry her?" Kitty asked.

"Gossip would suggest so," Miranda said. "Lord Morgrave wasn't even cold yet and the court was marrying his widow off to the king. Some were even suggesting the death wasn't from natural causes."

Kitty gasped and quickly glanced around. "Miranda, keep your voice down. If someone overheard you..."

Miranda looked to me. "Is it possible to kill someone and make it look like they died of heart failure?"

I bit my lip, warring with myself. I didn't like to lie but how much should I tell them?

"You know something, don't you?" Miranda said, inching toward me. "Out with it, Josie."

"I saw the body before Doctor Clegg did," I whispered. "He wasn't very thorough."

"And?"

"And that's all I can say. The captain knows my thoughts, but he forbade me to discuss it with anyone else."

"That doesn't include us," Kitty said, sounding put out.

Miranda's eyes brightened, and she sported a curious look on her face. "You *do* think he was murdered, don't you? Well, well. It seems someone paid Doctor Clegg to give a diagnosis of heart failure to hide the misdeed."

Kitty gasped. "Who?"

"The Deerhorns, of course."

Kitty gasped again and her gaze swept the trees behind us once more.

"Shhh," I hissed at Miranda. "For goodness' sake, don't say that to anyone. Not even your parents."

"I won't," Miranda said. "I promise. It would only get you into trouble, and I certainly don't want that."

Kitty gasped a third time and caught my hand. "Do be careful, Josie. Lord Morgrave was an awful man and better off dead, if you ask me. Finding out who killed him isn't worth the risk."

I reassured them both that I agreed.

Miranda patted my knee. "Good. Anyway, it's not certain the king will marry Violette. He might still do the right thing and marry Princess Illiriya. We have to hope so, anyway. Imagine if he doesn't choose her?"

"The Vytill representative will be most put out," Kitty said. "He was in the salon when Lord Morgrave's death was announced, and he looked positively ill over it. I thought he was going to faint."

"Forget Lord Barborough. It's the Vytill king we have to worry about. He won't take kindly to his plans being thwarted." Miranda cast a grave look at me. We both knew the future looked uncertain now.

"What about your husband, Kitty?" I asked her. "What will he advise the king to do now?"

"How would I know? He doesn't discuss politics with me. He thinks I'm not capable of understanding, but I am."

"He and the Duke of Buxton could try to prove that King Leon gained the throne through magic so he can be deposed," Miranda said. "Although deposing someone with magic at their disposal would be a difficult task."

"Do you believe in it?" Kitty asked. "Magic, I mean."

Miranda shrugged.

"Lots do, you know," Kitty said to me. "I've overheard some whispering about it in the salons. My servants believe it too, particularly after my maid heard the palace servants discussing it. What does your captain think?"

"He's not my captain," I said. "And I don't think we should discuss it anymore. Such talk is as risky as suggesting Lord Morgrave didn't die of heart failure."

I was relieved they both agreed with me.

We fell into silence, none of us particularly keen to leave. It was too hot even to walk back to the palace, and I wasn't prepared to say goodbye yet. I wasn't sure when I would next see them.

"Do you know where they took the body, Josie?" Miranda asked, quite unexpectedly.

"The cellar beneath the servants' commons," I said. "It's the coolest room. But the body won't keep long in this heat, even down there. He'll need to be buried soon."

Kitty's face drained of color and she increased the speed of her fan flapping. "Do we have to discuss this?"

Miranda ignored her. "I wonder if they'll send the body home to be buried on his estate."

"I wonder if the widow will return with the body," I added. "Or if she'll stay here to be near the king."

"She'll have to observe a period of mourning, surely," Kitty said. "It would be most unseemly if she didn't."

"But if she's gone for any length of time, the king's eye might catch another," Miranda said with a smirk. "There are many ladies circling him. She should be worried."

That was quite the understatement. The king had a wandering eye and was easily distracted by a pretty face and a sharp wit. He'd moved quickly from Miranda to Lady Morgrave and could certainly do so again.

"He has a son, you know," Kitty said idly. "Lord Morgrave does, from his first marriage. He's grown up, of course, and will inherit. I wonder what he thinks of his father's death."

Indeed. If anyone would want to see justice, it would be him. But he had to know his father was murdered first.

* * *

I PARTED ways with Kitty and Miranda when we reached the tip of the palace's southern wing. They entered the building while I continued on to the commons. Up ahead, in the shade of the building, stood Brant, talking to a footman dressed in the Duke of Buxton's livery colors. The footman nodded vigorously while Brant spoke in earnest. What could Brant possibly have to say to the duke's footman that was so important?

I was considering how to get closer and listen when someone emerged from the shadows and grabbed my arm. Lord Barborough jerked me around to face him.

"Let me go!" I cried, trying to pull free, and failing. I considered calling for help, but wasn't sure if Brant cared enough to come to my assistance.

"I see you've followed my advice and returned to the palace," Barborough snarled.

Kitty had said he looked ill upon hearing of Lord Morgrave's death, and I could see why. He sweated profusely and breathed heavily. There was also wildness in his eyes. Whenever I'd met him before, he'd seemed in ruthless control. Now, he looked like a man standing too close to the edge of a cliff in a storm.

"Are you unwell?" I asked, genuinely worried he might collapse. "Is it the heat?"

"Do you know what ails me, Mistress Cully? It's *you*." He shook me. "What have the servants told you?"

I shrank away but he pulled me closer. "N-nothing," I said. "I've not had a chance to speak to anyone."

"You lie. You've been to see the gardeners." He nodded in the direction of the greenhouse and pottage garden from which I'd come.

"I met with Lady Miranda Claypool and the duchess of Gladstow. Ask them if you don't believe me."

Mentioning two important names was enough to have him doubt himself. His grip loosened enough for me to jerk free. I stepped back, out of his reach.

"I want you to seek out the maids who clean the king's chambers," he said. "Ask them if they've seen any jewels. Not just ordinary jewels, but something...unique."

My heart thundered, crashing into my ribs. "Why?"

He glanced past me toward the commons. "Just ask them." He strode off and entered the palace.

I stared after him, my heart still hammering. He must know about the pulsing red gem in the king's possession. But how? Had he guessed? He hadn't suggested I ask the servants specifically about a gem before, so why now?

I turned and stopped short. The duke's footman had left but Sergeant Brant was still in the same spot—precisely where Lord Barborough had looked when he asked me about the jewel.

He turned and walked off. I picked up my skirts and hurried after him.

CHAPTER 4

*J*followed Brant to the servants' commons and hailed him as he crossed the internal courtyard. Other servants came and went in the busy area, carrying out their tasks with the efficiency Balthazar required of them. We were not alone, but it was still possible to have a private conversation.

"What do you want?" Brant snapped as he rounded on me. He was a solid, tall man with chiseled features that seemed to sharpen whenever he was angry. Which seemed to be often.

I drew in a deep breath and some courage with it. "I want to know why you were watching me just now."

"I was worried about your safety. Barborough looked like he was getting rough with you."

"How gallant." I didn't believe him for a moment, however. Brant possessed nothing as noble as gallantry.

He grunted and made to walk off, but I blocked his way. He bared his teeth at me. "Move!"

"Did you mention the gemstone to Lord Barborough?" I asked.

"Now why would I do that?"

I shrugged. "To enlist his help in solving the mystery surrounding the palace and your memory loss. He is supposed to be the expert on magic, although I doubt the claim."

He frowned. "He wrote a book about it."

"Anyone can write a book. If you want answers about magic,

ask a Zemayan. There are some on The Fist, although none in Mull since Tam Tao died."

His gaze pierced me, shredding my nerves. "Why did Barborough ask *you* about the gemstone? What's going on between you?"

I swallowed heavily. "If it was you, then you have just given information to a very dangerous man. It was a foolish—"

His hand whipped out and gripped my jaw, hard. I didn't move, didn't want to rile him further, but I did hold his gaze. I was terrified but I wouldn't let him see. "I haven't told him anything, Josie, and you make sure Hammer knows it, or you might find this pretty mouth of yours is no good for kissing anymore."

He let me go and stormed off. I sat on the edge of the fountain and drew in deep, ragged breaths until I felt a little calmer. Eventually I stood and headed to the garrison to fetch my pack. I'd had enough of palace intrigue for the day.

* * *

I THREW myself into work over the next two days. I called on both my patients and spent a while with the youngest, a first-time mother, preparing her for what to expect during childbirth. I prepared tonics and salves in my kitchen and foraged for herbs in the forest. Summer wasn't the best time, but it was something to do, and the weather had cooled enough that it was no longer unpleasant to be outdoors. I even helped Meg with the housework, earning myself an invitation to dinner.

I couldn't avoid the palace and Lord Barborough forever, though. Indeed, I expected to see him every time someone knocked on my door. I prepared a speech for him, keeping it vague enough that he couldn't verify the information. It remained to be seen if it would satisfy him.

While I avoided the dock, my work took me through the heart of the village. When the market was on, it was a hive of activity, with stallholders shouting over one another, shoppers attempting to bargain with them, and carts coming and going. Chickens clucked in cages and pigs snuffled around their makeshift pens. One even escaped, to the delight of the children who took up the chase. The palace guards were still in evidence, but they were few and far between.

Then, one morning, their numbers tripled. That, in itself, was an interesting development but not alarming. What worried me was the armor worn by both horses and men.

"Is everything all right?" I asked Erik, as he surveyed the marketplace from horseback. Most of the guards had passed by, but Erik and Max had stopped. They looked a little stiff in their armor, complete with helmet, breastplate, arm and leg protection.

"There was trouble last night," Erik said.

"I didn't hear of any trouble."

"In The Row."

"Is that where the other guards are going?"

He nodded but didn't take his gaze off the vicinity. It wasn't like the usually jovial Erik. He was rarely this serious.

"What kind of trouble?" I asked.

"A death."

"*Merdu.* Who died?"

"A man from The Row. He keeps women."

"A whore master," Max clarified. "An important man in The Row, apparently. He was stabbed in the throat."

"By whom?" I asked.

Both guards shrugged. "An unhappy customer?" Max suggested.

"There were fights, too," Erik said. "It is dangerous, but no one will tell the sheriff what happened."

Of course they wouldn't. The victim's people would dispense their own justice. They might have to wait for the guards to leave, however. With such a strong presence, only a fool would seek revenge now.

"Has the sheriff ventured into The Row?" asked Meg. I hadn't noticed her come up behind me. She was with the Bramm sisters, who looked horrified by our macabre discussion.

Max and Erik both sat higher in the saddle. Max smiled at Meg and Erik smiled at the two Bramm sisters. They perked up and smiled coyly back.

"He has," Max said, "with the captain and twelve of our finest at his back."

"How long will they remain?" I asked.

"Don't know. It's up to the captain."

The more brazen of the two Bramm sisters patted the armor covering the neck of Erik's horse. "Did *you* go into The Row?" she asked.

"Aye," he said. "Last night."

"That's very brave of you."

Erik shrugged and his armor rattled and clanked.

"Did you use your sword?" she asked.

"Aye."

"It's a big sword." She eyed the weapon strapped to his hip. Or thereabouts.

"Would you like to see it?" he asked.

The second Bramm sister grabbed the hand of the first. "Perhaps later." She steered her sister away from the guards.

They were swallowed up by a group of women who descended on them like wolves, attempting to get answers from them, I suspected. Now that I looked properly, there were lots of small groups gathered together at the edge of the market, talking intently. They looked worried. News of the trouble in The Row had spread, and it was still early.

"I like this armor," Erik said, tapping the sheet of metal covering his thigh. "The maids like it too, and that girl."

"She also likes pantomimes and dogs dressed in skirts," I said.

Max chuckled and Erik laughed too. "I do not know what is a pantomime, but dogs in skirts sounds amusing. Is it a local custom to do this to a dog?"

Max clapped Erik on the shoulder. "Josie means that girl likes silly, simple things."

Erik's grin widened and he peered toward the market where the Bramm sisters had disappeared.

Meg and I left the guards to their patrolling and entered the market too. I didn't need to buy anything, but I wanted to gauge the feeling of the villagers. The entire market seemed to buzz with the news of the whoremaster's murder. Some worried that the violence would spill out into the rest of Mull as the man's family sought retribution.

While Sheriff Neerim and his men were considered brave, no

one thought them capable of keeping the peace alone. It was only thanks to the palace guards that the violence had been contained. The king was praised for generously loaning them to the village, although some of the wiser souls realized the king had only loaned them because he worried for his own safety with Mull being so close to the palace.

"The problem is, what happens when the guards leave?" I asked Meg quietly.

She stared at me. "Why would they leave?"

"I meant leave The Row to return to the palace," I reassured her.

Meg fell silent, but I could sense her thinking through what I'd said. I didn't know why I'd said it. It slipped out. But the more I thought about it, the more I realized it was true. The guards would not only leave Mull one day, but they'd leave the palace, as would the rest of the servants. When they got their memories back, they would go in search of their lost lives, to rejoin loved ones and pick up the pieces left behind.

It remained to be seen how long they had to wait for that to happen. If it ever did.

* * *

I LEFT Meg and headed towards The Row. She wouldn't like me going near it, so I thought it best not to confide in her. I had to find out if Remy, Dora, Marnie and her family were all right. Fortunately, Quentin was on guard at the slum's entrance, not Brant or one of his ilk.

To look at Quentin's face, it was as if nothing were amiss. He smiled upon seeing me and greeted me with his usual exuberance. The armor, however, told the real story.

"You look hot in there," I said, tapping the metal plate covering his leg.

"I'm sitting in a pool of my own sweat." He squinted up at the sun. "But it ain't as hot as yesterday, thank Hailia."

"Thank Merdu," I told him. "The god controls the weather."

The other guard on duty at the entrance to The Row drew up alongside Quentin. I recognized him but didn't know his name.

51

"You shouldn't be here, Josie," he said apologetically. "Captain's orders."

"He's ordered everyone to stay away from the area?"

"Aye. He specifically mentioned you."

Dane knew me rather too well. "I wasn't expecting to go through, but I was hoping for some news of friends and patients who live in there."

"Captain thought you might," Quentin said with a twinkle in his dark eyes. "He told us to tell you they're not harmed."

"Oh. Well, that's very good of him to anticipate one of my questions. "

The second guard's eyebrows rose, disappearing into his helmet. "One of?"

"Have the tensions eased?" I asked, looking past them into the narrow street, where derelict buildings propped up their crumbling neighbors.

This part of The Row looked as it always had to me. Women sat in doorways while their children played in the gutter, and burly men loitered nearby, watchful. Deeper into the web of alleys not visible from the entrance, there would be families like Marnie's and Dora's, sheltering inside the buildings, all crammed together in a single room with their meager belongings. It was safer inside than out, but the rotting hovels were not homes.

"Too early to say," Quentin said.

Just as he spoke, Dane emerged from the shadowy depths on horseback. With his black horse, black clothing and somber expression, he resembled the mythical horseman who collected the souls of the dead. Children scurried out of his way and the adults watched, some warily, others with hostility.

"What are you doing here?" he asked me.

"Nice to see you too, Captain."

He merely glared back, waiting for my answer.

"I came to see if you've had word from Dora or Marnie. Quentin assures me they're fine."

"They are," he said. "Marnie and her family have been re-accommodated outside The Row. Dora and Remy are safe. I've told them to remain indoors."

"What's it like in there?" I asked.

"Tense, but the situation is stable, for now."

"What happened? Why was the man stabbed?"

He paused before saying, "It's an unseemly business."

I cocked my head to the side. "I know the man was a whore master and an important figure in The Row. What I don't know is, why was he killed?"

Dane turned a flinty glare onto Quentin and the other guard.

"We didn't tell her!" Quentin cried.

"I heard it elsewhere. Talk of whores and their masters doesn't bother me, Captain. Does it bother you?"

That glare turned icy.

Behind him, two riders emerged from the shadows, one in armor like all the other guards—except for Dane—and the other dressed in the uniform of the sheriff's office. I recognized Marnie's husband sitting tall on the horse. It would seem his apprenticeship had been shortened. Several of the women hissed as they passed, and some of the men rested their hands on their hips where weapons were most likely hidden by their loose shirts.

"They don't want you here," I said.

"That welcome is for the sheriff's man, not us," Dane said. "That's why Marnie and the children have moved out of The Row. Now that her husband is a lawman, it wasn't safe for them here."

It was sickening to think that some would target Marnie or the children because of her husband's employment—employment that he desperately needed to feed his family. But I was glad they were out of The Row. It was no place for them. If only Dora and Remy could leave too.

"Tell Dora to pack her things," I said on a rush of breath. "She and Remy can come and live with me. They have to get out of there."

He eyed me carefully. "Do you have the space?"

"My father's room is empty. They can share it. What I have is ten times what they do. Tell them or I won't be able to sleep at night."

"I will, but first I want to walk you home."

I glanced behind him again, trying to gauge the situation. How safe were they really?

Dane dismounted and touched my hand. The leather of his

riding glove was warm, supple. "They're fine, Josie," he said gently. "Let me take you home so you can prepare the room for them."

I closed my fingers around his, but he quickly withdrew. He led his horse forward. With a sigh, I matched his steps and we walked away from The Row.

"Why aren't you wearing armor like the others?" I asked.

"They don't respect armor in there."

"So they respect foolishness?"

"Are you calling me a fool for not wearing armor?" His mouth lifted on one side, and I was glad to see he hadn't completely lost his sense of humor.

"I wouldn't dare," I said, smiling back. "But your men are all wearing armor."

"I can't put their lives at risk."

We walked a few paces, so close that my shoulder almost bumped his arm. I expected him to move away and put space between us, but he did not. It should have given me hope that something still lay between us, but it didn't. I *knew* there was something between us. It was not being able to do anything about it that bothered me.

"So why was that man murdered?" I asked again. If flirting wasn't allowed, then I needed to talk about recent events to take my mind off his very tempting presence.

"He was a long-time resident of The Row, one of their so-called businessmen."

"So he was Glancian and a whoremaster."

He nodded. "None of his family or associates will say who they think did it, but the victims of the subsequent retaliation are members of a Vytill immigrant family. They set up in The Row recently and want to take over the women under the murdered man's jurisdiction. Marnie's husband, Jon, isn't surprised."

"Why?"

"One of the Vytill men tried to recruit him when they first arrived in The Row."

"Has the fighting stopped?"

"For now, but as soon as we leave, either the Glancians will attack out of revenge for the murder, or the Vytillians will take advantage of their leaderless rivals and make a play for the business."

"The sheriff can't keep the peace alone," I said. "Not even with his new recruits."

"Thankfully it's quiet at the palace. I can afford to keep a large presence in the village."

"Does the king understand the importance of having guards here?"

He hesitated before saying, "Balthazar and Theodore are explaining it to him. Hopefully he'll have no need to call us back."

"And you?" I asked as we reached my street. "Will you have to return to the palace or will you stay in Mull until things calm down in The Row?"

"I suspect I'll spend half my time here and half there."

"Then stop by for tea and cake when you have the opportunity."

His gaze fixed on my house ahead. "There won't be time for tea and cake."

"Of course there will be. You can't be on duty all day and night."

He stiffened. "I won't call on you. You have work to do and—"

"Nonsense," I scoffed. "There's hardly anything for me to do now. There are only two expectant mothers, and I haven't sold many medicines or salves these last few days. It seems rashes and warts have cleared up throughout the village, no children have fallen over and grazed themselves, and no one requires cough tonic. Hailia is smiling down on Mull."

"Are you in difficulty? Do you need money?"

"I'm fine," I lied.

"Your father left you with some savings?"

"He was a good father. Will you come in now for tea?"

His features settled into their hard planes and he looked away. "I can't."

Seeing him like this was frustrating after everything we'd been through together, and the secrets he'd shared with me. I missed the ease with which we used to talk. Silences used to be comfortable, now they were excruciating. I'd had enough. "Ever since that kiss you've been distant, cool," I said. "It's silly."

"I don't want to talk about it."

I rounded on him. "See? That's what I mean. You're pushing me away with both hands. You don't have to. We can still be friends."

"It's for the best this way," he said without looking at me.

"Why? Do you think I'm in danger of succumbing to your good looks and charm? I can assure you, your virtue is quite safe."

Another tilt of his lips proved his mood wasn't entirely sullen. "Thank you for the reassurance. I promise I'll stop by for tea, but not today. I'd best get back."

I watched him ride off, wondering whether he'd keep that promise, and whether either of us could continue as mere friends.

* * *

WHEN WORD SPREAD that the governor had called a meeting of villagers for late in the afternoon, I'd decided to attend with Meg and her family. No one expected there to be trouble, however, not with the guards still patrolling, but being in the company of others would give Dane less reason to scowl at me.

I spotted him on horseback in the village square at the front of the assembling crowd. Another twenty guards were spread out at the edges of the lawn, while the sheriff's men mingled on foot. The sheriff himself stood beside a stack of packing crates, talking to the governor. His gaze swept the vicinity as the governor spoke to him in earnest.

"What are *they* doing here?" Lyle muttered.

I followed his gaze to where four riders approached. Lady Deerhorn sat on her white horse with her nose in the air and her purple cape settled regally behind her. Lord Deerhorn rode a little behind his wife, and inspected the crowd with a look of complete authority, as if we were his biddable servants. He'd get a rude shock if he tried to order anyone about. Their two eldest sons, Lords Xavier and Greville, sported similar expressions of disdain. But while Greville didn't meet anyone's gaze, Xavier searched the faces in the crowd.

Until he found me.

His top lip twitched into a sneering smile. I swallowed down my rising fear and moved closer to Lyle and Mr. Diver.

I wasn't the only one to notice Xavier's interest. Lady Deerhorn's glare was so piercing that her son must have felt its prick. He joined her and seemed to make a point of *not* looking at me.

Dane had seen too. He shifted in the saddle and his horse wheeled around, restless. He calmed it with a hand to its neck, and a few soothing words, but didn't take his gaze off me.

I wished he'd speak soothingly to me. My nerves felt raw, my heartbeat erratic. I didn't like this. Calling a meeting at such a tense time seemed like a foolish thing to do. Most of the long-time Mullians had come to hear the governor speak, but there were many newcomers too and all of them men. The two groups stood on opposite sides of the green, eyeing one another across the narrow gap. They flung curses too, each blaming the other for their problems. The loudest was Ned Perkin and his group of troublemakers, Ivor Morgrain among them.

The voices became louder until finally one of the newcomers shouted at Ned. "We just want jobs!"

"You can't have *our* jobs!" Ned said. Then he spat at him.

The other man pushed Ned with both hands, and Ned pushed back. Ivor shoved a second man in the chest.

Dane carved a path through the crowd while Max and two other guards did the same from different directions. Dane reached down and grabbed the back of Ned's jerkin.

"At the front where I can see you," Dane ordered. "You too, Morgrain."

"Front row seats, eh?" Ned said. "Ain't I the lucky one?" Several of his friends snickered.

Ivor followed, drawing very close to me. "Nice to see you, Josie. Mind you don't get yourself into any trouble tonight. You ain't got no menfolk to take care of you anymore."

"Shut up, Morgrain," Lyle snarled. "I'll take care of her."

Ivor snorted a laugh then stumbled forward when Max pushed him in the back.

"Settle down, settle down," the governor called. He stood on the stack of crates so that those at the back could see him. "This meeting has been called to inform you all of what happened last night and what will happen next."

57

"We know what happened," Ned called out. "The Vytill scum murdered a Mull man."

Several men shouted him down so that the governor once again had to call for calm. The voices slowly died away, but the governor looked uneasy. Even though the hottest part of the day was over, his face and bald head shone with sweat, and his beard glistened.

"What happened in The Row isn't just the fault of the Vytill people," the governor went on.

A chorus of protests drowned out the governor's next words. He tried in vain to speak over them, but it was hopeless.

Lord Xavier appealed to his father, but Lord Deerhorn didn't say a word. He sat like a statue on his horse, looking very much like he wished he didn't have to bother with this meeting. It was Lady Deerhorn who nodded at her son.

"Silence!" Lord Xavier roared.

He moved his horse to the front of the crowd, but the jittery animal grew more agitated by the movement and noise. It twisted and turned then reared up. Hooves stabbed at the air, very close to the face of a woman. She screamed and put her arms up to defend herself. That only made the horse rear again.

"Are you trying to frighten your lord's horse?" Lady Deerhorn cried.

The woman was too terrified to answer. She cowered from the hooves, trying to push back into the crowd.

Dane rode up and grabbed the reins of Lord Xavier's horse as it reared again. Unable to hold on, Lord Xavier jumped off, stumbling before regaining his footing. Removing its rider seemed to calm the horse a little, and Dane was able to lead it away from the crowd.

Lord Xavier slapped the woman across the face. "Are you trying to kill me?"

The woman sobbed until a friend put an arm around her and steered her away. A hush fell over the crowd. Even Ned and Ivor looked shocked by what they'd seen. Aside from the woman Lord Xavier had raped a few years ago, the villagers never had much interaction with the Deerhorns. They only came into Mull to pass through it to the forests on the other side where the hunting was good. They owned many properties in the village but were absentee landlords, employing others to collect rents. Their presence at the village meeting was unusual but, considering the extraordinary circumstances, not a complete surprise. Slapping an innocent bystander was quite shocking.

The governor cleared his throat. "Back to the matter at hand: The Row."

"It's not just The Row," Ned called out. "Mull is crawling with the Vytill leeches."

"We ain't leeches!" someone on the Vytill side of the crowd shouted. "We want to work!"

"Aye!" his friends chimed in.

"There ain't any jobs!" Ivor shouted back.

"There could be if you did things properly. But you're hopeless. This place is so backward. It's like The Thumb was fifty years ago."

"Then move back there if you like it so much."

Such a stupid statement didn't even warrant a response from the Vytillians.

The governor raised his hands and called for silence again.

But Ned wasn't going to give it to him. "You gave our jobs to Vytill scum!" He stabbed a finger at the governor. "Mull's lawmen should come from Mull!"

"That wasn't my doing," the governor said. "Sheriff Neerim asked if he could put on more men and I agreed. I didn't know he was going to give half of those jobs to the Vytill."

Sheriff Neerim's jaw hardened. Some of his new Vytill men glanced uneasily at one another.

"You should be ashamed of yourself, Sheriff," Ned called out.

"Aye," agreed most of the Mull side of the crowd.

I bit my tongue to stop myself telling them that it made sense if they wanted to maintain peace among the Vytill immigrants. They would respect one of their own more than a Mullian.

I caught sight of Meg trying to urge her brother to speak up but he ignored her. She wouldn't dare ask her father. He was a good man and didn't join in with the shouts, but I could see he agreed with Ned.

"Let's not sway from the purpose of this meeting," the governor said over the top of the mutterings. "The reason I've called you all here is because we need to inform you of the council's plans for the area known as The Row. You all heard about last night's problem. Such a problem won't easily resolve itself. The two factions in The Row are now at loggerheads, and as soon as Sheriff Neerim and Captain Hammer withdraw their men, the filthy lanes will explode with violence. I cannot allow this! I *cannot* allow our good village to become the battle ground for these gangs." He paused and took stock. He had the audience's full attention. "After listening to the advice of our good Lord Deerhorn and his family, I have decided to rid ourselves of the scourge of that lice-infested place once and for all. We *cannot* have such lawlessness in our village. We don't want to live in fear of violence leaking into the rest of Mull. So we have decided to dismantle The Row and scrub its stain from our streets! We will pull down its grubby walls and shed light into its dark, godless heart! We will reclaim our village for the good people of Mull!"

It was a rousing speech and had most of the crowd nodding along, growing excited as the governor's voice rose higher and louder.

Behind him, Dane handed back the reins of Lord Xavier's horse. He frowned, while Lord Xavier's eyes gleamed. Dane must have had the same thought as me, and I could see from Sheriff Neerim's confused look that he too had questions.

"Removing the old buildings and cleaning out The Row will create new laboring jobs," the governor continued.

This created more murmurs. "How many?" asked a Vytill man.

"Not enough for all, alas, but for the strong among you, there will be work."

"And who will fund the clearance?" asked Peggy from the Buy and Swap Shop.

"It better not be us," someone said. "We can't afford another tax now. It's costly just to live in Mull."

"The Deerhorns have graciously offered a loan to the council to be repaid over five years."

"Under what terms?"

"The particulars are not your concern. Rest assured," the governor shouted over the murmuring voices, "the terms are fair to both parties."

"What will you build in place of the homes there now?" asked Selwyn Grigg.

"New houses, of course. Good, solid accommodation for families."

His words triggered a burst of relief from the crowd. Everyone talked at once, nodding and smiling. Someone shouted words of gratitude to the Deerhorns, while another praised the governor for his handling of the dangerous situation and his vision for the future of Mull.

Only Dane and the sheriff continued to frown, and I understood why.

"What will happen to those living in The Row now?" I asked Meg.

She shrugged.

"They can rent one of the new houses," Lyle said.

"With what money? Most of them have none and I doubt they'll benefit from the new jobs created to clear their own tenements. Particularly the women."

"I didn't think of that," Meg said. "Those poor women—and their children. Where will they go?" She took my hand, clearly thinking of Remy.

I hadn't told her that Remy and Dora were already safely tucked away in my house. But there were many other children in The Row who would not have anywhere to go when the governor destroyed their homes.

"They at least have a roof over their heads in The Row now and a community that looks out for them, in a way," I said.

"Tell them," said a slick voice in my ear. It made my nerves jump and my skin crawl.

"Go away, Ivor," I said.

"Tell them, Josie. Tell them they haven't thought about the poor orphans and widows. Tell the Deerhorns they're making a mistake." He shoved my arm. "Go on."

"Shut up," I snapped.

"Listen!" he shouted. "Everyone, listen! Josie Cully's got something to say."

I wanted to kill him.

The crowd turned to me, expectant.

"You all know Josie," Ivor bellowed. "All you respectable Mull folk do, anyway. For those that don't, this is Josie Cully, daughter of the last doctor. She's the midwife in the village, and she's got something to say. She doesn't think the governor's idea is very good."

The Vytill half of the crowd muttered their disbelief, but at least the long-term Mullians appeared to be listening.

"That's not what I said," I told them. "Ivor is stirring up trouble, as usual."

Ivor grunted while several people chuckled. Meg squeezed my hand. At the front, Dane had moved closer to the crowd, as had Lord Xavier. His mother sat on her horse behind him, her cold glare locked on me.

I drew in a measured breath. "I've attended expectant mothers and newborns in The Row," I said. "It's true that the conditions are terrible there, but if you clear away the homes they have, and replace them with new ones, will they be able to live in them?"

"They'll be able to rent them," Lord Xavier said. "My family doesn't discriminate."

"So the new houses will be as cheap as what they pay now?"

He snorted. "Of course not. They pay nothing. *Good* houses can be rented at the going rate."

"They can't afford the going rate. Those women are desperate, my lord. They may be living in squalor, but at least they have a roof over their heads. You can't take that away from them."

"Who cares?" Lord Deerhorn piped up for the first time. "They're all whores."

"That's not true, my lord," I said. "And those who are have turned to that life because they have no other way to feed their family."

"They can find employment, just like everyone else," Lord Xavier said. "Respectable employment. Then they can afford one of the new houses."

"Employment where? The only women who have respectable employment in Mull are those who work for their families and your servants." I could have added that no woman liked going into service for the Deerhorns but did not.

Lord Xavier lifted a nonchalant shoulder. "That is not our concern. We cannot help everyone, Mistress Cully."

My blood heated and flashed before my eyes. I knew I must remain calm but he was making it difficult. "Are your family helping anyone, my lord? Residents living in your tenements are facing rising rents. Every month, it goes up. The women from The Row will never be able to afford to live in a room in one of your new houses, let alone rent all of it."

Murmurs of agreement rippled through the crowd and heads nodded.

"That's not our fault," Lord Xavier said, his voice rising. "That's what happens when there is limited stock of a commodity. Prices go up. I don't expect an uneducated village girl to understand basic economics, but perhaps you can ask your husband, father or brother to explain it to you. Oh, wait. You're all alone, aren't you?"

Meg's grip tightened on my hand. "Don't answer him."

Several voices in the audience hissed their disapproval of Lord Xavier's crassness. Some even booed, albeit softly.

I caught Dane watching me. He no longer sat with ease on his horse, but looked as if he'd charge into the crowd at any moment. I gave him a small smile of reassurance, but it didn't dampen the intensity of his glare.

"We don't need to listen to people like this," spat Lord Deerhorn. He steered his horse away and rode off. Lord Greville followed him.

Lord Xavier smiled that slippery smile of his, until his mother moved up alongside him. "You have strong opinions, Mistress Cully," she said. "Do you have a solution to the housing problem?"

I looked at the mostly familiar faces surrounding me. They waited for me to speak for them, even Ned and Ivor. It was a strange sensation to be the center of attention and I wanted to shrink into myself and back away. I'd come this far, however, and felt compelled to go on and offer a solution.

"You could allocate some of the space that will be gained from clearing The Row for housing the poor. Perhaps a community house for women and orphans, and men with no hope of good employment."

Lord Xavier threw his head back and laughed, a brittle, cruel sound that shattered the air.

"We're not a charity," Lady Deerhorn said, her voice hard. "The temples do a serviceable job of that already, and of course we help unfortunates when we can."

Someone in the crowd barked a disbelieving laugh.

Lord Xavier rose out of the saddle and tried to see where it came from, but sat again without accusing anyone.

"You make it sound like the new houses will be owned by your family, my lady," I said. "Will they not remain in council hands? Are you not simply providing a loan to fund the clearance?"

A ripple of murmurs spread through the crowd, starting low but increasing as neither the governor nor the Deerhorns denied it.

"It's council owned land!" someone cried. "You can't sell it off."

The governor put up his hands for silence. "It's the only way! We can't afford to do it otherwise."

"Then don't do it!"

"It must be done. The Row's lawlessness is out of control. The filth is spreading. If we don't stem it now, who knows where it will end." That silenced some of the protestors, but not all. "The Deerhorn family have made a very reasonable offer!" the governor shouted over them.

"We all know how the Deerhorns treat their tenants in these times," someone near me spat.

Lady Deerhorn's nostrils flared. "Mistress Cully, are you suggesting that my family are raising rents to benefit ourselves? Because that's monstrous." It didn't seem to matter that I hadn't spoken. She only had eyes for me; it was as if the rest of the crowd didn't exist. "Rents rise because the cost of upkeep and daily living rises," she went on. "Yes, *our* cost of living rises, just like yours. We have an entire estate to run, with many servants. Do you know what that entails? Of course not. As my son so succinctly put it, you're just an uneducated girl. Do not judge something you don't understand. Clearing out that stinking hole called The Row will get rid of the gangs, the violence, the filthy vermin who prey on innocent villagers. Isn't that what you all want?"

Several people nodded in agreement, some of them the same

who'd agreed with me moments ago. One brave soul said, "But we don't want to set them loose in Mull, either."

Lady Deerhorn's lips pinched. She wheeled her horse around and barked at her son to follow her. They rode off.

My breathing was ragged and shallow as frustration and anger boiled inside me. Several people spoke to me, thanking me for voicing concerns. Some even told me how much their rents had risen since The Rift. It was far more than I'd realized. All were tenants of Lord Deerhorn.

I thanked Hailia that I didn't have to worry about rent when I now owned my own home. My father may have lost our savings, but he'd had the foresight and sense to buy that house when he married my mother.

The crowd dispersed, but not before Ivor accosted me. "When are you going to learn to keep that mouth of yours shut, Josie?" He walked off, chuckling.

"Ignore him," Meg said, looping her arm through mine.

I left with her, but not before seeing Doctor Ashmole and his wife, standing quite still as the crowd moved off. They watched me, twin stern expressions on their faces. Mistress Ashmole said something to her husband. He nodded and smirked before they also left.

Meg and her family remained to speak to friends, but I spotted Dane with his guards. "I'll be back in a moment," I told Meg.

I crossed the green, but Dane hadn't seen me. He rode off into one of the neighboring streets. I picked up my skirts and raced after him.

When I turned the corner, he wasn't there. Lord Xavier, however, was. He maneuvered his horse toward me and I backed up until I hit the stone wall of the building behind me.

"Look who's all alone," he sneered. "It's my favorite midwife masquerading as a doctor." He bared his teeth in a hard smile. "You've been naughty, Josie. Very naughty."

CHAPTER 5

"*We*'re not alone," I said. "There are still a lot of people about."

"No one will interrupt us," Lord Xavier said. "They wouldn't dare." His tongue darted out, wetting his lower lip. "What I've got to say won't take long. I simply wanted to warn you that Doctor Clegg told my mother something interesting the other day. Can you guess what it was?"

Merdu.

"He said you declared Morgrave dead." He leaned forward. "You can't do that, Josie. You're not qualified."

I swallowed.

"It's all right. Your secret is safe with us. We won't tell anyone—unless you cause problems."

"Why would I do that?" I asked, sounding bolder than I felt.

"Why indeed? Particularly now that my sister will be queen." His hand whipped out and grasped my jaw, forcing me to look up at him. "Good girl."

His thumb stroked my cheek then pressed into the bone. I winced but did not try to pull away. I met his gaze.

"Good girl," he murmured again.

"Xavier!" snapped Lady Deerhorn, riding up to us. "What are you doing talking to that girl?"

Lord Xavier released me. "Just having a little chat about our mutual friend, Doctor Clegg."

Lady Deerhorn's gaze narrowed. "It's time to go."

Lord Xavier pulled on the reins, wheeling his horse around. I skipped backward, but the horse bumped me, sending me careening into the wall of a nearby building.

I watched them leave, my heart in my throat, my whole body trembling. I hated that they scared me, hated that I had no power over them. I didn't like feeling so vulnerable.

I stayed there to gather my frayed nerves so I could face Meg without worrying her. But before I was ready, Dane rode toward me from the opposite end of the street. He quickened his horse's pace when he saw me.

"Josie?" he asked, dismounting. "You look shaken. Are you all right?"

I nodded and attempted a smile, but it must have failed. He frowned back.

"It's the meeting, isn't it?" he asked, gentler. "I saw what Morgrain did. You handled the situation admirably. I've had a word with him, and he regrets throwing you into the viper's nest like that."

"Regrets?" I echoed. "What did you say to him?"

"I told him it's one of my jobs to see that the king's favorites are treated with respect, and anyone who fails to do so will spend time in a palace cell until they understand the error of their ways. I went on to tell him the conditions in those cells."

"I'm not one of the king's favorites."

"Morgrain doesn't know that. Besides, the king does like you." He glanced past me toward the village green where his men maintained a presence to ensure peace as the crowd dispersed. "Meg's coming for you. I have to go." He touched my elbow. "Are you sure you're all right?"

I nodded.

"Go straight home and stay inside tonight. With word spreading about the governor's plans for The Row, it could get dangerous. The residents won't like it."

He went to mount his horse, but I grasped his hand. "Be careful, Dane. Please."

A wisp of a smile touched his lips before vanishing. "I've got the best men with me. We'll be fine."

He mounted and returned to the village green, nodding at Meg and her family as he passed.

Meg took my hand. "You look a little pale, Josie."

"I'm fine," I said.

"That idiot, Ivor. How dare he put you in that situation. He's very lucky it turned out the way it did, or I'd give him a piece of my mind."

"*I'll* have words with him," Lyle said, patting my shoulder.

"As will I," Mr. Diver said. "It was irresponsible. The Deerhorns are unpredictable and can't be reasoned with."

"Although you made a wonderful attempt, Josie," Mistress Diver said. "But next time, it's best if you bite your tongue. People like the Deerhorns don't want to be told the truth, and nothing will change, anyway."

"Not if we don't try," Meg said.

"Be sensible, child. Putting your neck out only gets your head lopped off. It's foolish to try and change something that can't be changed. It'll only put a target on your forehead."

Meg shook her head and increased her pace. I walked faster to catch up to her, as did Lyle.

"Everyone thinks you were so brave," he said to me. "They're all impressed you told the governor and the Deerhorns what's what."

"It was foolish," I said. "Your mother is right. It's safer to say nothing."

"And let them get away with raising the rents?" Meg asked. "With turning the poorest people out of their homes and into the streets? No, Josie. You did the right thing. Someone has to tell them what they're doing is irresponsible—cruel, even." She hugged my arm. "I'm proud to call you my friend. And don't worry, no one in Mull will let anything bad happen to you. The Deerhorns wouldn't dare."

A cold knot formed in my stomach and tightened. Meg didn't know the Deerhorns like I did.

* * *

AFTER A RESTLESS NIGHT, I managed to fall asleep a little before dawn, waking in the late morning when a visitor knocked. I threw a shawl around my shoulders and opened the door a crack. Dane stood there looking tired but well, thank Hailia. His horse was tied to the bollard. It was a good sign that he intended to come in.

Even so, he hesitated when I opened the door wider. "I have to get back," he hedged.

"You can spare some time for tea," I said. "I'll also cook eggs if you haven't eaten breakfast." Thankfully one of my patients had paid me only yesterday with the eggs laid by her hens.

"Eggs would be good," he said, stepping inside. "Did I wake you or do you always dress late?"

I smiled, relieved to see his mood wasn't too grave. "I'll put the tea on then change. I had trouble sleeping. You haven't slept at all, have you?"

He scrubbed a hand over his jaw, shadowed with stubble. "Is it that obvious?"

"Only to someone who knows you well."

He paused inside the kitchen door and looked surprised at the thought. Then he unfastened his sword belt and leaned the sword against the wall. "Are Dora and Remy still here?"

"They must have gone out. There's no one home but me."

I indicated he should sit then checked the contents of the pot hanging over the fire. There was enough mildwood tea for both of us, left over from my attempt to calm my racing heart during the night. It only required warming.

"Have any of your men slept?" I asked, stoking the coals. "Or was there too much to do?"

"It was a busy night. It's better now, calmer. The guards' shift changed not long ago and fresh replacements are on duty."

"Why didn't you return to the palace with the last shift?"

"I'm needed in the village."

I wondered if the king agreed with that. "So this is your time off?"

He cast me a weary smile. "It was either here or the beach, but I thought I'd have a better chance of tea here."

I smiled back. "And eggs." I fetched the eggs from the larder, carrying them in two hands. My shawl slipped, dragging my nightdress with it, revealing my bare shoulder.

Dane's gaze warmed. He shifted in the chair and swallowed.

I set the eggs down carefully on the table near him. When I looked up, he was still staring. A slight flush colored his cheeks, and I felt my own face heat.

I was torn between wanting to encourage him to kiss the bare skin of my shoulder, and wanting to help him be the honorable man he was trying to be. In the end, he decided. He looked away.

I fixed my nightdress and shawl. "I'll change before I make breakfast."

When I returned to the kitchen, I thought he was asleep. He sat in the same chair, his eyes closed, but opened them when I entered.

I unhooked the pot and poured the tea into two cups. "What was it like, last night, in The Row?" I asked, passing him a cup.

"There were pockets of trouble. They're angry about the governor and Deerhorns' plans for their homes, and they voiced those concerns to us. Loudly."

"Violently?"

He paused. "There were some fights between the Mull and Vytill factions, but it's possible that was left over from the murder. The two sides still hate each other, just as much as they hate the sheriff, the governor, the Deerhorns and everyone else they think is against them."

"Dora described it as a cooking pot with a lot of ingredients thrown together, and the fire blazing beneath."

"The governor and Deerhorns are throwing on more fuel." He shook his head. "Sheriff Neerim and I tried to warn the governor but they went ahead with the meeting anyway."

"It was irresponsible of them to announce their plans now when the tensions were already high in The Row after the murder," I said, settling the pan over the coals.

"Irresponsible, yes, but clever, in a way. Now they can pretend they're ridding the village of gangs, dispersing the two warring factions, weakening them." He rubbed his hand through his hair and gave another shake of his head. "But it will only force them onto the other streets of Mull where good people live."

I cracked an egg into the pan. "The Deerhorns don't care, but the governor should."

"I don't think he has a choice. He's their man and they know what they're doing. They know they can quickly build poor quality housing, and charge high rents."

I cracked another egg and watched it slide into the pan then cracked another four. "The villagers won't let them get away with their scheme. The Deerhorns don't control this village, although they like to think they do."

"You expect trouble?" he asked.

"I'm sure there will be secret meetings held in the village over the next few days, discussing the good and bad of the idea. I suspect they'll all reach the same conclusion we have—that there will continue to be fights, no matter where the gangs are, and the poorest need to be housed or they'll be on the street."

"Your speech last night opened a few eyes to their plight," he said with a tilt of his lips.

"It was hardly a speech. Just a few choice words to remind them there are others less fortunate. "

I watched the eggs cook rather than look at Dane. Seeing him smile like that lifted my spirits a little too high. I'd begun to think I'd been foolish to speak up at the meeting, but he made me feel as though my opinion mattered. Being this close to him, alone, and knowing what he thought, only made me want to sit on his lap and throw my arms around him.

"There's bread and cheese in the larder," I said briskly.

He disappeared into the larder, returning with half a loaf of bread and a small wedge of cheese. "The timing couldn't be worse," he said. "There is tension at the palace too."

"And the king allows you to be here?"

"He isn't aware of it. The servants are talking about magic and the gem, but only among themselves, and no one dares gossip about Lady Morgave in front of him."

I slid some of the eggs onto a plate and handed it to him before joining him at the table with the remainder. "What are the servants saying?"

"They're wondering if the king used magic on them." He sliced off two pieces of bread and offered me one, then cut slices of cheese.

"Are they angry?" I asked, watching him.

He placed two of the fried eggs and two slices of cheese between the bread. "Not yet, but they will be, if Brant keeps stirring them up."

"So he'll be spending a lot of time on duty in the village?"

"You do know me well."

I watched him bite into his breakfast. He closed his eyes, apparently enjoying the taste. "That looks interesting," I said.

He frowned then studied his food. "You've never tried it like this before?"

"I've never put cheese and egg together with bread. I thought you'd just eat it all separately. Have you always eaten it like that? I mean, ever since you can remember?"

He nodded and took another bite.

We finished our breakfast in silence but neither of us made a move to get up from the table. He seemed in no hurry to finish his tea, and I was in no hurry to see him go.

"Speaking of Brant," I finally said, "I saw him as I left the palace the other day. He and Lord Barborough shared a look, just as Barborough was asking me about the gemstone."

"When were you going to tell me you spoke to Barborough?"

"Don't look so cross. This is the first opportunity I've had to inform you."

His frown deepened.

"I think Brant told Barborough about the gem," I went on. "Perhaps Brant was asking him if he knew something about it, in his capacity as magic expert."

"The fool," Dane muttered into his mug. He sipped then added, "Speaking of Barborough, you need to be prepared for a visit from him. His time here is running out. He'll get more desperate for answers."

"Is the king sending him home?"

"Probably. The king and Lady Morgrave get closer by the day. They don't bother to hide their affection for one another since she became a widow. She sent the body home and decided to stay at the palace. A wise choice, considering the fickle nature of the king."

"Is *she* encouraging him to send the Vytill and Dreen representatives away?"

"It seems so. The king tells his ministers and the lords that he hasn't decided on a wife yet, but in private to Balthazar, Theodore and myself, he's talking about Lady Morgrave becoming queen."

"The lords and ministers aren't stupid," I said. "If the king is more affectionate with his mistress in public, surely they'll realize which way he'll jump."

"They're aware, as are both foreign representatives. The Dreen lord is worried and Barborough is furious, but I'm not sure if that's because he doesn't want to fail his king or because he hasn't solved the mystery of the palace yet."

I suspected the latter. Magic seemed to be all Barborough cared about.

"I'm also sure it was he who started the rumor that Lord Morgrave was murdered," Dane went on. "Although the king hasn't heard it yet."

I gasped. "Has my name been mentioned in connection with the rumor?"

"No." He leaned forward and touched my arm. "You have nothing to fear there, Josie. My men are the only ones who heard what you said, aside from Doctor Clegg, and they've been sworn to secrecy."

I smiled weakly. "I suppose they fear you enough not to cross you."

He withdrew his hand, and I felt awful for suggesting he'd use violence against his own men. I'd meant it as a joke, but it was too close to the truth.

I cleared my throat. "More tea?"

He held out his cup. "Thanks."

I poured the tea and handed back the cup. "Thank you for the company," I said. "It's nice. I hope you found it a good alternative to the beach."

"I do." He accepted the cup. "But you have company now, with Dora and Remy. What's it like with a child in the house?"

"I've hardly been here at the same time as them. I wonder where they've gone today."

"Hopefully to forage for food. Your larder contains mostly medicines."

"I have eggs, cheese and bread," I protested.

He looked at the crumbs on his plate then fished out some coins from his pocket. "Take it," he urged when I refused. "If you don't, I'll never come back, not even for tea."

I took the ells. "Will Balthazar want it accounted for?"

"He gave all the other guards enough money to buy food during our shift. So it's only right I give it to you." He smiled. "He's very strict, not to mention thorough. Not an ell goes unaccounted for. Theodore and I think he had something to do with money in his former life. Perhaps a lender or merchant."

"I'm convinced he was a smuggler," I said, lightly. "He's good with codes and money, and he's very organized. He's not so good with people, though."

"I can't imagine him fleeing very quickly from the authorities."

We laughed. It felt good to laugh with Dane, especially after the tensions of the meeting and the tension between us. It gave me hope that we could manage friendship without needing anything more. Until desire flared again.

There was a knock on the door, and I went to answer it. I was about to tell Dora that she didn't need to knock while she lived here, but it wasn't her or Remy. It was one of my patients, complaining of a pain in her belly. I led her to my father's workshop and checked her before sending her off with nothing more than a smile and reassurance that all was well.

I returned to the kitchen to see Dane sitting exactly where I'd left him, his arms crossed over his chest and head bowed. Dark hair fell across his forehead, and his eyes were closed. He breathed deeply and evenly.

I resisted the urge to kiss the top of his head, and left again so he could sleep in peace.

* * *

CONSIDERING the tensions in the village, it was a surprise to see Kitty and Miranda on my doorstep the following day. It seemed Kitty had made her own way from the carriage to the house without the coachman carrying her over the dirt as he had on her previous visit. She also wore sensible brown shoes. This was a planned visit then, and Miranda hadn't tricked her.

"Come in," I said, stepping aside.

Kitty, being the higher ranked of the two, should enter first, but she hesitated and glanced up and down the street. Miranda gave her a little push.

"I thought it was supposed to be dangerous in the village," Kitty said, stepping inside. "But it's very quiet."

"The presence of the guards and sheriff's men are keeping things calm," I said. I decided not to tell her about the meetings, the angry residents, and the regular fights breaking out in The Row between the two factions. I didn't want to worry her. "If you thought it was going to be dangerous, why did you come?"

"To see you, of course." Miranda paused in the kitchen doorway upon seeing Remy and Dora. "Oh. Good morning."

Dora looked up from the pot she was stirring over the fire and hastily performed a curtsy. "Bow to the ladies, Remy."

Remy grinned and bowed deeply.

"How adorable," Kitty cooed. "What a charming young man. Is he a relative, Josie?"

I made the introductions. Upon hearing their titles, Dora found an excuse to leave and she hustled Remy out, despite his protests.

Kitty frowned. "What did we say to upset her?"

"Nothing," I assured her. "You make her nervous. Come and sit down. Would you like tea?" I inspected the contents of the pot Dora had been stirring. It smelled delicious with the extra herbs she'd gathered the day before steeping nicely.

"We can't stay long," Miranda said. "My parents and Kitty's husband think we're riding around the estate. We've been forbidden from entering Mull after word reached the palace of the riot."

"It wasn't a riot," I said. "Just some fights restricted to The Row."

"Tea would be lovely," Kitty said, taking a seat at the table. "I don't have to leave in a hurry. Miranda is just being polite, but the truth is, my husband doesn't care where I am these days." She stared down at her gloved hands in her lap. "He doesn't care about me at all."

Miranda touched her shoulder and cast me a grim look. "I'm sure that's not true, Kitty," she said. "He loves you dearly. He hovers over you and likes to show you off."

"He *used* to," Kitty mumbled. "Not anymore."

Miranda sighed and sat too. "He has been very busy lately, and he has a lot on his mind since the death of Lord Morgrave."

Kitty sniffed and did not look up. I doubted she was upset by Morgrave's death, nor the affect it had on her husband's plans. Something else bothered her.

I poured tea into cups and passed them around. "Whatever the reason, I'm glad you both came. I enjoy your company."

Kitty gave me a wan smile. "You are a dear, Josie. We have come for a reason, as it happens. Tell her, Miranda. I'll only get it muddled if I try."

Miranda daintily set down the cup and regarded me with her earnest blue-gray eyes. "We overheard Lord Barborough from Vytill talking to both the dukes." She leaned forward and lowered her voice. "About magic."

My fingers tightened around the cup. "What specifically did he say?"

"That the king used magic to create the palace. That he shouldn't be on the throne because he used magic to trick King Alain into believing he had an heir."

"Shocking, isn't it?" Kitty whispered. "I mean, Miranda and I wondered if magic created the palace, but we'd never go so far as to suggest the king isn't the heir."

"As the Vytill king's representative, Lord Barborough must feel safe," Miranda said. "Or he wouldn't have suggested such a thing."

Or he knew his audience well enough to know they wouldn't reveal what he said. "He also knows he has limited time left here," I added, recalling what Dane had told me only yesterday. "With Lady Morgrave now free to marry the king, he must know he'll be sent back to Vytill soon."

Miranda and Kitty nodded gravely.

I was reminded of Lord Xavier's request for me to spy on the Duke of Gladstow for him. This was precisely the sort of information he wanted me to find out from Kitty. Thankfully his mother had stepped in, and they no longer thought it important to spy on the dukes now that Lady Morgrave was likely to become queen. Still, it worried me that I was in possession of the information. What if Lord Xavier defied his mother and decided he wanted me to spy, after all?

"How did you overhear their meeting?" I asked.

"Miranda was helping me choose an outfit for riding," Kitty said. "We were in the wardrobe when we heard voices in the bedchamber. It was such an odd place to hear men speaking that we decided not to reveal ourselves."

"People only meet in bedchambers for utmost privacy," Miranda said. "No other room in the palace is entirely safe."

"And what did the dukes think of Lord Barborough's accusation?" I asked.

"They scoffed at first. They told him he was a fool for believing such nonsense. Then Barborough listed the reasons why he suspected magic. He was very convincing."

Kitty and Miranda exchanged knowing glances.

"He convinced both of you, too?" I asked.

Kitty nodded. Miranda met my gaze levelly. "It makes sense, but it seems so...fantastical. When magic was first suggested to me, by my maid some weeks ago, I dismissed it. When Kitty wanted to look for clues pointing to magic around the palace, I went along with it to pass the time of day. I didn't truly believe it. But now, hearing someone of Barborough's standing talk about it with such credibility... I think I believe him."

"My husband and the Duke of Buxton believe now, too," Kitty said. "They certainly seemed very interested and asked a lot of questions."

"Of course they're interested," Miranda told her. "You know why."

Kitty covered her ears. "Don't say it. I can't bear to think of Gladstow being involved in, in..."

"Treason," I finished for her.

Kitty looked as if she would be ill. "He's going to get himself into awful trouble if he keeps listening to that horrid Lord Barborough. If the king found out, Gladstow would lose his head."

"Then perhaps you can get yourself a kinder husband," Miranda said.

"Miranda!" Kitty cried, lowering her hands. "I can't believe you'd say such a thing."

"He isn't treating you very well, lately. You've been moping about the palace, and I know he's the reason. Tell us what's wrong. Perhaps we can help."

Kitty shook her head and sipped her tea. "It's nothing. I'll be all right."

Miranda sighed.

I wondered if the Duke of Gladstow's change toward his wife coincided with seeing Miranda's mother again after so many years. He claimed to still be in love with Lady Claypool, although he'd behaved despicably toward her on the night of the revels. Neither Kitty nor Miranda knew about that, and it was best it stayed that way.

I decided to return the discussion to less personal matters, lest I say something I shouldn't. "Why are you telling me about Barborough meeting the dukes, anyway?"

"We didn't know who to tell," Miranda said with a fluid shrug of her shoulders. "We don't want to get the dukes into trouble, but we do want to know what those at the palace think. You know the servants better than we do, Josie."

"You're very friendly with the guards," Kitty added. "One in particular."

I didn't like lying to them, but I couldn't tell them about the memory loss. I wouldn't break my promise to Dane.

"We know the servants have discussed the idea that magic created the palace," Miranda said. "But only among themselves. My maid, Hilda, overheard them, but they wouldn't speak directly about it to her. She says they keep to themselves, and none of the visiting servants can glean any information from them about their backgrounds. Don't you think that's odd?"

"Since you're friends with the guards, we thought you could ask them," Kitty said. "I think a direct approach would work best in this case, don't you, Miranda?"

"Most assuredly." Miranda smiled that beautiful smile of hers, the one that had captured the king's heart soon after her arrival, and had all the men in the palace desiring her.

It didn't work on me. "I'm not that close with the guards. If the servants won't talk to your maids, the guards are unlikely to talk to me, either."

"They *must* be hiding something. They *must* know what created the palace."

"Or they're scared."

"Of what?" Miranda asked.

"It's treason for servants to suggest magic put the king on the throne, just as much as it is for dukes."

She nodded, and I was glad my reasoning had got through to her. As curious as she was, she wouldn't endanger anyone by pressuring them for answers.

"I think it's best if we don't mention it again," I said. "Let the pieces fall where they may."

Miranda sat back with a sigh. "I don't like doing nothing."

"Sometimes doing nothing is the best course for everyone."

"I cannot imagine my husband doing nothing if he thinks magic is involved," Kitty said. "Nor the Duke of Buxton."

It was a sobering thought, and one that had us sitting in silence as we finished our tea. I only hoped Dane was right, and the dukes wouldn't dare try and overthrow the king if they believed he possessed magical powers. Looking at Kitty's worried face, however, I wasn't sure we could trust the dukes to be sensible.

CHAPTER 6

I hoped to get word to Dane in The Row that I needed to speak to him. He needed to know that Lord Barborough was meeting with Glancia's two dukes in secret, attempting to stir them into action against King Leon. I wasn't sure what he'd do with the information, but the more information he possessed, the better.

The problem was, he wasn't in The Row, according to Erik. The Marginer was on duty at the slum's main entrance, along with another guard, and informed me that Dane was at the palace.

"The king wanted him," Erik said.

"Why?" I asked.

Erik shrugged those massive shoulders of his, causing his armor to clank. "He is jealous? He likes Hammer near. He does not like to share him."

The other guard rolled his eyes. "You make it sound like something it ain't."

Erik frowned. "I do not understand."

"Obviously." To me, the guard said, "The king thinks the captain of the guards should be at the palace, not here. He thinks the village is the sheriff's concern."

"You two are still here," I pointed out. "What about the rest of the men on duty in The Row?"

"There ain't as many of us. The sheriff reckons the situation is under control."

"Is that what you think?"

"We do not think." Erik tapped his helmet at his temple. The metal plate covered his forehead tattoos but not the twisted ropes of hair. The ends stuck out and cascaded down his back. "We just take orders." He looked past me and smiled. "Good. We go home now."

Ten guards rode toward us, their armor glinting in the sunlight. I didn't realize until they joined us that Sergeant Brant led them. He eyed me from beneath his helmet.

"What are you doing here?" he barked as most of his men continued through to The Row.

"Talking," I said.

"Civilians should be moved on quickly," he told Erik and the other guard.

"Come, Josie," Erik said. "I take you home."

"She can make her own way. She's just a civilian now, and she's been no help to us."

Erik straightened in the saddle. "She has been much help. She helped me, and Quentin—the king, too."

Brant looked around before saying, "I mean with our memories. She hasn't found a cure."

"Maybe we are not sick," Erik shot back. "You know this, Sergeant. You say that magic made us like this. That is not Josie's fault. She cannot cure us if there is no cure."

Brant moved up alongside Erik. "Go away, Marginer. I don't want to see your ugly face for the rest of the day."

Erik grunted. "You need Balthazar's spectacles."

"And a mirror," muttered another guard too far from Brant for him to hear.

I walked away, hoping that might diffuse some of the tension between them. I didn't get far when Erik, the guard who'd been on duty with him, Max and seven other guards rode up to me.

"Are you all right, Josie?" Max asked. "Erik told me what Brant said."

"Fine, thank you." I smiled up at him. "Are you returning to the palace now?"

He nodded.

"May I come? I need to speak to the captain."

Erik patted the saddle in front of him. "Give me your hand."

Since no one else offered, I put out my hand to Erik, and he hoisted me onto the saddle in front of him.

We set off at a walking pace, leaving Mull behind. The guards always attracted attention in the village, but even more so dressed in armor. Friends stared and asked in horror why I was under arrest. I was relieved once we reached the open road. We passed fewer people I knew, although there were still numerous delivery carts heading to and from the palace, as well as travelers going into the village.

Erik and Max rode at the front of the cohort of guards, maintaining a steady yet unhurried pace. Two more guards quickened their pace to join us. I could see from their faces that they had something to say to me, but neither wanted to speak up.

"Out with it," Max finally ordered them.

"If it's a medical matter," I said before they could speak, "you may wait until we're alone."

"Why?" Erik asked. He rode with one hand on the reins, the other resting on his armored thigh. He rode with even more ease than Dane, his body moving fluidly with the horse. Marginers were said to be good horsemen, and I could believe it.

"Because it might be private," I told him. "Not everyone likes to talk about their ailments in public."

"Like my wart? Do you have warts on your little friend too?" Erik asked the guards.

"No!" one cried.

The other clicked his tongue. "Why do you have to mention your cock in every discussion, Erik?"

"Because it is important to me. Like food is to you, Ray."

The guard named Ray glanced down at his armor plated stomach.

"And like Josie is to Hammer," Erik added.

I swiveled to see him better. "He talks about me?"

"Of course."

"What do you two want?" Max barked at the guards.

Ray cleared his throat. "We were thinking about how we asked you to find a cure for memory loss that first day you came to the garrison, Josie. We wanted to know if you're still looking for a cure."

"I am, but it's not easy. I'm not sure there is a cure."

"Not of the medical kind, you mean?" asked the other guard.

I nodded.

He dropped his head. "So you think Brant's right and magic did this?"

"I don't know. I'm sorry."

"Some of us thought about asking the new village doctor," Ray said.

"Merdu, don't do that. You can't trust anyone."

Max pointed a gloved finger at Ray. "Do *not* discuss this with outsiders. Not without the captain's permission."

"Aye, sir," the second guard said. He dropped back to ride with the rest of the guards but Ray remained.

"It's just that the new doctor only recently arrived from the college in Logios, didn't he?" he asked.

"I believe so," I said.

"So his knowledge is up to date. He'll know if something like this has been reported in recent years, whereas Doctor Cully wouldn't." He chewed the inside of his cheek and gave me an apologetic shrug.

"Ray!" Max snapped. "Don't be disrespectful."

"It's all right," I told him. "I would say the same thing, in his position. While I can't be certain Doctor Ashmole isn't aware of a cure, I highly doubt it. Something like this, happening to so many at once, would have made news all over The Fist." I smiled gently at him. "Mull isn't that much of a backwater anymore."

He smiled sadly back. "I won't ask him if you think it best not to."

"I do."

The guards went directly to the kitchen when we arrived at the palace, and I made my way to the garrison alone, hoping to find Dane there, or ask one of the guards where to find him. The garrison was empty, however, so I headed back to the commons. It was a pleasant day and many nobles were out, crossing the fore-courts on their way to the coach house or stables beyond the gate, or being carried in a sedan chair. Others merely ambled in small groups, seeming to have nowhere to go. Most were women, of course. The king had asked for eligible ladies and their parents to be presented to him at court, not their brothers, hence so few young noblemen were present. Those who had come had defied the king's orders or, in the case of the Deerhorns, were near neighbors and invited out of politeness.

That was why Lord Barborough stood out. Being in his thirties, he was a rare find at court, and I would have suspected more of the ladies to flirt with him, simply for something to do. But almost every time I saw him, he was with men or alone.

He was alone now, standing near the end of the southern pavilion at the edge of the large forecourt. He saw me and pushed off from the wall. I picked up my pace and hurried past the pavilion. Once in the breezeway between pavilion and commons, I felt safe. The area was frequented by servants hurrying between the main service building and the palace. I belonged among these people and blended in. The well-dressed and aloof Barborough did not.

I glanced behind me and was relieved to see that he hadn't followed. I headed into the kitchen only to be shouted at by the cook to get out of his domain. One of his assistants took pity on me and told me the guards were in the servants' dining room. It wasn't mealtime, so they sat alone at one of the dozens of long tables, sharing a platter of chicken.

Max raised his tankard of ale when he saw me. Ray beckoned me over and Erik offered me a chicken leg, but I declined. He poured me a cup of ale instead.

"The captain wasn't there," I told them.

"He might be attending the king at his picnic," Max said. "The kitchen hands told us they've been busy all morning preparing a feast for the king and thirty of his favorites."

"They're in the garden somewhere," Ray said. "You might as well eat with us while you wait."

Erik passed me the plate of chicken again. I was starving. My meager diet had been made even more pathetic since the arrival of Dora and Remy. Dora refused to eat most of the time, but I couldn't let her go hungry, so I assured her I had money to buy more supplies from the market and even told her I'd dined out at The Anchor the night before so she wouldn't worry. She and Remy had spent two days foraging in the forest for berries or edible mushrooms, but hadn't come home with much. Every woman in the village foraged these days. The forest was almost as busy as the dock. A mere year ago, I could search for ingredients for my medicines and not come across another soul all day.

I ate with the guards and considered keeping some of the chicken for Remy and Dora, but there was nothing left by the time they finished. I returned with them to the garrison afterward. Some sat at the table and continued to nibble at the cheese and bread supply, while others left altogether to get some rest in the adjoining dormitory.

Max seemed to want to stay and talk to me, however, and he waited until we were alone before moving his chair closer. "How is Meg?" he asked. "And her family?"

"Fine," I said.

"She looked upset after the village meeting."

"She was angry that Ivor Morgrain forced me to speak up." I smiled. "She gets indignant when her friends aren't treated well."

"She's a good woman."

"She is."

He sighed. "I wish she'd talk to me."

"Give her time."

"She won't even look at me."

I touched his arm. "Don't give up if you truly like her."

"If she won't talk to me, how will I get to know her?" He sat back, breaking our contact. "I s'pose it doesn't matter. I can't start something with her until I know more about myself anyway."

It was my turn to sigh and slump into the chair. "I understand."

The door opened and Dane strode in with Quentin. They both looked surprised to see me, although Dane hid it better. He unbuckled his sword belt and hung it by the door, but Quentin forgot. He held his arms out and I stood to embrace him.

"Is one of the maids with child?" he asked. "It's Gruda, isn't it? I knew she'd be the first."

"No one is with child," I said, laughing. "And don't say that to Gruda's face."

He grinned. "I wouldn't dare. She scares me." He tore off a chunk of bread and stuffed it into his mouth. "I'm starving," he said around the mouthful. "All that food at the picnic, and I weren't allowed to eat any. I had to stand there and watch. It ain't fair."

"Josie," Dane said with the stiffness he'd adopted when speaking to me lately. I missed the interlude at my house when he'd returned to his usual friendly self. It had been too brief.

"Captain," I said, matching his tone. "May we speak alone?"

"Of course." To Max, he said, "Anything to report from the village?"

"Nothing of note, sir. Everything has calmed down considerably since my previous shift."

Dane nodded approval.

"Sounds like it's all blown over," Quentin said, still chewing.

"Or they're biding their time." Dane collected his sword belt and opened the door for me. "Will Balthazar's office suffice?"

I nodded. "He should hear this, anyway."

We didn't speak as we walked along the corridors, and the tension shrouded us. I scrambled to think of something to diffuse it, but everything sounded pathetic in my head.

I was grateful to reach Balthazar's office. Dane opened the door without knocking and the master of the palace didn't seem at all surprised.

"What is it, Hammer?" he asked, without looking up.

"Josie needs to speak with us," Dane said.

Balthazar regarded me over the rim of his spectacles then his gaze shifted to Dane. He grunted. "You two look unhappy. Care to confide the reason?"

"I've just come from the king's picnic," Dane said, as if that explained his mood.

Balthazar removed his spectacles and placed them on the desk. He clasped his hands together over his stomach. "How terrible. You had to listen to talk of parties, theater, and fashion. The ladies flirted outrageously with the king, although some of them made eyes at you when he wasn't looking."

I arched my brows at Balthazar. Beside me, Dane shifted his weight from foot to foot.

Balthazar merely smiled. "How is the grieving widow?"

"She fed the king strawberries while he rested his head on her lap. She laughed at his jokes, even the terrible ones, and didn't discourage his roaming hands."

"No wonder you're in a bad mood after witnessing that." Balthazar waved a hand at the tray with the jug of wine and cups on the table by the wall. "Have a drink."

"Later. I want to hear what Josie has to say."

Balthazar indicated I should sit. "Has something happened in the village? More unrest?"

"It's relatively quiet," I said, "although there's an undercurrent of tension. But that's not why I came. I had a visit from Kitty and Miranda."

Balthazar's bushy brows wriggled like grubs up his forehead. "That is interesting. It must have been important for them to venture into the village at a time like this."

"They overheard Lord Barborough speaking to the two dukes in the bedchamber Kitty shares with her husband. He was telling them his theory about magic and the creation of the palace."

Balthazar expelled a breath then went very still. It resembled the last moments of a dying man and would have been alarming if he hadn't suddenly sat forward with more vigor than I'd expect from him. "Did the dukes seem to believe him?"

I nodded. "And now Kitty and Miranda do too. They won't discuss it with anyone," I assured him. "They know how dangerous such talk can be."

Balthazar appeared to be lost in thought and no longer listening.

"It was a logical move for Barborough to make," Dane said. "With Lord Morgrave out of the way, and Lady Morgrave likely to become queen, Barborough had to change tactic. It wouldn't surprise me if it was a directive from King Phillip of Vytill."

"What do you mean?" I asked.

"With an alliance between Glancia and Vytill through marriage looking less and less likely, King Phillip will need to take over Glancia another way."

"He'll want the dukes to overthrow the king," I finished. "Then he'll swoop in while they're squabbling."

"It remains to be seen if the dukes are foolish enough to fulfill their part. They don't know the king doesn't have access to the sorcerer's gem anymore."

If they did find out, they wouldn't waste time accusing the king of being an imposter and gathering their forces against him.

"You're both forgetting something," Balthazar said. "Lady Morgrave isn't queen yet." A wicked gleam brightened his eyes. "Thank you for informing us, Josie. Hammer, you need to watch the dukes."

Dane nodded.

"The captain has his hands full at the moment," I said. "Can't you or Theodore do it?"

Balthazar smirked. "How considerate of you to worry about him."

"Exhaustion can lead to health problems."

"Ah. Professional concern then, is it? Forgive me, I didn't recognize it, what with the way you two look at one another."

"That's enough, Bal," Dane warned him. To me, he said, "I won't be personally watching them. One of Buxton's footmen is spying for me, and the maids who clean Gladstow's apartments report in whenever they discover something of interest."

"Oh," I said, feeling foolish. Of course he had spies all over the palace.

"It's all right, Josie," Balthazar said. "We'll have you thinking like us in no time."

"Don't listen to him," Dane said. "We're not all like him, suspicious of everyone and questioning everything."

"Not to mention cantankerous," I added. "And a know-it-all."

Balthazar grunted. "Not all." He picked up his spectacles and put them on. "If you don't mind, some of us are busy."

Dane and I left him, only to be met by Theodore rushing along the corridor. He was out of breath by the time he reached us. "Thank goodness you're still here, Josie. The king wishes to see you."

"Me? Why?"

"He has a pain in his chest."

I hesitated. The king had asked me to see to his medical problems before, and I'd always complied. He was, after all, the king. But it really shouldn't go on. It *couldn't*.

"Perhaps Doctor Clegg can attend," I said.

"He asked for you." Theodore set off, expecting me to follow. "You too, Hammer. And hurry. He's in a strange mood."

"He was happy when I left him," Dane said, walking beside me.

"You know how quickly he can change. Why are you here anyway, Josie?"

"I'll tell you later," Dane said.

Theodore glanced over his shoulder at us to make sure we followed.

"How did the king know I was at the palace?" I asked.

"When he complained of chest pains, Lady Morgrave suggested he call for Doctor Clegg, but he said he'd rather have you. A footman overheard and informed the king he'd seen you at the palace."

We headed up a set of stairs then along another corridor. "How long has he had the chest pains?" I asked.

Theodore paused at a door. "This is the first I've heard of it. After what happened to Lord Morgrave, he's worried."

I was about to remind him that Lord Morgrave hadn't died of heart failure but realized, from his expression, that he didn't need reminding. But the king hadn't heard the rumors, and he certainly didn't know that I believed Morgrave had been poisoned.

"Be careful what you say to allay his fears," Dane warned me quietly.

Theodore pushed open the door and we found ourselves in a large salon where ladies clustered in small groups by open windows, talking and flapping their fans. A few tried to catch Dane's eye, and failed, but the rest ignored us.

We passed through the blue and white tiled antechamber housing a throne, then onto the opulently furnished sitting room and games room where more noblewomen gathered. They looked hot and bored. One elderly lady had fallen asleep on a velvet sofa, her head tipped back and mouth ajar. We passed through the king's private dining room, where he could dine with dozens of his closest friends, then another room before reaching the library and office. Dane nodded at the guard standing by the door to the king's bedchamber as Theodore knocked.

The king bade us enter. I performed a low curtsy, only rising when the king ordered me to do so.

"Dearest Josie," he said, taking my hand in both of his. "I am so glad to see you again. Your beauty is a sight for sore eyes."

"You flatter me, Your Majesty. I've seen the ladies here at court and there are many beauties."

"True." He leaned closer and whispered, "But the greatest beauties possess more than a pretty face." He squeezed my hand then let it go.

I cast a sideways glance at Dane. He remained by the door, his arms crossed over his chest, his gaze hooded. "You wanted to see us, sire?" he asked.

The king pointed to me. "Josie first. You two, wait outside."

"No," Dane said. "As with the last time, I won't leave Josie alone with you. She has a—"

"A reputation to uphold. Yes, yes, I know." The king sighed. "You're no fun, Hammer. No fun at all." He flopped onto the big bed and stretched out his arms. "Unfasten my shirt, Josie."

"I'll do it," Theodore said, coming forward. "It's my job to dress and undress you, sire. You don't wish to make me obsolete, do you?"

The king lifted his chin so Theodore could untie his cravat. "You know I can't do without you, Theo, so stop fishing for compliments. It's tiring."

"Yes, sire."

The exchange was somewhat awkward, particularly while Theodore undressed his master. The process of removing the cravat and unfastening the hooks on the king's jerkin seemed to take forever.

"Did you enjoy your picnic, Your Majesty?" I asked to fill the uncomfortable silence.

"I did, until the pain started." He winced and swallowed heavily. "There it is again. It's excruciating. Here." He rubbed his chest. "Hurry up, Theo. I could die waiting."

Theodore finished unlacing the shirt and drew it over the king's head. The king's dark hair, dampened from sweat, formed spikes on the top of his head.

"Describe the pain," I said, placing a hand over the king's chest. His heart beat at a healthy speed.

"It's a burning feeling that rises into my throat."

"Have you felt the pain before?"

"These last few days. It's not constant, but comes and goes."

"After eating?"

"Yes. What is it, Josie? What's wrong with me?"

I asked him a few more questions before declaring he had no serious illness. "You're quite healthy, but you shouldn't eat so much rich food. That's what's giving you the chest pains and burning sensation."

He frowned. "Are you sure?"

"Yes."

"It's just that Violette told me her husband seemed healthy before he died. He didn't experience any symptoms."

I stood back to allow Theodore to dress the king.

"Yet I *do* feel a pain in my heart," the king went on. "Surely that's an indication of something."

"It is," I said. "It's an indication that you shouldn't eat so much of the cook's delicious food. Ask him to give you more vegetables, fish and lean meats, rather than cakes and sweets."

The king straightened, drawing in his stomach, although he didn't succeed in hiding the paunch. "I'm not a glutton."

"That's not what she meant," Dane said.

The king relaxed again once his shirt covered his body. "I think I'll ask Doctor Clegg some questions."

"Please do," I said.

"Do not mention you asked Josie first," Dane warned him. "You know the law, and she's not above it. Not even when she works for you."

The king sniffed. "I must get around to changing that law. Theodore, make a note of it. I'll mention it in the next council meeting."

"Yes, sire. And might I add that I think it's an excellent idea. Josie should be allowed to get her qualification from Logios, just like the men."

The king pushed Theodore away as the valet tried to re-tie his cravat. "Stop fussing, Theo. I'm going to rest for the remainder of the day."

Theodore bowed. "Very good, sire. We'll leave you in peace."

"One moment, Hammer. I want you to fetch something." The king glanced at me. "The cabinet that used to be housed in there." He flapped a hand toward his wardrobe. "Bring it to me."

I froze. Theodore also went very still, except for his gaze. It darted between the king and Dane.

"Of course," Dane said smoothly. "I have to leave for the village now, but I can tell one of my men where I hid it, and he can bring it to you."

"No! Merdu, don't tell anyone where it is. That's why I entrusted *you* with it." He glanced at me again then away. "I simply want to see my family heirloom. It gives me comfort. Hammer, forget the village. That's the governor's problem, not mine. Fetch my cabinet."

Dane bowed. I waited for him to make up another excuse, but he did not. He simply followed Theodore and me out of the room.

We headed back the way we'd come in silence, finally breaking it when we reached the service corridor. Theodore closed the door to the salon and collapsed against it.

"What will you do, Hammer?" he whispered. He squeezed the bridge of his nose and added, "Merdu. It hasn't arrived yet."

It took me a moment to recall that "it" was the replica jewel being created by a Tilting jeweler. "It hasn't?" I asked on a groan. "But what will you do?"

"Distract him," Dane said.

"How?" Theodore hissed.

"You could give him the real one," I said. "Just this once. Let him see it inside the cabinet then put it back."

"And what if he wants to use it?" Dane asked. "We don't know what the gem does, but we have to assume it holds formidable power. Why do you think he wants it now?"

Theodore shrugged, but I was beginning to make sense of it. "Because he's afraid for his life," I said. "Lord Morgrave's death has rattled him and now he thinks he has a heart condition too. If that gem holds power, he might use it to make him healthy again. But he's not sick, so it doesn't matter."

"What if he uses it to do something else, something we haven't thought of?" Dane asked. "It's too much of a risk. I don't want to give him the gem. Not if there's something we can do to distract him."

"I ask again," Theodore said, "How?"

"A party. Something grand. He likes revels." Dane set off.

Theodore and I raced to keep up with his long strides. "But Balthazar needs time to prepare," Theodore said. "The party needs to be tonight or your plan won't work."

"Then Balthazar had better start now. Shall you tell him or will I?"

"You're armed; you do it."

We reached a fork in the corridors, and Dane stopped. "The garrison's that way, and Balthazar's office is this way. Are you coming with me, Josie?"

"As much as I'd like to see Balthazar lose his temper with you, I'd better leave. I suspect you're all about to get very busy."

Theodore clapped Dane on the shoulder. "Good luck. He won't be happy."

"When is Bal ever happy?"

I left Theodore in the garrison and headed outside, intending to leave immediately, however Lady Deerhorn stopped me before I even reached the forecourt. She must have been waiting for me.

I tried to move past her, but she grabbed my arm. "What are you doing here?" she hissed in my ear.

"Making a private call," I said.

"You can't do that. Wait until the sheriff hears."

"It wasn't a medical call."

"No? Then why did the king send for you?"

Merdu. Gossip spread faster than fire in the palace. I pulled free and lifted my chin. "Ask the king."

She struck me across the face.

I stumbled backward and put a hand to my cheek, too shocked to protest.

She advanced on me, and I stumbled backward to keep out of her reach. "Did you tell him your lies about Morgrave?" she said through clenched teeth. "Is it *you* spreading the rumors about Morgrave's death not being from heart failure?"

"No."

"I know you disagree with Clegg's diagnosis. He told me himself."

My back hit the wall of the palace. I was trapped. Lady Deerhorn's eyes lit up with a wicked, cruel gleam. "I asked you a question and I expect an answer. What have you been saying?"

My hands started to shake so I fisted them at my sides. I thrust out my jaw in a show of defiance when all I felt was powerless. "Nothing about Lord Morgrave's death." I didn't want her to see my fear, but my shaking voice betrayed me. "I can assure you, the king still thinks Lord Morgrave died of heart failure. The rumors haven't reached his ears."

Her lips stretched into a tight smile. "If he does find out, I'll know who to blame." She edged aside, allowing me to pass.

I ran off toward the pavilion, only glancing back when I felt safe. She was no longer there.

I blew out a shuddery breath and took a moment to gather my wits in the shadows. Lady Deerhorn must be very worried that I'd give the king my opinion of Lord Morgrave's death to accost me in the open like that. She knew he trusted my medical knowledge. It was the most damning proof we'd had that her family orchestrated the murder.

I considered returning to the garrison to tell Dane but decided against it. Lady Deerhorn might still be waiting nearby.

Instead, I headed for the gate. Hopefully one of the coachmen would drive me back to Mull. I didn't feel like walking, not after that meeting. There were too many trees lining Grand Avenue which would provide a good hiding spot for someone who might wish to jump out at me. I'd had my fill of surprising encounters for one day.

I was stopped before I reached the gate, however, but not by a Deerhorn. A footman dressed in a visiting nobleman's livery asked if I was the midwife. I didn't recognize his uniform as belonging to one of the main houses of Glancian nobles, but there were so many that I didn't know them all.

"I am," I told him.

"Will you return with me to the palace, miss?" he asked, head bowed. "It's my lady. She has need of you."

"Did she specifically ask for a midwife? Not a doctor?"

He nodded and glanced around. Then he stepped forward and whispered, "She says it's something of a delicate nature that only you can help with."

"Show me the way. The back way," I added, as we walked to the palace. "Through the service corridors."

We entered the palace through a service door and followed the series of winding corridors and staircases to the second floor that housed the attic apartments where Miranda now lived with her family. We headed south and finally emerged into a corridor painted in cool blue and cream. Large blue vases stood sentinel beside each of the dozens of doors along the corridor, all containing a spectacular display of summer flowers. Despite an ornately plastered ceiling, there was no gold leaf in sight in this part of the palace. There were certainly many paintings in gold frames, including one very prominent one of the king at the end, standing with one hand on his hip, the palace in the background.

It was hot and airless this far up in the palace. I didn't know how the nobles could stand it. My first directive to the woman, if she proved to be with child, would be to get as much fresh air as she could.

The footman knocked lightly on a door then opened it. He smiled and asked me to go through. I stepped across the threshold, but he didn't follow. He shut the door, revealing Lord Barborough standing there.

Before I could even gasp, he slammed me back against the door, knocking the breath out of me. He pressed his arm against my chest, pinning me. I coughed and tried to pull free, but with all his weight bearing down on his arm, I couldn't move.

"Time has run out, Josie." He eased back but when I tried to move, he slammed me into the door again. "I have lost my patience with you."

CHAPTER 7

*M*y vision blurred and my head hurt as Lord Barborough shoved me against the door a third time. "P-please, my lord," I begged. "Stop."

"Do you have any information for me?"

"Yes," I said, my voice cracking.

"Then why didn't you come and find me?"

"I was on my way."

He wrapped his fingers around my throat and thrust his face close to mine. The smell of cloves didn't hide the stink of his breath. "You were leaving."

I struggled and pushed against his chest, but that only caused him to tighten his grip. My throat ached, and my eyes bulged.

"I-I have something for you," I croaked.

He let me go. I bent forward, coughing and gasping in as much air as possible.

"Well?" he snapped.

I drew in several deep breaths to give myself precious moments to remember the lies I'd fabricated with Dane, Balthazar and Theodore.

"I'm waiting," he barked.

"The maids I've spoken to all have different stories of how they got here. One came from a village in the south of Freedland, another from the north, and another from Dreen. They heard about the palace requiring maids and came here to apply. Some were without family in their homeland, others were glad to leave behind abusive relatives. All wanted to make the long journey for a new start."

"Without knowing if they would be offered a position?"

"It's what they said, my lord."

He folded his arm over his chest and grasped his other, limp one at the elbow. "What prior experience did they have of being in service?"

"Two of them claimed to have worked for noble families in their homeland."

"Which noble families?"

"I didn't ask, my lord."

"Why not?"

"I don't know the noble houses of other kingdoms, so their answers would have meant nothing to me."

He stepped closer and sneered. "You're lying."

"No!"

"Freedland doesn't have nobles anymore. Those who didn't lose their heads during the revolution were stripped of their titles."

Merdu, I was a fool. How could I have made such an obvious mistake? "I-I mean prominent families, not nobles. They worked for the rich."

"Stupid girl." He raised his hand to strike me.

I flung my arms over my face and ducked.

"You're lying to me," he snarled. "Why? Why are you keeping the truth from me?"

"No, sir, I'm not lying! If they are lies, then I am the one who has been lied to. They don't like talking to outsiders. I can't befriend them." I turned the door handle at my back.

He slammed his hand against the door, an inch from my face. "I haven't finished with you yet. Stand over there." He jerked his head to the center of the sitting room, away from the door.

I did as ordered, keeping him in my line of sight. My heart thumped madly in my chest, but I still had my wits. I glanced around for a weapon, and my gaze fell on the candlestick on the desk. I inched my way toward it.

"Stop there!" he snapped. "No further."

I stopped too far away from anything that could be used as a weapon.

"Don't treat me like a fool, Mistress Cully." His voice was steadier and his eyes no longer held the glint of madness. Yet he looked as if he would spring toward me if I dared move.

"You frighten me too much for me to risk lying."

He looked satisfied, either with my answer or the effect he had on me.

"I've tried my best, but the maids are not very forthcoming with information. I'm an outsider. They don't trust me."

"And the captain of the guards? Does he trust you? Rumor has it you two are intimate."

"We're not."

"I've seen you together. You must know something about him."

"Nothing about his past. I've tried asking him, but he brushes off my questions and changes the subject. I've tried…encouraging him to take me to his chambers, but he sleeps in the room next to the king and won't take women there. I'm sorry, my lord, but what else can I do?"

He strode up to me and thrust his finger at my face. "Try again, and again, and again," he snarled. "Until you learn something useful. Search the maids' rooms, the master of the palace's office, anything! Merdu, I thought you were smarter than this." He paced the floor in front of the door like a restless guard dog.

"And I thought you fair and reasonable," I shot back.

He didn't seem to hear me as he continued to pace and mutter under his breath. "He won't be happy… I need answers…"

I eyed the door. I couldn't reach it without him catching me. I needed to draw him away from it or make him let me go of his own free will. Fighting him off wouldn't work. Even with one functioning arm, he was stronger than me.

"My lord, if I may ask," I ventured. "If magic were involved, shouldn't it be best left alone? Meddling might be dangerous."

"It might be," he agreed. "But the truth must be discovered, whatever the cost."

"For Glancia's sake?" I asked, pretending not to understand what was at stake for his king and Vytill.

"For *my* sake."

"Yours?"

He looked at me and I saw real panic in his eyes. I'd thought it was madness, but now I realized he hadn't lost his mind. He was scared of something. Scared enough to confide in me, perhaps the only person in the palace he *could* confide in.

"If I don't return home with information, I'll be executed," he said.

I gasped. "Is that how your king punishes those who fail?"

He looked away. "It was the agreement we came to after my predecessor died."

According to Kitty, Lord Barborough had murdered the man originally chosen to be Vytill's representative to Glancia so that he could come here and study the palace and magic for himself. If that rumor were true, it would explain why Barborough's life was in danger if he didn't succeed in gathering information. King Philip must have used the threat of execution for murder to make Barborough do his utmost, either to organize a marriage alliance or find out if King Leon used magic. Perhaps both.

If the rumor were true, it meant Barborough was more desperate than I realized. And more ruthless.

I inched toward the door. "I have to leave now. I'm expected elsewhere."

He stared at the floor near his feet and did not look up.

Then I stepped too close. His hand whipped out and grabbed my elbow. "Very well," he said with a calmness I didn't expect. "I'll let you go. But you now have a new task. Forget the information gathering. I want you to find the gemstone."

I concentrated on looking innocent. "A what?"

"Don't pretend you don't know what I'm talking about. I know you've heard of the king's magic gem."

"You're mistaken. I—"

He shook me violently. "*Enough* of your play acting! You are aware of the gem. That is a fact."

I swallowed. "I am aware of it, yes. But I don't know what it does."

"It controls the sorcerer."

My heart rose. "So whoever possesses the gem can ask the sorcerer for three wishes?"

"No. Only the person who *found* the gem can. The one who merely possesses it can't take that power away. But the one who found it must have the gem in his possession to use his wishes."

That's why the king wanted the gem back—he did want to use one of his wishes. Unfortunately it also confirmed that Dane couldn't take the sorcerer's power for himself.

"Find the gem for me, Mistress Cully."

"But if you can't take the sorcerer's power for yourself, why do you want the gem?"

"That is none of your concern. You simply need to find it. Do you understand?"

"Yes."

"Find it and bring it to me. You have two days." He let me go.

I opened the door and ran my finger along the wall until I found the hidden entrance to the service corridors. Once inside, I let out a long, shuddery breath.

Then I went in search of Dane.

He wasn't in the garrison, but Quentin assured me he would return soon and invited me to wait. "Did you hear?" he asked as he handed me a cup of ale. "There's going to be a party tonight."

I drank deeply, settling my nerves a little. "Will it involve theatricals and music like the last one?"

He shrugged. "Balthazar hasn't told anyone his plans."

That was probably because Balthazar didn't know what they were yet. "You're lucky that you get to see it. All those beautiful dresses, the music and dancing."

"The food. Lots and lots of food. If we're lucky, they won't eat it all and we'll get the leftovers tomorrow. That's if the kitchen staff don't keep it to themselves. Cooks are the worst gluttons."

I smiled, feeling a little more myself again. The garrison felt safe, and Quentin's innocence was refreshing after the intrigue and danger of Lord Barborough.

"Have you seen how fat they're getting?" said one of the other guards resting his booted feet on the table. "They never used to be so big."

"Whatever they did before they came here, it wasn't working in a kitchen," said the second guard.

"Not with as much good food leftover anyway," Quentin added thoughtfully.

The first guard lowered his feet to the ground and sat forward. "Some of us were real scrawny back then. Do you remember?"

The second guard frowned. "Aye, I do. On that first day, I was starving. When they fed us, I ate until I threw up."

"So did I," Quentin said. "But I also remember that not everyone was skinny. Many were, but not all."

Did that mean they hadn't all come from the same place? Had they lived quite different lives? Other evidence would suggest so. Some men had scars on their backs, others didn't. They were from different countries on The Fist Peninsula, some of mixed nationality, and even The Margin was represented in Erik, but most seemed to be from Freedland or appeared to have Freedland blood in them. Some had cultured accents and were educated, while others couldn't read or write. Finding a common trait between all of them was impossible.

The door opened but my heart sank to see Balthazar, not Dane. He limped into the garrison, leaning heavily on his walking stick. He clutched a leather folder.

"Why are you still here?" he asked me.

"I need to speak to the captain," I said. "Have you seen him?"

"He's gone to the village."

I sighed. "Then I'd better go too."

"Is it important that you speak to him?"

"Of course, otherwise I wouldn't have remained. Contrary to what you think, Balthazar, I don't particularly like being in the palace lately."

He narrowed his gaze. "If you return to the village, you might miss him. He wasn't going to be gone long. He had a quick meeting with the sheriff and governor."

"Then I'll wait here, if that's all right."

He tapped his finger against the folder and his gaze shifted between each of the guards then finally settled on me again. "This works out perfectly. You're just the person I need, Josie."

"Me?"

"You've got the right amount of authority without being over-bearing." He leaned his walking stick against the table and opened the leather folder. He pulled out a piece of paper and handed it to me. "Read this then follow the instructions, one by one."

The paper was a list of directions to give to members of the outdoor staff. "This is a palace servant's job," I said. "They won't listen to me."

"Take a guard with you. He'll vouch for you and help you find the people you need."

Quentin shot to his feet. "I'll do it."

"Why not just let him do it alone?" I asked Balthazar. "Or one of the footmen or maids?"

"The footmen are all busy delivering invitations and the maids have to do last minute laundry duties. This lot are hopeless. I don't trust them to do the job properly."

"Oi!" one of the guards protested. "You calling us stupid?"

"Yes," Balthazar said.

The guard opened his mouth to protest then shut it again. The other chuckled.

"Go on!" Balthazar made a shooing motion at me. "Time is running out. I have to go to the kitchen and deliver instructions to the cook."

I headed into the service corridors clutching the paper, Quentin at my heels.

"Where's the first stop?" he asked as he strapped on his sword belt.

"The menagerie," I said glancing at the paper. "I didn't know the palace had one."

He pulled a face. "I hate that place."

"Why?"

"It's full of birds and strange creatures."

"Aren't they in cages?"

"Not all of them."

We exited the palace on the western side where the formal gardens looked empty. Most of the nobles must have received their invitations and were busy preparing for the evening. Only a few gentlemen strolled around, talking quietly in small groups, while a clutch of women hurried towards the palace as if they were late for an appointment.

We walked past partitioned gardens with perfectly trimmed

hedges and topiaries, fountains, lawns and slender trees, toward Lake Grand. The sun still hung high in the sky but scudding clouds kept it from becoming too hot. I expected to skirt the lake but Quentin headed towards the boat landing and the four gilded gondolas moored there. A gondolier sat in each boat, some lazily slumped over the pole, while one lay back, his straw hat covering his face.

"Take us to the menagerie, Tallen," Quentin said to a youth.

"Walk, you lazy oaf," Tallen said. "These gondolas are for the guests, not you."

"Mistress Cully is a guest."

Tallen looked me up and down then sniffed. "She ain't a lady guest. We only take—"

"Shut up, Tallen," said another of the gondoliers. He dipped his pole into the water and maneuvered his craft into the gap between Tallen's gondola and the landing. "Hop in, miss. I'm Kenny, Head Gondolier." He touched the brim of his hat. "At your service. Careful, now. Take Quentin's hand."

Quentin assisted me into the boat and I settled on the bench seat. Quentin stepped one foot in, accidentally pushing the gondola away from the landing. With one foot still on the landing, his eyes widened as his legs spread.

"Help!" he cried.

"Jump in," Kenny said. "No, wait!"

His warning came too late. Quentin jumped and fell into the water. Tallen and the other boatmen hooted with laughter. Quentin scowled back at them.

"Let's try that again," Kenny said, trying to contain his grin. "Take Mistress Cully's hand."

Quentin climbed back onto the landing. I stood, settling my feet a little apart for balance, and put out my hand. Quentin took it.

"Bet that happens all the time," he said, stepping into the gondola without incident this time.

"Nope. Never."

"Then you moved away on purpose."

"Mistress Cully managed to get in just fine."

"I was born and bred on the coast," I said, sitting down. "I'm used to boats. This one is quite lovely." I ran my hand over the golden serpent head on the boat's bow. It was smooth and warm.

"I think I was too," Kenny said as he maneuvered us away from the landing. "I feel comfortable on boats. All of us gondoliers do."

Quentin gripped both sides of the boat and watched the water slide past. "Not me."

"I see now why Balthazar asked someone else to deliver his messages," I said, watching Kenny put his back into another stroke. The gondola slid effortlessly across the glassy lake surface. "I can't imagine him walking this far or climbing into one of these."

"Are you helping Balthazar organize the party?" Kenny asked. "The guests disappeared as soon as word reached us. What's Balthazar got planned?"

"You think he tells us?" Quentin said.

"There is an instruction for you on here, Kenny," I said. "He wants all gondoliers working from dusk."

I had begun to piece together Balthazar's plans from his list. There were another two stops we had to make. Firstly to the menagerie; then we had to find the head gardener. From what I could glean from the instructions, the menagerie would be the main site for the evening's entertainments.

Lake Grand was larger than I realized. It was shaped like a t, and it was down the shorter cross-canal that we traveled, finally alighting at another wooden landing after what felt like an age.

When I commented as such to Quentin, he told me it would have taken twice as long to walk. The formal gardens close to the palace had given way to a more rambling structure here, with tree-lined gravel paths winding through groves where waterfalls plunged into clear pools, and rockeries provided seating where the views were best. Finally the trees opened up to reveal a gatehouse and stone wall. Beyond it, something shrieked.

Quentin jumped. "I hate this place."

Several birds responded to the shriek using their own unique calls. It sounded like dozens of musicians tuning up. Quentin covered his ears as we strode through the gate.

The other side was rather disappointing. I'd expected to see animals, but it was just a path cutting through a lush green lawn edged by high stone walls. The building at the end of the path was quite a sight, however. It was made of the same biscuit colored stone as the palace with a gilded balcony rail circling the first level. Like the palace, the domed roof was black slate. A gold spire shot from the center of the dome. As we drew closer, I realized the spire was in fact a spear, and the golden statue of a man held it aloft. It was impossible to tell from a distance if the statue depicted Merdu or the king.

The birds continued to welcome us with their cacophony but I still couldn't see them. Inside, positioned around the edges of the octagonal building were eight large cages, each housing a collection of exotic animals. Three contained different types of monkeys while the remainder housed lizards and snakes, an eagle, a large cat with pointed ears, something small and furry that peered out of its burrow, and a creature sleeping while hanging upside down from a branch.

"Quentin? That you?" asked a woman of middling age. Unlike the maids and other female staff, she wore pants and a jerkin over a shirt. Her hair was dark, with threads of gray through it, cascading in a thick plait down her back. "What're you doing here? You hate this place."

Quentin hadn't taken his eyes off the eagle's cage. "Balthazar's got a message for Wes. Is he here?"

"I'll fetch him." She waited then finally gave a shrug. She thrust out her hand to me. "Looks like he's not going to introduce us. I'm Deanne, one of the keepers."

"Josie," I said. "From Mull."

"The doctor?"

"Midwife," I clarified. "My father was the doctor."

"Right. Sorry."

I wasn't sure if she was apologizing for the mistake or offering sympathy for my father's death. She walked across the mosaic floor and left via a door opposite.

I peered through the cage with the sleeping animal inside. "What a lovely creature. I wonder what it is."

"Don't put your fingers in!" Quentin slapped my hand away from the bars.

"It's asleep," I told him.

"It could be pretending."

"Why would it do that?"

"So it could make a meal of your finger." He glanced at the eagle in the next cage. "Some of these move real fast, and have enormous teeth and claws. I've seen them eat other birds they've caught mid-air." He pulled another face. "It was enough to turn me off my dinner."

"Where are the rest of the animals?"

He nodded at the door through which Deanne had left. "Most are out there in the seven courtyards around this building. You can view the courtyards from a balcony or you can wander through them. The birds are harmless, so Wes reckons, but I've seen their beaks and I ain't going in. There are other animals in pens not far away, but the guests don't see them."

"Why not?"

"Those animals end up in the kitchen."

A short man with thinning gray hair entered with Deanne. He smiled at me, revealing gaps where his teeth were missing.

Quentin wrinkled his nose and stepped back. "You stink, Wes."

"Hazard of the job," he said. "I'm Wes." He put out his hand to me only to withdraw it. "Sorry. Don't touch me. I've been cleaning out the ostrich courtyard."

My brows arched up my forehead. "Ostriches? On The Fist?"

He grinned. "I heard they're not common."

"They don't exist here at all. I've only read about them in books."

"Want to see them?"

"Yes, please."

"Can't," Quentin said. "No time. Balthazar would skin us if he knew we were standing around sightseeing."

"Just a quick look from the balcony," Wes said, leading the way.

"Balcony?" Quentin echoed. "That's all right then."

We climbed a set of stairs to the next level and walked out onto the wraparound balcony. I peered down at the enclosure directly below where six large birds with long necks and reed-thin legs stalked about.

"Ostriches," Wes announced. "They're flightless."

The enclosure was wedge shaped and positioned next to the yard enclosing the path we'd walked along. At one side of the ostrich enclosure was a narrow pavilion made of the same biscuit colored stone as the other buildings on the estate. Two fountains in the middle of the enclosure offered drinking water for the ostriches and the other birds that inhabited it. I recognized a variety of ducks and peacocks, but others were unknown to me.

Wes directed us along the balcony to the next enclosure where pelicans were given the same freedom as their flightless neighbors.

"How do you ensure they stay here and not fly off?" I asked.

"They have everything they want here," Wes said. "Water, food, safety from predators. This is bird paradise."

I wondered if magic had anything to do with it too. They were, after all, as much a part of the sorcerer's plans as the servants.

We continued around the balcony, and Wes pointed out each of the birds in the remaining wedge-shaped courtyards that radiated out from the octagonal central building. I recognized some but not all. I liked the pink flamingoes the best.

"Their fountains pump out saline water," Wes explained. "But none of the other birds like their water salty so that's why the flamingos have the enclosure to themselves."

"You're very knowledgeable," I said as we returned inside.

"We all know our jobs here in the palace."

"Yes, of course."

"So what are these instructions of Balthazar's?" he asked.

I showed him the list. "He wants you to clean out the enclosures and cages, and prepare the animals for a parade."

"What!" he exploded. "I can't do all of this before nightfall!" He shook the list at me then at Quentin. "There isn't enough time!"

"Balthazar's orders," Quentin said, jerking his head at me to indicate we should leave.

Wes shoved the list at Quentin. "Tell him I can't do it. Not for tonight. He needs to think of something else for his party."

"There isn't time," I said. "Balthazar has to work with what's already at the palace. He can't get dancers, musicians or gymnasts at such late notice." I took the list from Wes and read Balthazar's instructions. "According to this, the animals have to be dressed in costume." I re-read it in case I'd misunderstood Balthazar's scrawl. "Costume?"

Wes pressed his fingers to his temple. "He means the jewels, beads and other paraphernalia in the menagerie storeroom. We've never used them before, but there are all sorts of things to fit the animals. He wants me to parade them in front of the guests like baubles."

"Some of them perform tricks," Deanne said. "The eagle will catch a live mouse, for example, and the cat can jump through flaming hoops as well as any trained dog. It is a better spectacle with music."

"I'll suggest it to Balthazar when I return to the palace," I said. "Perhaps it's not too late to gather musicians from Mull."

Wes sighed and appealed to the dome ceiling. "Just when it was getting interesting, I have to put it off to entertain pampered aristocrats."

"Shhhh," Deanne hissed. "You knew there was a party tonight."

"I wasn't expecting it to involve me and my animals."

"Let me organize it," Deanne said.

Relief flooded Wes's face. "You're a marvel, Deanne." He hugged her and she hugged him back, smiling.

"I'll have the others help me," she told him. "You return to the surgery."

"Surgery?" I asked.

Wes waved a hand in dismissal. "I'm dissecting the cat that used to share the cage with that one." He indicated the large feline with the pointed ears. It resembled the cats roaming Mull's streets in many ways, yet it was different, with a rounder shape of its eye, and mottled markings on its fur, not to mention those impressive pointed ears. "It died yesterday, and I want to study it. I've looked all over the books, both here and in the palace library, and there is very little information on the internal structure of animals. I'd like to add to my knowledge and this is the only way to do that."

"I understand," I said.

"This is only the second animal that has died here, so it's a unique opportunity," Wes went on. "It must be done before the body decomposes, which won't take long in this heat."

He thanked Deanne again, making her blush, then he raced out of the building. Deanne also made her excuses and rushed off to organize the animals.

Quentin studied the list of instructions as we exited the

menagerie through the gate. "Next stop, the head gardener. Problem is, I don't know where to find him. He could be in the greenhouse, the orchard, the potting shed, or any of the formal gardens."

"Are the gardeners visible to the guests or king during their walks?"

"No." He snorted. "Can't have the servants being too obvious."

"This is the best time of day for walking, isn't it?"

"S'pose." He looked to the sky. The sun had advanced considerably while we were making our way to the menagerie.

"Then the gardener won't be in the formal gardens where the nobles could see him. Where does he do the potting, grafting and the like?"

"The greenhouse."

We both sighed. The greenhouse was all the way back near the palace.

The exercise did me good, however. It helped shed the last remnants of anxiety from my encounter with Lord Barborough as I talked with Quentin, mostly about medicine and surgery. There were no lulls in the conversation; Quentin was too chatty, and I was too eager not to allow myself time to reflect on my abduction.

By the time we found the head gardener, the shadows had grown long. Like the rest of the gardens, the greenhouse was deserted of noblemen and women. It didn't feel empty, however, not with so many fruit trees. They were potted in large square containers and arranged in rows to form avenues from one end of the building to the other. The trees were tall but didn't even reach half way to the vaulted ceiling.

We headed along one of the avenues toward the statue at the end, but found no one. I heard clipping and followed the sound to the next avenue, where a gardener trimmed an orange tree. He directed us to the potting shed adjoining the greenhouse, and it was there that we found the head gardener, Lewis.

He read through Balthazar's instructions and groaned. "Does he know how much work this entails?" He handed the paper back to me, smudged with soil.

"What does it mean change the color?'" I asked, pointing at the line on the paper.

Lewis removed his straw hat, scratched his bald head, and slapped the hat back on. "It's supposed to be a secret. Bal won't like me telling people his ideas, 'specially to someone not from the palace."

"Josie is here all the time," Quentin said. "She's one of us. Besides, I want to know too. Come on, Lew, tell us, if only because it'll annoy Bal and he's making you do so much extra work."

Lewis pouted as he considered that. "Changing the color means just that: changing the colors of the flowers. According to those instructions, the guests will be taken to the menagerie. The route from the lake to the building will be lined with flowers all of the same color, but when they leave, the flowers will be a different color."

"Wow," Quentin murmured in awe. "How do you do that? A dye on the petals? You'd have to use a spray. Dabbing each petal will take too long."

"They're not dyed." Lewis's smile turned smug when Quentin and I failed to offer another suggestion. "It's easier to guess when you realize all the flowers will be in pots."

"You swap the pots!" I said.

"Correct. It'll be done while the guests are all inside. They won't even see us. Some won't even notice the difference, despite the lighting."

"But that's a lot of pots. We've just walked from the lake to the menagerie and it's not a short distance. You'd need hundreds."

"A thousand, and a lot of men to move them in a short space of time. After Balthazar warned me he wanted to do this for a party, I practiced it. But only once. I thought he'd give me more time to practice again if he was going to use the idea."

"You could tell Balthazar you need more time," I said. "You can do something simpler tonight instead."

Both Lewis and Quentin snorted. "You don't know him," Lewis said. "It's easier to mobilize all my men than get Bal to change his mind."

Lewis left to gather his gardeners, and Quentin and I returned to the garrison. It was a relief to see Dane there, addressing the guards. He paused upon seeing me but continued giving his orders for the evening's roster.

Afterwards, he pulled me aside. "You seem to always have trouble leaving here when you're supposed to." Going by the firm set of his jaw, he wasn't trying to make light of it.

"Lord Barborough stopped me."

His gaze drilled into me for a long moment. "I'll walk you to the coach house."

Once outside, we headed towards the training ground rather than the forecourt. No one was using the space for sparring, and we were quite alone.

"Did Barborough hurt you?" he asked.

Barborough's rough handling had stopped hurting long ago, but the memory of it hadn't. My throat constricted at the thought of his hand wrapped around it. "No," I lied.

He stared into my eyes, and I knew he'd see the truth if I didn't look away. He caught my chin, however, and forced me to meet his gaze.

His nostrils flared. "Return to the garrison." He walked off.

I ran after him. "Where are you going?"

He didn't answer.

I caught his arm. "Dane."

Using his real name seemed to get through to him, but fury continued to simmer in his eyes. "Go back to the garrison, Josie. I'll come for you."

He shook me off and strode away, back straight and fists clenched at his sides.

CHAPTER 8

*J*couldn't let Dane confront Lord Barborough. It was too much of a risk. I caught his hand again.

"Stop! Calm down, Dane!"

He tried pulling his hand free, but I clung to it. He rounded on me. "Let go, Josie."

"No."

He sucked in a breath. "He can't keep getting away with bullying you. He has to be stopped."

"Not yet."

He tried walking off again so this time I raced past him and shoved him in the chest with both hands. He blinked at me.

"You're going to ruin everything," I growled at him.

He looked past me to the training yard exit and clenched his jaw. "I'm going to tell him to end his harassment."

"And how will you do that? With a punch to the jaw? And then what will happen?"

He gave no indication he was listening but at least he no longer tried to leave.

"If you charge into Barborough's rooms now, he'll know I've been deceiving him all along," I said. "He'll know we've been colluding to feed him false information."

"It's time he knew. It has to end."

"We don't know what he'll do next. He might leave in the

middle of the night and then we can no longer spy on him or he might retaliate."

He suddenly grasped my shoulders. "I'll take care of you. You can stay at the cottage."

"No, Dane," I said, gentler. "No. I have patients who need to find me. Listen." I drew his hands away and held them. "He's more dangerous than we thought. He admitted to killing his predecessor so he could take his place here."

His focus sharpened. "I'd heard the rumor, but I assumed it was an exaggeration."

Now that I had his attention, and he seemed a little calmer, I told him how Barborough had tricked me into going to his rooms and demanded I find the gem. "Brant must have told him about it," I finished.

Dane rubbed his gloved hand over his mouth and chin. Where before he was all fierce anger, he now simply looked worried. "What did you tell him?"

"That I would do my best to find it. I couldn't refuse him."

"You did the right thing."

"He's desperate for information about magic. If he doesn't succeed in finding a magical connection between King Leon and the palace, King Philip will execute him for murder."

"The gem can prove it."

"Possessing the gem will also stop King Leon from making more wishes. According to Barborough, the sorcerer's power is contained within it, but only the one who found it and freed the sorcerer can use the power."

"The king," he said heavily.

"He needs to hold it to use the power. That's why he wants it back. He wants to use one of his wishes to heal himself."

Dane folded his arms over his chest and tapped his thumb on his arm, a restless figure of pent-up power. "Theodore informed me the king is feeling better," he said. "That, coupled with preparations for the party, have helped him forget about the gem."

"Until he feels ill again," I added.

"How often will he get the pains in his chest?"

"After every meal, if he indulges. If you can control his diet, he'll get better, but it'll take time. He won't improve overnight."

"Then we must continue to distract him and reassure him until the fake gem arrives." He cast a glance toward the gate. "It better arrive soon."

"In the meantime, there's tonight's party," I said as we walked out of the training yard together. "I wish I could see it.

"You're not staying."

"I know. After last time, when Lady Deerhorn saw me and reported me to the king, I can't be caught again. Still, it would be—"

"No!"

I sighed. "Is that why you're personally escorting me to the coach house?"

"And waiting until your carriage is no bigger than a speck at the end of Grand Avenue."

I laughed and would have looped my arm through his if things were different between us and we had not sworn to keep our distance. I glanced sideways at him, only to find he was watching me. He quickly looked away.

"How are things in the village?" I asked.

"Fine, or I wouldn't be sending you back there."

"I can't go anywhere else. My patients need me. One of them is a first-time mother, and she's nervous."

"Babies have never been born without a midwife's assistance?"

"I won't shirk my responsibility, Captain." I'd almost said his name but stopped myself. We were passing too close to some maids carrying ladies' gowns. "Anyway, the village is quiet, so this discussion is pointless."

"You still have to be careful. Avoid The Row and keep your mouth shut. Don't say anything to offend the governor. He's the Deerhorns' man."

Speaking of the Deerhorns reminded me of Lady Deerhorn accosting me in almost the same spot we now passed. I didn't tell Dane she'd warned me not to inform the king that Lord Morgrave had been poisoned. He had enough to worry about, and I didn't plan on telling the king what I'd seen and smelled in that sedan chair.

Dane nodded at his men on duty at the gate and they saluted

him. "Balthazar says he asked you and Quentin to organize the party for him," he said to me.

"We just delivered some messages," I said.

"He likes you. He trusts you."

"I trust him too," I said, realizing it was true. I no longer suspected the master of the palace was involved in sorcery. He was as much in the dark about his past as any of the servants.

"You don't quite understand," Dane said. "Balthazar trusting you is an important step for him. He doesn't trust anyone except Theodore and me. Not even the other servants."

"Why not?"

"Do I need to remind you of what Seb the footman did? What the others in the cells have done? What the king is doing?"

"I see your point." After a few steps, I added, "Tell Balthazar I'll be happy to help him whenever he wishes it. If he needs an assistant, send someone to fetch me."

"Nice try, Josie, but the less time you spend at the palace, the better. While Barborough is here, anyway. Besides, you have a lot of expectant mothers who need to know where to find you, so you like to remind me."

"Not as many as you'd think."

He frowned at me. "Enough that you can live off the fees?"

"I'm also an apothecary," I said.

"Do you still sell a lot of remedies, even now after...?"

"My father's death?" I filled in for him.

I nodded my answer, but now that I thought about it, the last few days had been quiet. While we'd never sold medicines in great numbers, the tisanes, herbal teas, poultices and salves had been a good supplemental income. But that had recently dried up to almost nothing.

Dane ordered a carriage to take me home and, true to his word, he waited until I was inside. He went to shut the door but paused. He met my gaze. "Thank you for stopping me from confronting Barborough." He rested one hand on the doorframe and the other on the velvet covered seat beside my skirt.

I rested my hand beside his. The movement caught his attention but I couldn't tear my gaze away from his face. His features had softened over the course of our walk, flaunting his handsomeness to full effect.

"My temper got the better of me, and I couldn't see reason." He waited, perhaps expecting me to say something, but I was too mesmerized by the quiet vulnerability in his voice to speak. "Hammer," he suddenly bit off.

He went to move away, but I caught his hand. He looked up at me, his blue eyes huge.

"Not Hammer," I said. "Not to me." I let him go, expecting him to move away.

But he leaned in and kissed my forehead. Just as I closed my eyes and willed him to kiss me on the lips instead, he pulled back. The door shut and the coach drove off.

I turned and watched him standing on Grand Avenue between the coach house and stables, until he was a mere speck.

* * *

THERE WAS A PROTEST OVERNIGHT. According to Meg, who came to visit, protestors had taken to the village square to object to The Row being torn down and new housing replacing the derelict structures.

"They don't want prostitutes and gangs on the streets." She gave Dora an apologetic shrug. "Sorry. I know you're not all like that."

"It's all right," Dora said, tucking her hair behind her ear with a small, jerky movement. "Many are, but rarely by choice. They do it out of desperation."

Meg chewed her lip, a deep frown scoring her forehead. "It's awful. Really awful."

"Were the protests peaceful?" I asked.

"Lyle says so."

"He went?"

She nodded. "Many agree with your sentiment that the replacement housing should be affordable. And the protestors want something set aside for the very poor and orphans, those who have nothing."

"Both sides agree with you," Dora told me. "Them that live in

The Row and out of it. Nobody wants to see folk living in gutters. The roofs of what the poor have now might leak, and the walls are barely standing, but at least they have roofs and walls. Hailia bless you, Josie, for giving me and Remy somewhere to live away from all that."

"You're welcome to remain as long as you need," I said. The house had never looked so clean. Dora couldn't pay board, but when she wasn't foraging for food and herbs in the forest, she was scrubbing floors or dusting. It was marvelous, until I realized I had very little else to do. After paying visits to the two expectant mothers, I'd taken stock of the larder. I'd sold few medicines recently and had no need to make more.

"Were Ned Perkin and his followers at the protest?" I asked.

Meg scoffed. "Of course. Whenever there's trouble, Ned and his friends are nearby, beating their chests. But they were quiet, so Lyle told me. They didn't speak for or against the clearance."

Like most Mullians, Ned wouldn't want to see The Row's rougher residents forced into the streets where they could prey on villagers. But since most of The Row's newer residents were Vytill migrants, he wouldn't want to take their side either, out of selfish pig-headedness. I felt no sympathy for his dilemma.

"No one wants to demolish The Row and build expensive housing in its place." Meg said. "No one except the governor and Deerhorns, and only because they'll profit from it."

"It's council land," I muttered. "They can do what they want with it, including sell it to the Deerhorns. No one can stop them."

"*We* can." Meg set down her cup. "We must keep protesting the clearance, or keep pushing for low-cost housing if they do insist on clearing it. They can't go against the wishes of the entire village."

Dora and I exchanged grim looks. Like me, she knew Meg's idealism had no grounding in reality. The Deerhorns could do what they wanted. It didn't matter if all of Mull was against them. They had the governor on their side, and probably other members of the council too. Their votes could be bought.

"Do you know what the governor had the gall to say once the protestors dispersed?" Meg went on. "He was overheard saying that we should be glad to get rid of The Row, that its buildings are falling apart. He doesn't understand that we're not fighting for the buildings; we're fighting for the people."

Dora touched Meg's hand. "Thank you."

Meg seemed surprised to be the subject of gratitude. Surprised and a little embarrassed. She sipped her tea, hiding her face behind the cup.

"No one would realize you're such a rebel at heart," I teased her. "Everyone thinks you're so meek and amenable. But Dora and I have seen your true nature come out today. You'd make Ned Perkin quake if you two ever had an argument."

Meg grunted. "Hardly."

"Perhaps not quake, but you could certainly beat him in a debate."

"The problem with men like Ned is they don't bother with debate," she said. "They make statements with clubs and fists, not words."

"And those kind of statements win," Dora muttered.

"Then we have to hope Ned continues to watch on and do nothing," I said. "Now, who wants cake?"

"I'll get it," Meg said, entering the larder before I could stop her. "You have a lot of medicines in here, Josie," she called out.

"Nobody's buying them."

She brought the cake out on a board and sliced it up. There was just enough for three with a little left over for Remy. It was a cake Meg's mother had brought over the day before, and it had been our dinner. I planned to buy fish today with the few ells I had left. Remy needed proper food for a growing boy, and hopefully there'd be something left after the best of the day's catch was sold. Considering the help I'd given Gill Swinson's daughter after she was raped, I hoped he might sell me a fish at a discounted price.

"Why is nobody buying your medicine?" Meg asked.

"That's what I'd like to know. You haven't heard any rumors?"

She handed me a piece of cake. "Like what?"

"Like Mistress Ashmole is making her own medicines and selling them to Doctor Ashmole's patients?"

"No one will buy off her. They'd rather come to you. Those who've known you all your life, I mean." She passed a plate to Dora. "Doctor Ashmole isn't very well liked. I've heard his manner is abrupt and his wife's is worse. Oona Dwyer invited her for tea, but all Mistress Ashmole did was complain about Mull the entire time. Apparently she hates it here and wants to go back to Tilting, where they lived before Logios. And no one wants to see Doctor Ashmole. Apparently his hands are as prickly as his manner."

"Prickly hands?" Dora echoed.

Meg merely shrugged.

"What about his diagnoses and treatments?" I asked.

"Nobody's died after seeing him, if that's what you mean."

She looked so serious that I spluttered a laugh, and they both laughed too.

We finished our cake and I tidied up, returning the board to the larder. There wasn't much space for food among the medicines, but it didn't matter since I had so little to eat. I stood in the doorway, hands on hips, and frowned at the rows of labeled jars and bottles of different sizes, the bunches of herbs hanging from the rafters to dry, and the small drawers filled with powders.

"Meg," I said over my shoulder. "Are you sure Mistress Ashmole isn't making and selling her own medicines?"

She came up beside me. "I was only guessing she isn't because no one would buy off her when they can get them from you. My mother will know for certain."

"She wouldn't have mentioned it?"

"You know my mother," she said with a roll of her eyes. "She doesn't like hurting anyone's feelings, and that includes delivering bad news. But if we confront her directly, she'll have to tell us."

Meg and I went across the road and found Mistress Diver in the kitchen, one hand massaging her lower back, the other stirring a pot hanging over the hot coals. I planned to make polite conversation first, but Meg launched straight into her question.

"Mama, is Mistress Ashmole making her own medicines?"

Mistress Diver stopped stirring and chewed her lip.

"Mama?" Meg prompted. "I know that look. Tell us what you've heard."

Mistress Diver had always been such an honest, upstanding person, and it seemed she couldn't lie to us now, not even to save my feelings. "Apparently she is making her own. I don't buy from her, mind. I only buy from you, Josie. I don't believe a word that woman says."

I frowned. "What is she saying?"

She resumed her stirring. "Nasty lies. It's best if you don't hear them. It'll only upset you."

Now my curiosity was really piqued. "It won't upset me," I assured her. "I'd rather know what she's saying so I can prepare myself. Wouldn't it be better if I heard it from you rather than in the marketplace?"

Mistress Diver still hesitated.

"Tell us, Mama," Meg said. "Do you want Josie to hear it from Arrabette Fydler?"

Mistress Diver's lips pursed at the mention of the sharp-tongued Arrabette. "Very well, but don't take it to heart, Josie." She set down the spoon and rubbed her hands on her apron. "I learned only yesterday that Mistress Ashmole is making and selling her own remedies to her husband's patients. I won't tell you who told me, but I will say she's a good woman who's too trusting some-times. She believes everything she's told without question. Anyway, when I asked her why she'd buy medicine from Mistress Ashmole and not you, someone she's known all her life and who needs our support now, she told me the doctor and his wife have been...saying things."

"What things?" Meg asked, indignant.

"That Josie's remedies don't work."

"They can't say that! It's not true!"

"We know that," Mistress Diver. "But some in the village are fools. The Ashmoles are saying that it was your father who guided you, Josie, and that without him, your medicines no longer have the healing properties they once did."

"Bollocks," Meg spat.

Mistress Diver glared at her daughter. "They're using Josie's lack of education against her." She turned to me. "Your father was the trained doctor, not you, and the Ashmoles are claiming that an uneducated girl can't possibly carry on the work without him."

"She's hardly a girl at her age," Meg muttered.

I sat heavily on a chair, not quite certain what to make of the news. Surely Mistress Ashmole hadn't put it quite so baldly, or

Mistress Diver's friend exaggerated. "But medicines are sold by apothecaries all over The Fist, many of them the uneducated wives or daughters of doctors. It's not a requirement to have been to a Logios college to study."

"Try telling that to simple village folk," Mistress Diver said.

"Simple is right," Meg spat. "Simple, backward, provincial. Some folk here are everything the Vytill migrants claim. I'm ashamed to call them my friends and neighbors." She sighed and slumped into the chair next to me, all her fire suddenly gone. "How can they believe the word of someone they hardly know over you, Josie?"

"Because they're scared," I told her. "They don't want to take a risk with their health or the health of their family, and they trust someone who has attended college. It's why we have the college system." I knew how the villagers could be when they fell ill. They'd do everything in their power to make their loved ones better again, even if it was at the expense of someone they'd known their entire lives. Besides, many wouldn't know how dire my situation had become since I was still the village midwife.

But for how much longer? Would Mistress Ashmole take over that as well?

* * *

As much as I wished the gossip didn't affect me, it did. I couldn't rise above it, nor could I push it to the back of my mind and get on with my day. The real problem was, I had no work to distract me.

I spent some time with Remy in the afternoon while Dora returned to The Row to take fresh water and medicine to the only friend she'd made there. Remy was a quick learner but his level of education was very low.

When Dora returned, I questioned her about the situation in her old neighborhood as we sipped our tea.

"The guards are still on duty at the entrance," she said. "It was difficult to get in, but they eventually allowed it after I convinced them I used to live there. There were fights between the two factions last night over the food the palace sent. Apparently the fights were contained, but no one thinks peace will last. Everyone is worried the situation will escalate and fear skirmishes will turn into a war."

"Was anyone injured?"

She nodded. "Some of the men have knife wounds."

"Have they had their wounds checked by Doctor Ashmole?"

She shook her head. "A man went to fetch him to take him to his brother who got a cut on his leg, but Doctor Ashmole refused."

"Did the brother take the wounded man to Doctor Ashmole instead?"

"You don't understand, Josie. The doctor refused to see anyone from The Row, either there or in his surgery. He said if he tends to one man's wounds, that man's enemies might take offence and come for *him*."

Doctor Ashmole was a coward. My father wasn't the bravest man in Mull, but he went into The Row if needed, and he never turned anyone away.

I stewed for the rest of the day. The more I thought of Doctor Ashmole's cowardice, and his wife's lies, the more my blood boiled. I could hear my father's words in my head, telling me that I was too impetuous and emotional sometimes. He'd been right—I was—but knowing that didn't help settle my nerves.

I left the house as the buildings cast their long shadows over the streets and the sun had lost most of its heat. After all, why deny my nature? If I was impetuous, then so be it.

Doctor Ashmole's house was located on the edge of Mull, a good walk from my street. It wasn't the most convenient place for his older patients, particularly as his house was located in a dip. Even after several dry days, there was still a muddy puddle outside his front door. One of his neighbor's chickens wandered past as I knocked. It clucked and pecked at the ground, then tried to run away as a young boy gave chase. Both chicken and child squealed when he caught it.

Mistress Ashmole opened the door and her mouth pinched upon seeing me. I thought she might slam the door in my face, but perhaps politeness got the better of her. She invited me inside, but not before shouting at the child.

"Stop that noise! This is a doctor's surgery. We require peace and quiet. Honestly," she muttered, closing the door. "The children in this village are wild."

She did not invite me further into the house, but remained standing in the small sitting room at the front. It was sparsely furnished with no cushions on the wooden chairs and no rugs covering the stone floor. It was spotless, however, and the two silver candlesticks on the mantel gleamed.

"I'm glad you're here," Mistress Ashmole said before I could speak. "You've saved me a journey. I need your recipe for Mother's Milk."

I blinked in surprise. "I'm not selling the recipe. You're welcome to purchase a few bottles, however."

"I require the *recipe*, Mistress Cully. Don't make a scene. My husband has a patient. Please bring the recipe by tomorrow morning."

I couldn't quite believe what I was hearing. If she had the nerve to expect me to agree then she certainly wouldn't think twice about spreading nasty rumors about me. "Mother's Milk is a pain suppressor developed by my parents over many years. It's complicated and expensive to reproduce but very effective, particularly in surgery."

She thrust out her chin. "I'm not asking for a lecture, I'm asking you to give me the recipe."

"And I'm telling you, you can't have it. I will sell what I can make to you."

Her nostrils flared, reminding me of Lady Deerhorn when she was affronted. "You have no need of it!"

"On the contrary. My only source of income is from the sale of medicines and midwifery work. Since Mother's Milk is too dangerous in the hands of ordinary folk, I can only sell it to your husband. So either you buy it from me, or you make your own."

"You would deny my husband's patients? You would have them endure the pain of surgery?"

"No, Mistress Ashmole, *you* would, if you refuse to buy it from me. When you change your mind, I'll have a bottle of Mother's Milk waiting for you. Until then, your husband will have to perform surgery the way they still do in the medical colleges—with a bottle of strong spirits."

She turned on her heel and opened the door again. She didn't even bother with a "good day."

I hadn't finished yet, although I knew my request would fall on deaf ears. If she wouldn't give in on the Mother's Milk, she wouldn't give in on anything else.

"I came here to appeal to your husband's sense of duty, to ask him to attend to patients in The Row," I said.

"And risk his life?" she scoffed. "You're a silly fool, Mistress Cully. As was your father, so I've heard. *We* are not fools."

I bristled but stamped down on my rising anger. "They won't retaliate against you if you help one of their enemies."

She suddenly laughed, a barking sound that shook her thin shoulders and stretched her lips into a narrow gash. "It has nothing to do with retaliation and everything to do with their ability to pay. Most folk in that den of vice don't have an ell between them, and those who can afford my husband's services are vile and godless. He certainly won't be helping *those* kind of people."

"'Those kind of people?'" I echoed, sounding as foolish as she claimed me to be. "But…your husband is the village doctor. He *has* to treat everyone who comes to his door."

"He doesn't have to do anything of the sort. He can refuse anyone, for any reason." She opened the door wider and waited for me to exit.

I stared at her, not quite sure what to say. It was one thing for Doctor Clegg to limit his services to only the elite, but Doctor Ashmole was the village medic. It was his duty to attempt to heal everyone.

I was about to tell her I'd inform the college, but stopped myself. That would do no good. The college in Logios was finished with Doctor Ashmole, and what he did after obtaining his education wasn't their concern. The problem was, I couldn't complain to the governor of Mull or council members either. They would probably take his side and be happy to see The Row's people die of starvation, illness or their wounds. There wasn't a soul in the whole of Glancia who could order Doctor Ashmole to treat everyone in the village equally.

Mistress Ashmole cleared her throat and drummed her fingernails against the door.

"And another thing," I said. "I've heard what you're saying
about me and my medicines. It must stop. You know very well that
apothecaries don't need to go to any of the colleges."

"I don't know what you're talking about, Mistress Cully. If you
don't mind—"

"How dare you disparage me around the village! All my remedies are made from the same recipes we used when my father was
alive. There's nothing wrong with them."

She snorted in derision.

"Stop your campaign against me," I said. "Stop your lies."

"If your medicines work then you have no need to worry, do
you?"

I was about to say more but bit down on my tongue. She would
never admit to lying and gossiping about me. I was wasting my
time.

I stepped across the threshold but left one foot inside so she
couldn't shut the door all the way. "If you believed your own
words, you wouldn't be wanting Mother's Milk, would you?" I
said, forcing a smile. "I wonder what everyone would think of
your skills as an apothecary when they hear that you're desperate
for my recipe?"

I marched up the street and didn't look back. The sensation of
her gaze burning a hole in my back didn't fade until I reached
home.

* * *

PROTESTS AGAINST CLEARING The Row were held again that night,
but I remained at home with Dora and Remy. The following morning, Meg told us the protest hadn't been altogether peaceful. Ned
Perkin had finally picked a side, and it wasn't the side that favored
the Vytill migrants.

"He wants the clearances to go ahead," Meg said. She spoke to
me from the front doorstep, having refused to come in. She was
supposed to go straight home from the market. "Ned says it'll force

The Row's Vytill faction to leave Mull because they won't want to live on the street and no landlord would rent a house to them."

"What did everyone think of that?" I asked.

"Many agreed with him."

"No doubt Ivor was one of them."

"He was right by Ned's side."

I glanced over my shoulder toward the kitchen, where Dora and Remy were practicing their reading together. "And what about the other residents in The Row? Did anyone speak for them? Did anyone question what will happen to them after their homes are destroyed?"

"Lyle said some did." She hoisted her basket higher and rested it on her hip. "That's when the scuffles broke out. Ned didn't like anyone disagreeing with him. He threw the first punch."

Ned Perkin had always wanted things his way and never liked being challenged. His answers often involved fists, always arguing, and never reasonable discussion. "Was anyone badly hurt?"

"Two had minor cuts. It could have been worse, but the captain broke up the fight."

"He has men here still?"

"Not many, and those patrol The Row at night. I mean the captain himself broke it up. He was there with the sheriff, overseeing the protest. It seems the sheriff thought it would be a peaceful protest again and took the opportunity of the guards patrolling to send his men home for some much-needed rest."

"Did the captain get hurt?"

Her slow smile turned wicked. "He might have. Perhaps you ought to check on him. I'm sure he'd like your attention."

"I'll agree to see the captain if you come to the palace with me to see the sergeant."

That wiped the smile from her face. "I'd better go home. Mama is waiting for these pathetic vegetables." She lifted the cloth on her basket to show me the wilted lettuces and shriveled potatoes. "There was no meat, chicken or fish left that we could afford, so it's broth for dinner again. Have you got enough, Josie?" She glanced past me then leaned closer. "Can you afford to keep your guests much longer?"

"We're fine, Meg. Don't worry. I have eggs, and Dora is a

marvel at making things last." It was a lie, but I couldn't let Meg worry. She would only tell her mother, who would then insist on feeding us—something the Divers couldn't afford to do.

Meg sighed. "One day, this will all settle down and there'll be balance and order in Mull again. There'll be enough work for everyone who wants it when the docks have finished expanding and the harbor is dredged. Food will be imported in greater quantities, bringing the prices down, and of course more houses will be built. It's only a matter of time."

I shared her optimism. I truly did. But I suspected we would disagree on how long it would take. She thought it would be a matter of weeks, months at the most, but I suspected it would take years before equilibrium was restored to Mull. One thing we both agreed on—our sleepy village was gone forever.

I spent the afternoon trying not to think about visiting the palace to check on Dane. Meg had planted the seed in my head, and by the end of the day, it had grown roots and flourished. I did not succumb to my need, however, and was rather pleased with myself for being strong.

Lyle knocked on the door just as dusk began to settle. Like his sister, he also didn't cross the threshold. "I just got home from work," he said. "Meg told me to come here and tell you what I just told her before we sit down to dinner."

"Oh?"

"The crier has just announced that The Row won't be cleared. Governor's orders. They've backed down."

"What will be done about the area instead?" I asked.

He shrugged. "Looks like you got what you wanted."

"Affordable and decent housing for the poor is what I wanted. Doing nothing is only a slight improvement on the clearance idea."

It was a victory, I supposed, although it didn't feel like one. The Row still harbored criminals, the factions within it still fought for control, the poor still went hungry, and the houses still looked like they'd fall down in a strong breeze. But at least those houses offered shelter.

"Thank you, Lyle. Go home and enjoy your dinner."

He cleared his throat and a rather strange look came over his face. I realized what it meant too late, and couldn't stop him. "Do you want to go for a walk with me?" he asked. "Just a quiet walk with a good friend, nothing more."

Nothing more? I failed to see how an unwed man and woman walking aimlessly around the village could be viewed as anything other than the first stages of courtship, but I didn't say so. Lyle was like family, and deserved to be let down gently. I scrambled to think of an excuse that wouldn't offend or hurt him.

"Thank you, but I think it's best if I stay home at night."

"No one will dare harm you if you're with me."

Meg's brother wasn't a big man and certainly not a fighter. Walking with him was no guarantee of safety. "I think I'll just stay home," I said. "Thanks anyway."

He nodded grimly and walked off. He hadn't got far when he suddenly stopped and turned back to me. "You shouldn't be so choosy, Josie."

"Don't, Lyle," I said on a sigh.

My plea might as well have fallen on deaf ears. "Meg says you're half in love with the captain of the guards, but you mark my words, he's not for you. You're a nice village girl." He swallowed, and I got the impression he'd swallowed his next words altogether.

I cocked my head to the side. "And he is what?" I prompted.

He squared his shoulders. "They call him Hammer. Doesn't that tell you all you have to know about him?"

"No, as it happens. And how do you know that's not his real name?"

He grunted. "Don't be a naive child, Josie. You're smarter than that."

I didn't wait to see him enter his house but I heard the door slam. I hoped he didn't tell his parents that I'd rejected him. Mistress Diver was like an aunt to me, and I didn't want to upset her. She wouldn't understand why I'd turned down her son.

Meg would, though. She knew I couldn't see her brother as a suitor.

It was dark when the knock I'd been expecting ever since Lyle stormed off sounded on my front door. Dora didn't want me to answer it, that late in the evening, but I suspected it would be Mistress Diver, come to ask me to reconsider Lyle's offer of a walk. If not her then one of my patients' husbands.

It took my eyes a moment to adjust to the dim light outside. The moon had slipped behind the clouds and my candle did nothing to push back the darkness. Whoever it was must be wearing black, because he was little more than a shadow. A horse snuffled and I could just make out its silhouette near the bollard.

"Captain?" I said.

A tall figure stepped in front of me, very close, and I lost my balance. An arm reached out and circled me around the waist, drawing me close.

It wasn't Dane. His smell, the rhythm of his breathing, his size, were all wrong. I held my candle higher and gasped.

Lord Xavier stared down at me. When I tried to move away, he grabbed my backside with both hands and crushed his body against mine. His cock protruded through the layers of clothing and his hot breath moistened my cheek.

Then he kissed me.

CHAPTER 9

I pushed at Lord Xavier and smacked his chest, his shoulders. But that only made him tighten his hold and press his lips harder to mine. I jerked my head to the side, breaking the kiss, if that's what the mashing of our mouths could be called.

"Let me go!" I spat.

He chuckled low in his throat. "My, my, aren't you the fierce little—"

"Josie?"

I almost cried with relief when Lord Xavier let me go at the sound of Dora's voice.

"Who're you?" he barked.

Dora shrank back into the kitchen, her eyes huge with fear. Remy tucked himself against her side, and she clutched him to her.

"Dora and Remy are my friends," I told Lord Xavier. "They're staying with me."

His tongue flicked over his lower lip as he regarded her.

"Please leave," I said, opening the door wide.

He chuckled again, but it didn't have the cockiness of earlier. "You liked it, Josie," he whispered. "I could feel how rapidly your heart beat."

"That was fear."

He licked his lips again as he straightened. "You can protest all you want, but I know the difference between desire and fear."

I leveled my gaze with his. "I've asked you to leave. Please do so."

"Or you'll do what? Scream?" He grunted. "The sheriff's men won't touch me."

"But the king's men will."

He chuckled again. This time I was very sure it was all showy bravado. "I came here to congratulate you," he said. "You won. The governor has bowed to your wishes and won't go ahead with clearing The Row."

I said nothing. Telling him that I wanted the residents of The Row to be given proper, affordable housing would only invite him to engage in conversation. I wanted him to leave as soon as possible.

"Well done, Josie." The sinister thread through his voice shredded my nerves. "Your words the other night made the villagers change their minds. But it also made you a very powerful enemy. My mother is furious."

"Your mother had decided before that night that she didn't like me."

His gaze searched mine. I forced myself not to look away. "The funny thing is, she would like you if you weren't so common. You have a lot of the qualities she admires. As do I."

His gloved finger stroked my cheek to my jaw and his hungry gaze followed it. I pulled away and he grasped my breast. I slapped him. He pushed me.

I fell against the table by the door, knocking off the candlestick I'd set down. The flame went out. Dora gasped and rushed to my aid.

"Oi!" Remy shouted as he charged forward. "Don't hit ladies!"

Dora grabbed his hand to keep him back, but Lord Xavier was already striding through the door. I lurched to my knees and slammed it shut. Dora slid the bolt across then sank to the floor beside me. We clasped each other's hands.

Remy remained standing, the light from the kitchen behind him casting his face in shadow. "I don't like him."

"Stay away from him, Remy," I said. "Him and his family."

"Go and put some tea leaves in the pot." Dora's voice trembled but she managed a reassuring smile for her son. "Good boy."

Neither she nor I stood. Her legs must feel as weak as mine.

"Are you all right?" she asked.

"Yes." I reached for the candle and stood to light it. "Thank you, Dora. I don't know what he would have done if you weren't here."

"Don't think about it."

Easier to say than to do.

"He's a Deerhorn, isn't he?" she asked.

"Lord Xavier, the eldest."

"I've seen him," she said. "He goes to one of the girls in The Row."

"I thought he used the maids for that."

"This woman has a particular reputation. She accepts it rougher than the others."

The man was vile, yet he and his mother had the gall to suggest the people in The Row were the revolting kind. Thank the god and goddess for Dora's presence tonight. Now that Lord Xavier knew I no longer lived alone, he wouldn't try that again. Not here.

I hoped.

* * *

WHEN A MESSAGE CAME for me the following morning, summoning me to the palace, I jumped at the chance to go. I was restless at home with nothing to do, and the shadow of Lord Xavier's visit hung over me. I needed to get out. Besides, I was curious as to why Dane wanted to see me. The message hadn't offered a reason.

I hitched a ride on the back of a cart heading in the direction of the palace, but it wasn't until I was almost there that I began to worry. There'd been no name attached to the note. The only person who would summon me to the palace but not write his name would be Lord Barborough. He'd given me two days to find the gem, and those two days were up.

I jumped off the cart and headed to the stables, where I asked a groom to escort me all the way to the gate. From there, I spotted Erik on patrol and asked him to walk with me to the garrison.

"You are here because king is ill?" he asked as we walked.

I scanned the faces of the passing nobles and squinted into the shadows, but could not see Barborough."I don't know why I'm here," I said. "Is he feeling unwell?"

"Aye. Theodore is worried. Hammer is happy because he does not have to go with him for rides or walks all the time."

He pushed open the door to the garrison. Inside, Quentin sat at the table, a book open in front of him. Another guard sat too, his arms crossed over his chest and eyes closed.

He opened his eyes and sat up straighter. "A drink, Josie?"

"No, thanks. Do you know if the captain will be back soon?"

"Nope. Sorry." He poured himself an ale and drank the entire cup before replenishing it.

Quentin pulled out the chair beside him. "Come and help me, Josie. I don't understand this bit."

He was reading the medical book I'd given him some time ago, and the page was open to skin conditions. "Is this what Erik had?" He pointed to a drawing of a lump on the back of a hand.

"It's similar but his was specific to the genital area. You'll find it under the section on male genitalia and its diseases."

The other guard made a gagging sound. "That's disgusting."

"Did Erik show it to you?" I asked Quentin.

Quentin flushed. "He offered."

"He asked," Erik countered.

"I did not! I said I'd like to learn more about doctoring, and he took his clothes off. Right in this room."

"It's true," the other guard said. "I saw it. I didn't touch it, like some." He flashed a grin at Quentin.

Quentin's face flushed even brighter. "I, er, needed to maneuver it so I could see the lump."

"His hands are rough," Erik said. "Not as rough as mine or some of the maids, but it was not pleasing to me."

"Some of the maids have callused hands too?" I asked.

"Aye," Quentin said, sounding glad to move the conversation in a different direction. He showed me his palms and the old, hardened calluses. He didn't have as many as Dane. "They're not as bad as they used to be. My hands had cuts and sores at first. So did almost everyone else."

"Even the women," the guard said.

"Not Balthazar," Erik said. "And not all the maids."

It wasn't something I'd given much thought to, before now. I wondered what it meant about their pasts. As with other characteristics, it wasn't universal for all the servants.

Erik turned to leave just as the external door opened and Brant strode through. He paused upon seeing me then cast a glance at the other guard. His gaze finally settled on Quentin. Quentin tensed.

"Milo," Erik said to the guard, "take over on patrol from me."

"I just got off duty," Milo whined.

"I will do your next duty."

Brant removed his sword belt and hung it up before pouring himself a cup of ale. "He wants to stay here and protect Hammer's two pets personally. Seems I can't be trusted around them." He drank the entire contents and refilled the cup. "Go on, Milo. Off you go. That's an order."

Milo strapped his sword belt around his waist and headed out, but not without shooting a glare at Brant.

Brant pulled out the chair beside me and sat. He could have chosen one of a dozen other chairs, but it seemed he wanted to torment both Quentin and me.

He reached across me and grabbed the book then tossed it on the floor. "This ain't going to teach you to be a better guard."

Quentin got up and went to fetch the book, but Brant beat him to it, pressing his foot on the cover, close to Quentin's fingers. He smirked down at the smaller, younger man.

"Get off it," Quentin said. "It's Josie's, and you're damaging it."

"Make me." When Quentin didn't move, Brant said, "Go on. Try and knock me off. You've got to learn to beat a bigger man. You've got to learn a lot of things."

Quentin's fingers recoiled and he swallowed heavily.

I stood and held out my hand. "And you have to learn that taunting a smaller man doesn't impress anyone. Give me the book, please."

Brant snorted. "You think I'm trying to impress *you*? The captain's whore?"

A flash out of the corner of my eye warned me to step back. I got out of the way just as Erik flung himself at Brant. They fell to the floor together, somehow neither injuring themselves enough to stop them throwing punches.

Erik's longer reach helped him, but Brant was bullishly strong and withstood the pounding. Bleeding from the nose, he grabbed Erik's hair and wrestled him off.

Quentin scrambled away, and I thought he was going to fetch other guards, but he grabbed one of the swords by the door and clutched it in both hands.

"Stop!" he shouted, hovering too far away from the two fighting men to strike. "Stop, Brant, or I'll strike!"

Brant sat on Erik's chest and grasped the front of his doublet. Erik reached up and wrapped his long fingers around Brant's throat, but it didn't affect the sergeant. He pulled his fist back and punched Erik in the jaw. The back of Erik's head slammed against the flagstones and his eyes rolled up into his head. Brant wound up for another punch.

"You're going to kill him!" I cried.

I didn't see Dane enter but I heard his barked command. "Enough, Sergeant!" He charged past Quentin and using only one hand, ripped Brant off Erik before he could lay another punch. Dane's other hand clutched a small wooden box.

Brant stumbled to his feet and took a swing at Dane, but Dane dodged it. He struck a short, sharp punch that landed on Brant's jaw. Brant's head snapped back but he was able to regain his footing and settle his stance. He bared his teeth at Dane.

"Don't," Dane warned him. "Or there will be more severe consequences."

"There'll be consequences anyway, won't there?" Brant snarled. "Think I care if you take me off the roster? You going to give me the shittiest tasks again? Go on, assign me to prison duty. I don't care."

"You'll go to the prison, Brant, but you won't be on duty."

Brant stared at him and slowly lowered his fists. He wouldn't fight Dane. He knew he wouldn't win. The last time they'd fought, he'd come off second best.

"You can't imprison me!" Brant cried. "*He* started it. Ask them. Go on, ask them."

Dane looked to Quentin. "Who threw the first punch?"

Quentin looked away.

"Answer me!" Dane shouted.

Quentin swallowed. "Erik tackled him after Brant insulted Josie." He gave Erik an apologetic shrug as the Marginer sat up, rubbing the back of his head.

I knelt and inspected it. There was a lump but the skin wasn't broken. "Do not fight on stone floors," I told them. All of them. "If someone strikes their head as they fall, it could kill them."

Quentin appeared to be the only one listening. Brant and Dane glared at one another while Erik got to his feet.

"He is scum," Erik spat. "He should not be in the same room as Josie."

I tended to agree. Every time I was in Brant's company, there was an argument or a fight.

"Stop trying to lift her skirts with your concern, Marginer," Brant sneered. "She's only got eyes for Hammer." He wiped the back of his hand over his cut lip, smearing the blood so that his mouth appeared to stretch into a gruesome grin. "Go on, Hammer. What's my punishment? What's his?"

"Erik will be on prison duty," Dane said. "You will hand in you sword and uniform and wait for further instructions from Balthazar regarding your new role."

A deep pit of silence swallowed us for a long moment, then Brant barked a harsh laugh. Erik and Quentin exchanged glances.

"You can wait in the dormitory," Dane said.

"Why am I being punished more than him?" Brant blustered. "He started it."

"Go to the dormitory and wait for me there. I'll return with Balthazar's instructions."

Brant shook his head, over and over. "You can't do this. I'm supposed to be a guard. No one changes duties."

"You'll be the first. See it as an experiment. If you suddenly vanish or die, we'll know it's not allowed."

Quentin pressed his lips together to suppress his smile.

Brant's fists closed and I worried Dane would have another fight on his hands. But Brant merely turned to me. "What if I apologize?"

I was so stunned I almost laughed, thinking it were a joke. But I was glad I didn't. He looked serious.

"Go ahead," Dane said.

Brant cleared his throat. "Sorry, Josie. I shouldn't have called you..." His gaze flicked to Dane. "I shouldn't have said what I did. It isn't true."

It was more than I'd expected. Much more. It sounded sincere, too. "Thank you," I said. "Apology accepted."

He didn't wait for Dane's final ruling on his fate but walked through to the guards' dormitory and shut the door.

"Are you all right?" Dane asked me.

I nodded without taking my gaze off the door. "Is being a guard really so important to him that he'd swallow his pride so completely?"

"It would seem so."

"Or he really did regret his words," Quentin said. "Maybe he wanted to apologize anyway, and this offered him a way to do it. His pride is pricked a bit, but not deflated completely like it would be if he'd apologized unprompted."

"I doubt that's it," I said, frowning at the door again. "Brant doesn't like me enough to regret calling me names."

"Some people have strange ways of showing their feelings."

I blinked owlishly at him.

Erik snorted. "Brant does not feel good emotions, only bad. Anger, hate, fear. And pride. Much pride. He will not like being gardener or footman. That is enough for him to take his words back." He rubbed my shoulder. "He cannot say that about you in front of me."

I touched his chin and inspected the bruise developing around his eye. "Next time someone calls me something you don't like, please just turn the other cheek."

He pointed to his face. "This cheek?" He slapped his backside. "Or this cheek?"

Quentin muttered something under his breath as he bent to pick up the book. Erik chuckled but suddenly stopped. I followed his gaze to see Dane glaring at Erik.

Erik cleared his throat. "I will return to duty."

"I don't know about you two," Quentin said when he was gone, "but I need a drink. Josie?"

I shook my head and regarded Dane. He still held the box. He'd not let it go throughout the entire exchange. Either it contained something very important or he hadn't been too worried about Brant. I suspected it was the former. I also suspected I knew what was in it.

"Did you send a message to me to come to the palace this morning?" I asked him.

He frowned. "No. You were summoned?"

"Anonymously."

His frown deepened. He looked down at the box in his hand. "I was on my way to Balthazar's office. Come with me."

We left via the internal door, but as soon as it closed, Dane took my hand, halting me. The flames from the flickering wall torches danced wildly in his eyes, and the shadows sharpened the planes of his face.

"What did Brant say to you?" he asked.

"It doesn't matter. I wasn't offended."

He inched closer and his hand skimmed up my arm. His face was so close to mine that if I stood on my toes and leaned in just a little, I could kiss him. A kiss from Dane would banish the last vestiges of my anxiety, and the foul memory of Lord Xavier's lips crushing mine. A kiss from Dane would make everything so much better.

I stood on my toes. I leaned in. My lips parted.

Dane filled my vision. His eyes became warm, his breathing quickened. Then his lips skimmed mine, so tenderly that I ached from the longing of it. My longing, and his.

His hand rested on my waist then circled me, holding me against him. I gripped his shoulders, aware that I'd vowed not to do this, not to tempt him or be tempted. Yet I couldn't stop. The achingly tender butterfly kiss only made me want to break every promise I'd made to stay away.

But before I could deepen the kiss, he stepped back and set off along the corridor.

I blew out a shuddery breath and tried not to regret the loss of his touch. He'd done the right thing by walking away. His willpower was stronger than mine.

I tried to dampen the fuse of desire as I followed him, but I failed. So I searched for something to say instead to break the tension.

"Why are we going to Balthazar's office?"

He held up the box. "This just arrived and I sent word for Theodore to meet me there. If Barborough is looking for you, I can't send you out alone and I have to attend this meeting. You might as well come along."

It was hardly a welcoming invitation, but I wouldn't refuse it. I wished he didn't talk as if the kiss had been as banal as scheduling patrol duty.

"Finally!" Balthazar said when we entered his office. "I could have died of old age waiting for you. Why is she here?"

"Good afternoon to you too, Balthazar," I said, taking the vacant seat beside Theodore.

The king's valet gave me a small but fleeting smile as his fingers tapped out a rhythm on his thigh.

"There was an incident in the garrison," Dane said. "You need to find Brant work elsewhere in the palace. He won't be returning to guard duty."

Theodore's fingers stilled. Balthazar sat back and regarded Dane.

"No," I said, shaking my head. "You can't do that, Captain. He apologized."

"He causes too many problems. This was just the latest. He needs to be punished, and to someone like Brant, the only punishment that will have any effect is to remove him from a position of authority and to take away his sword."

"But you can't go back on your word."

Dane's gaze narrowed to slits. "Why are you defending him?"

"I'm not, but you told him you wouldn't banish him from the garrison if he apologized to me."

Dane's jaw hardened. The man was stubborn.

"I'm not disagreeing with you for Brant's benefit but for yours," I said. "If you remove Brant from guard duty, your men might no longer respect you."

"You're telling me how to manage my men?"

"Advising, not telling."

Theodore made a strangled sound which I realized, when I looked at him, was a smothered laugh. Dane turned his frosty glare onto him, and Theodore quickly sobered.

"It doesn't matter what either of you think," Balthazar said. "I'm not assigning him different duties. The sergeant needs to be with other guards. I can't let him loose among staff with no combat experience. He won't take orders from them, and they won't be able to control him if he loses his temper. I have a strong suspicion that's why he's with you, Hammer."

Dane shook his head. "I disagree."

"Noted. Now, can we ask why you called this meeting, and with Josie in tow, too?"

"And be quick," Theodore added. "The king's resting now but he'll need me when he wakes. He's been demanding today."

"Is that because he still feels unwell?" I asked.

Theodore nodded glumly. "It's the same complaint. He thinks he's going to die after every meal." He looked to Dane. "He demanded I fetch you but I told him to wait until after his rest. He wants the gem, and I don't think we can distract him this time. He was very distressed."

"The party didn't work?" I asked.

"It did, for a time," Balthazar said. "It seems the positive effects have worn off."

"And his poor dining habits have returned," Theodore added.

Dane set the box down on the desk. "You don't have to distract him anymore."

"It arrived?" Theodore asked as Balthazar reached for the box. "Thank the god and goddess."

Balthazar opened the box and plucked out the blood-red stone. It didn't glow or throb like the magic gemstone from the king's cabinet, but it looked the same in every other way.

Balthazar turned it over to inspect it then held it to one of the candles, the only light in the windowless room. "The jeweler matched the drawing perfectly."

"Who drew it?" I asked.

"One of the servants is artistic."

"The same one who sketches our faces for Laylana," Dane added. "We found a curtain in one of the salons that matched the color of the gem and sent the jeweler a piece along with the picture."

"No one noticed the missing fabric," Theodore said, taking the gem from Balthazar. "Shall I take it up to him now?"

"No," Dane said. "The king doesn't know we've opened the cabinet and seen its contents."

Balthazar rested his elbows on the desk and steepled his fingers. "He thinks we're obedient servants who wouldn't dare look inside his personal cabinet. Hammer, you'll have to take the cabinet to him and let him open it."

"After you've swapped this fake gem for the real one," Theodore added. He handed the gem back to Dane, who pocketed it. "Go immediately. He's going to wake soon and—"

The door burst open and the king charged in. I scrambled to my feet and curtseyed, but I doubted the king even noticed me. His furious glare was directed at Theodore.

"I woke up and you weren't there," he said.

Theodore bowed. "I'm sorry, sire."

"That's it? You're sorry!" The king moved further into the room. Behind him, a footman hovered in the corridor, looking like he wanted to be anywhere but there. He must have told the king where to find Theodore and escorted him. I wondered if the king knew his way around the palace like the staff, or if the corridors were a maze to him as they were to me.

"We apologize for inconveniencing you, sire," Balthazar said.

"You could have sent someone to fetch Theodore," Dane added. "There was no need for you to come all this way in person."

"And not catch him at whatever he's up to?" the king snapped. "Not catch all of you?" He looked around the small office with its map of the palace estate on the wall, the sideboard with the jug of wine and cups, the paperwork covering Balthazar's desk. His gaze skimmed over the empty box, dismissing it as unimportant as he dismissed everything else he saw. "What's going on?"

"It's a small matter of a servant," Dane said. "One of my guards. Nothing to concern yourself with, sire."

"If it's a small matter, why do all three of you need to be here?

Theodore has nothing to do with the guards. And why is Mistress Cully here?"

"I came to the palace to see how you fared, Your Majesty," I said, lowering my gaze in deference. "You were in pain last time I saw you, and I wanted to know if you felt better after a few days of eating a more healthful diet."

I glanced up when he didn't immediately answer, only to see him blinking rapidly at me. "You were worried about me?" It was the most vulnerable and humble I'd seen him for some time. When I'd first met him, he'd seemed like a youth out of his depth, a young man who needed reassurance and guidance. But he'd changed. Seeing him now, perhaps the insecure youth still lurked beneath the conceited, selfish man after all.

"Yes, sire," I said with a kind smile. "How are you feeling?"

"The pain has returned today, worse than ever." He pressed a hand to his chest, and his brow furrowed. "I don't think anything can be done. You were not able to help, and Doctor Clegg's medicine did nothing for me."

"No medicine can cure you, sire, although the pain could have been alleviated with the right tonic. Did Doctor Clegg use his own medicine?"

"He had it sent from the village apothecary."

"Aren't you the village apothecary, Josie?" Balthazar asked.

"The new doctor's wife makes her own medicines," I told them.

"Then she isn't very good," the king said. "Bring me one of *your* tonics, Mistress Cully." He rubbed his chest and winced. "The pain is almost unbearable."

"I'll send a bottle as soon as I get home," I said. "But it won't cure you. Do you understand? Only a change in diet will."

"I have ordered the cook to change it," he whined.

"Perhaps not enough."

"Or perhaps you're wrong and the problem is worse than you think. That would explain why Doctor Clegg's tonic didn't work. Hammer, I asked you to bring me my cabinet days ago. Why haven't you?"

"My apologies, sire," Dane said. "I'll fetch it now."

"I'll come with you. I want to know where you hid it."

Dane paused. "It's a considerable walk."

"Prepare three horses," the king said over his shoulder to the footman, still hovering in the corridor. "Make it four. One for Mistress Cully too."

"Why?" Balthazar asked as the footman left.

"I want her to check me afterwards."

"After what?" Balthazar asked, innocently.

The king dismissed him with a wave. "Theo, come with me. I need to change into something appropriate for riding."

The king and Theodore left, shutting the door behind them. I blew out a long breath as I sat heavily.

"You'll need excellent sleight of hand, Hammer," Balthazar said. "Don't let him see you swap it."

"Let's hope I was a conjurer in my previous life," Dane said.

"That's not amusing."

"I'm not laughing. Don't worry, Bal, I know what I have to do."

"I can try to distract him at the appropriate moment," I said.

Dane regarded me coolly. "I'm going to the stables. Wait here. I'll send someone to collect you."

Balthazar plucked his quill pen out of the stand. "She can wait here if she sits quietly. Quietly means no speaking, no sniffing, no coughing, no loud breathing."

I rose. "I'll come with you, Captain."

"Pity," Balthazar said lightly. "I'll miss your company."

"Liar."

He smiled at me and I smiled back.

"Careful, Bal," Dane said. "Flirting at your age could be bad for your heart."

Balthazar's smile vanished. "Go away. I'm busy."

Dane laughed softly as he shut the door behind us. "I'd prefer it if you went home," he said to me. "Being seen around the palace will only anger Barborough."

"I feel safer here, with you," I said.

He frowned, and I wondered if he was thinking the same as me —that my home was no longer a sanctuary.

"Besides, King's orders," I said cheerfully. "Do we have to ask a gardener for a shovel?"

"There's a shovel at the cottage. Do you still have the key for the gate?"

I'd attached it to a thin strip of leather and tied it around my neck for safekeeping. I pulled the key out of my bodice, over my head, and handed it to him. He placed it around his own neck and tucked it beneath his doublet before leading the way outside.

He walked close to me and scanned the vicinity, no doubt looking for Barborough. We reached the front gate without spotting him or being stopped.

"Has Lord Barborough left the palace today?" Dane asked the guards on duty.

"No, sir," one said.

"Let me know if he does."

We continued toward the stables, keeping pace with two sedan chairs. The ladies in the sedan chairs talked to one another loudly to be heard across the gap. They were gossiping about an acquaintance's wig.

"Did you know the governor changed his mind about clearing The Row?" I asked Dane.

He slowed his step to allow the sedan chairs to move ahead, out of earshot. "When?"

"Yesterday."

"He went against the Deerhorns' wishes?"

"It seems so."

We walked on in silence and I thought that was the end of the conversation; of all conversation. But as we reached the stable building, he said, "Something's not right. The governor is the Deerhorns' man. Stopping the clearance wouldn't be his idea; it would be theirs. But why would they stop it?"

"To keep the peace in the village? There have been protests every evening since the governor announced the clearance."

"Peaceful protests."

"There were fights. You broke up the one Ned Perkin started."

"That was nothing. Certainly not enough to worry the sheriff or change the governor's mind. The Deerhorns are up to something, but I don't know what."

I wasn't convinced. The governor might be the Deerhorns' man but he wouldn't want to see the protests escalate. The protestors might not pose a problem now, but as time went on, they could become more violent. Nor would he want to see his village overrun with the whores and thugs who used to be contained to The Row. He probably thought leaving the slum was a wiser course.

The king arrived at the stables in a sedan chair some time after us. Theodore walked behind, carrying a velvet-covered stool that he set down in the stable courtyard. A groom led the king's horse to the stool and stood by, holding the reins.

The king stepped onto the stool and mounted the horse. He winced as he settled in the saddle and pressed a hand to his chest. "Where to, Hammer?"

Dane mounted Lightning, his usual horse, and I was given Sky. Theodore's horse didn't look particularly lively either, and he held the reins as awkwardly as I held Sky's. The king was only marginally more comfortable than either of us.

We followed Dane out of the stable yard, toward the palace, and turned northerly to meet the Tilting road. No one spoke. The chatter of birds in the forest to our right and the thud of hooves on the packed earth were the only sounds. For someone who didn't like awkward silences, it strained my nerves.

It was a relief to reach the gate that led back into the palace grounds and through the overgrown arbor to the cottage. The sight of the pretty little house with its rambling garden was a soothing tonic. I took a moment to breathe in the sweet scent of the flowers while the men went on ahead, led by Dane.

"Wait here," Dane said, dismounting. "I'll fetch the shovel."

"I didn't know this was here," the king said, looking around. "Did you, Theo?"

"No, sire."

"I wonder how Hammer did. Hammer?" he called out. His horse's ears twitched and it walked forward. The king grasped the reins tighter and made shushing sounds.

"I stumbled upon it," Dane said, returning from the side of the cottage carrying a small shovel. He stopped at the spot where the cabinet was buried and removed his doublet. He threw it over a shrub then rolled up his shirt sleeves.

"Violette would like this place," the king said. "But it's too far from the palace. Theo!"

Theodore dismounted and assisted the king down from his

horse. I dismounted unaided and let the reins go. Sky joined the other horses, nibbling on a bush.

"This was a good place to hide it," the king said, hands on hips as he watched Dane dig. "No one would come all the way out here."

"Not even the gardeners," Theodore said, inspecting the long arm of a climbing rose that had been allowed to grow unchecked. It looked as if it had been neglected for years, yet it hadn't existed here mere months ago.

Sometimes it was easy to forget that the palace hadn't been here long. In a place of such wild beauty, it seemed as though the only kind of magic were the laws of nature.

I watched Dane dig. The muscles in his forearms bulged with each thrust, and those in his shoulders bunched beneath his white shirt as he threw the dirt to the side. I wasn't the only one captivated by the sight. Both Theodore and the king watched him rather than the hole he was making.

The hole was quite deep by the time he set the shovel aside and knelt on the ground. He reached in and pulled out the cabinet, brushing the dirt off. He set it down and picked up his doublet, and checked the pocket.

He frowned.

"What is it?" the king asked. "Open it!"

"I can't find the key," Dane said. "I had it when I dismounted, but now I can't find it."

The king squeezed the bridge of his nose. "I'm surrounded by incompetence."

"It must be here somewhere," Theodore said, searching the ground near his feet. "Perhaps over by the horses. Sire, will you help me look. Josie?"

Well done, Theo.

By the time we reached the horses, Dane called out that he'd found the key. He handed both key and cabinet to the king, and the king opened the cabinet.

The king snatched up the gem inside and clasped it to his chest. "Thank Merdu." He kissed the gem.

"It's beautiful," I told him. "King Alain must have treasured it."

"What? Oh. You're right, he did. My grandfather gave it to me

146

when we met. If you don't mind, I'd like to be alone. Go stand with the horses. And face the other way."

None of us witnessed what the king did next. By the time he called out that he was satisfied, knowing the gem was safely hidden, he'd returned it to the cabinet.

"I'll keep the key this time, Hammer." The king patted the pocket of his doublet. "Let's return. Violette will be waiting for me. She says she pines for me when I'm not there. She is a beauty, isn't she?"

"Seeing the gem has certainly lifted your spirits, sire," Theodore said. "You look better."

"I feel better. The chest pains are gone. It seems you were right, Mistress Cully, there was nothing to worry about. I won't be needing you to check me after all."

It would be pointless to remind him to eat well. He believed himself to be cured by magic. Although the fake gem held no magic, he believed it did. What more evidence did we need that he hadn't lost his memory? Whenever one of the servants who'd lost their memory went near the real gem, it had throbbed and glowed. It couldn't have done that for the king, ever, or he would have realized this one wasn't real when it didn't do it for him now.

"Rebury the cabinet, Hammer," the king directed. "I have to piss. Theo, go through there and make sure no creatures lurk in those bushes." He indicated the forest beyond the cottage clearing with a flick of his wrist.

Theodore set off but stopped when a twig in the direction he was heading snapped. Leaves rustled.

"Wait here," Dane ordered. He drew his sword and sprinted toward the sound.

I reached for Theodore's hand, needing the comfort as I watched Dane plunge into the bushes. Theodore's fingers gently squeezed mine.

Dane disappeared from sight.

A moment later, a shouted curse punched the air, sending birds screeching from the trees.

My heart plunged. The shout had come from Dane, and it was filled with pain.

CHAPTER 10

I crashed through the forest underbrush, stumbling over my own two feet. Branches scratched my face, tugged at my hair and clothes, but I didn't care. Nothing mattered but Dane.

Relief made my head feel light when I saw him sitting on the ground, alive. His foot was caught in an animal trap, the sharp teeth biting into his ankle above the boot. Blood dripped onto the leaf matter and dirt.

I fell to my knees beside him. My hand skimmed over the bunched muscles in his jaw before turning my attention to the trap. "Don't move."

"We'll pry it off," Theodore said, picking up a stick.

The king knelt beside me. His breathing was labored, his face damp from sweat. "No need. This type has a small catch. Remove it and the trap springs open." He tugged on the catch until it came away, releasing the spring.

Dane hissed as the teeth withdrew from his leg.

"Don't move," I said again as he tried to get up. "Let me stem the bleeding first."

I gently rolled up his pants leg and inspected the wound. The teeth had torn through flesh and lower calf muscle, but didn't appear to have reached the bone. I needed to clean the wound and inspect it properly to be certain.

I tore off a strip of my own underskirt at the hem and tied it tightly above the wound before tying another strip around the wound itself. The blood flow had already begun to lessen by the time I finished, thank Hailia. He would not bleed to death.

Dane tried to get up, but I pushed him back down.

"Theodore, help him to stand," I said, indicating he should take Dane's other side.

"I can do it," Dane said.

"I don't want you putting pressure on that leg. Put your arm around my shoulders."

"Move aside, Mistress Cully," the king said, nudging me out of the way. "Ready, Theo?"

Between them, they assisted Dane onto his good foot and headed back to the horses. Once in the saddle, Dane looked more comfortable, although his leg must have been throbbing.

"Theo, the cabinet," the king said. "Make sure it's well buried."

Dane tossed my cottage key to Theodore. "Lock the gate when you're done."

We left the valet and set off along the path, through the gate, to the road. I glanced often at Dane, but either the pain had subsided or he was a master at masking it.

"What in Merdu's name made you run off like that, Hammer?" the king asked. "It was probably only a pheasant."

"Probably," was all Dane said.

"You think it was poachers?" The king clicked his tongue. "Thieves. I'll inform Balthazar to order the foresters to search for traps before anyone else is injured."

"No one else will get hurt," Dane said. "Nobody ventures that far from the palace."

"Damned poachers."

"The trap was most likely set by our own foresters, sire. They catch the wildlife and send it to the kitchen."

"Those things are dangerous. I never liked them."

Dane eyed the king from beneath lowered lids.

"Somehow I remembered about the release catch," the king added quickly. "Isn't it odd how little things come to you yet you can't remember anything else?"

Dane faced forward again.

Theodore rejoined us before we reached the palace and handed the key back to Dane. Then he and the king peeled away to return to the stables. I rode with Dane through the gate, all the way to the garrison entrance, escorted by one of the guards.

Dane refused his assistance to dismount, and he refused to be helped into the garrison. He limped to a chair, sitting with a small groan. Quentin and Max frowned at him as he rested his injured foot on another chair.

"What happened?" Max asked.

"You're bleeding!" Quentin looked to me. "What do we do? Get bandages? Do you have some of that milk stuff for the pain?"

"I have nothing on me. Quentin, ride to my house. Tell Dora what's happened then bring back my medical pack. Grab the bottle of Mother's Milk from the larder, and bandages from my father's surgery. Everything else I need will be in the bag."

"I don't need the Mother's Milk," Dane said.

"You are truly the most stubborn man I've ever met. Now sit still. I'm going to remove the boot."

"I can do it."

"Did you hear me say *sit still*?"

He grunted, but at least he didn't try to remove the boot himself.

"What happened?" Max asked again.

"Forester's trap," Dane said. "Just a small one, probably for rabbits."

"Max, fetch clean water and cloth," I said as I unlaced Dane's boot.

As the sergeant left the garrison, I gently pried the boot off, earning another hiss from Dane. I cupped his calf above the wound, where I'd tied the tourniquet, and the muscle slowly relaxed.

"On a scale of one to ten, how painful is it?" I asked.

"Bearable."

"Can you wriggle your toes?"

He wriggled them and showed no signs that it hurt.

"Can you move your foot from side to side?"

He did as asked, again giving no indication that it pained him.

"Now move the foot up and down. Good," I said as he did it without wincing. "There's no major damage. I'll know more for certain once the wound is clean, but I'd say you've got nothing worse than a few cuts. You're lucky. I've seen men left with permanent limps after being caught in a trap."

He swore under his breath and shook his head. "I was a fool. I know the forest is full of them."

"It was the last thing on your mind."

"Even so."

"Do you think someone was there or was it just a pheasant, as the king suggests?"

"Someone was there."

Then that someone had seen the cabinet's hiding place, and if they didn't already know it contained the gem, they did now. "Where is the real gem?" I asked. "Your doublet?" We'd left the doublet behind but Theodore had picked it up. It must still be with him. "Dane?" I prompted when he didn't answer. "The real gem *was* in the cabinet. Wasn't it?"

He hesitated. "I removed it some time ago. I thought it wise to separate the gem from the cabinet. The cabinet was easy to find."

"Good thinking, I suppose, but I wish I'd known. I was worried the king would see you replacing it with the fake one. So where is it?"

"Safe."

I didn't press him. I knew he wouldn't tell me, no matter how many times I asked.

"I trust you, Josie," he said. "I just don't want you put at risk. It's best if no one but me knows. If the king realizes we gave him a fake today, he can't pressure anyone into giving up the location of the real one."

"He can pressure *you*."

His gaze connected with mine. "That's a risk I can afford to take."

Three guards entered and came to inspect the wound, only to be growled at by Dane. "You have work to do. And don't mention this to anyone. Understand?"

They filed out again.

"It's all right to admit you're in pain," I said. "It's not a weakness."

"You think that's why I don't want them talking?" At my shrug, he added, "No one must know about this."

"You think people won't continue to respect or fear you if you're injured?"

He tilted his head to the side. "I don't want anyone knowing you're performing a medical task."

"Oh." I stared down at the wound. "I see. Thank you."

"Besides, no one fears me," he muttered.

I smiled wryly.

Max returned carrying a basin with a cloth over his arm. Behind him, Balthazar limped in.

"I hear I have to lend you my stick," Balthazar said, brandishing his walking stick. "Will his foot fall off, Josie?"

"No," I said with a smile.

"Then what's all the fuss about? The sergeant made it sound like a disaster, but it seems you're enjoying Josie tending to you, Hammer."

Dane glared at him but didn't rise to the bait.

Balthazar leaned on his walking stick and peered down at the wounds as I cleaned them. If he hadn't made a small sound in the back of his throat, I wouldn't have looked up and seen his face drain of color.

"Max, get Balthazar a chair," I said.

Balthazar didn't say a word as Max helped him to a chair. He rested both hands on his walking stick and lowered his head.

"Take some deep breaths," I told him. "And don't watch."

Max placed cups of ale beside both Balthazar and Dane then fetched another for me.

"How did you get your foot caught in a trap?" Max asked. "Or am I not supposed to know?"

Dane told them about the rustle in the bushes near where the cabinet was buried, pausing only once when I cleaned the blood away from the deepest cut. The hand resting on his thigh curled into a fist before he resumed the story.

"I think someone was watching us," Dane finished.

"Should you remove the cabinet altogether?" Balthazar asked.

"The gem is a fake. It doesn't matter if someone digs it up. It'll be no use to them."

Theodore entered and enquired after Dane's injuries.

"I'm fine," Dane said, shifting as if he intended to his leg off the chair.

I caught it by the calf. "Don't move yet. Not until I've sutured the wounds."

"They don't need suturing."

I arched my brows. "Clearly you weren't a doctor before losing your memory, otherwise you'd know you need stitches. Since you're not a doctor, kindly keep your medical opinion to yourself. Now sit still until Quentin returns with my pack."

He folded his arms over his chest, but thankfully he didn't protest further.

Balthazar chuckled. "I knew he'd be a difficult patient."

"Probably as difficult as you would be," I shot back.

"The king wants me to report on your condition, Hammer," Theodore said. "He was asking after you. He was very worried."

"Speaking of the king," Dane said, "I think it's time we confront him. We should tell him we know about the gem, the magic—"

"No." Balthazar shook his head. "Not yet."

Dane blew out a frustrated breath. "The plan was to learn as much about magic as we could before confronting him, but we've learned almost nothing."

"Not true. We know about the wishes, the sorcerer, and the gem. What we don't know is what happens to us if the king dies."

"We're not going to kill him!" Theodore cried. "Just ask him some questions."

"You agree with Hammer?" Balthazar asked. "Listen. If we confront him, he'll deny it. If we present all the evidence we have, he'll either continue to deny it, or he'll feel as though we've backed him into a corner. Do either of you know what he'll do then?"

Silence.

"Neither do I," Balthazar said. "He's unpredictable."

"This can't go on," Dane said. "I need to know my past." His gaze lifted to mine before darting away.

"Lord Barborough is still here," Theodore said. "I propose we take him into our confidence and tell him about our memory loss."

"No," both Dane and I said together.

"He's more dangerous and unpredictable than the king," Dane added.

"I don't think he'll give you the answers you need," I said. "He knows nothing about the memory loss or he would have asked me if it were true. I agree with the captain. It's time to confront the king. He's the only one with answers."

"This isn't your decision to make, Josie," Balthazar said. "You're not involved."

"I am involved."

Balthazar sighed. "Young people," he muttered.

"We could search Barborough's rooms," Theodore offered. "For books or notes."

"I already have," Dane said. "I found nothing of interest."

Theodore threw his hands in the air. "Then what do we do? Wait for the king to make a mistake? To accidentally give us a clue about our backgrounds?"

The master of the palace pushed to his feet. "We do nothing, for now. Confronting him is a bad idea. At the very least, he'll dismiss us."

"He won't do that," Theodore said. "He relies too heavily on us."

"You believe that? Even now, with Lady Morgrave exerting influence over him? The Deerhorns will see that we're replaced with people they can control. People who won't let us near the king. And then where will we be? We'll have no answers and no way of getting answers. We'll also be cut off from the rest of the staff."

"Then what do you propose?" Dane asked.

"Leave it with me. I have a plan." Balthazar limped out of the garrison, Theodore on his heels.

There was nothing for us to do but wait for Quentin to return. The wounds were clean and the bleeding had stopped. Dane sat calmly, although he looked troubled. That could have been from the discussion rather than the pain, however.

Max rose and inspected the roster on the wall.

"You'll need to be in charge out there," I told him. "The captain will be off duty until—"

"No." Dane shook his head. "I'll remain on duty."

I crossed my arms. "How?"

"You could borrow Balthazar's stick," Max said, helpfully, only to follow it with an apology when Dane gave him a withering glare.

"I'll limit walking to a minimum," Dane said. "I can continue to ride into the village."

I rolled my eyes. "While you're there, please do see Doctor Ashmole."

"Why?"

"Because I don't like him and I can't think of a better way to annoy him than to inflict a stubborn patient upon him."

He crossed his arms too.

Max glanced between us, smirking.

Quentin returned with my pack, and I set to work suturing Dane's wounds. It wasn't easy. He tensed every time the needle went in and either grunted, hissed, or swore under his breath.

"Sit still," I told him. "You didn't want Mother's Milk so now you have to face the consequences."

He drew in a fortifying breath. "Just get it over with. Please."

Perhaps it was the plea in his voice, or the fact he looked vulnerable, but my heart tripped. My frustration at having a recalcitrant patient vanished. I set down the needle on the cloth and placed both hands on his leg above the wound. I caressed his calf with my thumbs.

"I know it hurts," I said gently. "But it'll be over soon. Sooner if you can be still."

He gave a short, sharp nod.

Standing behind Dane, Quentin held up the bottle of Mother's Milk.

Dane frowned then suddenly turned, but Quentin had already tucked the bottle behind him again.

"Quentin, pour another drink for the captain," I said. "I think he's going to need it. Not much," I added as he took the cup to the sideboard. "Just a little." I hoped he remembered I'd only used a small amount when I'd sutured Max's arrow wound when we'd first met. Diluted in ale, he could put in more, but not much.

I waited for Dane to drink the ale. When he only sipped, I told him to drink it all. "It'll numb the pain."

"This won't get me drunk enough," he said but drank it all anyway.

I pretended to clean and inspect the needle then re-threaded it while I waited for the effects of the Mother's Milk to take hold. When I noticed Dane relax, and his eyelids droop, I finished suturing the other cuts.

He didn't fall asleep, however. When I finished and smiled at him, he scowled back. "You put Mother's Milk in my ale."

"Yes."

"Quentin, you're taking over from Erik on prison duty."

"No, you're not," I told Quentin. "He was only following my orders," I said to Dane.

"I'm the only one who gives orders to my men." There was no anger in his tone, no resentment, only tiredness. He wouldn't make Quentin do prison duty, and Quentin must have known it because he didn't look worried.

I stood and patted Dane's shoulder, resisting the urge to kiss the top of his head.

With a speed I didn't expect from someone under the influence of Mother's Milk, he trapped my hand beneath his. "The key," he murmured.

I crouched and he removed it from around his neck and placed it around mine. It brought our faces very close. When our gazes connected, it was as if the sorcerer had placed a spell on us. Everything else ceased to exist for me in that moment—the room, his injury, Max and Quentin. There was only Dane and his handsome face, his blue eyes and strong jaw.

Then the garrison door opened, and Dane looked away, breaking the connection. The leather strip slid through his fingers, but before he let go, he brushed his thumbs along the underside of my jaw. "Thank you," he whispered.

I stepped back, feeling as if I'd just woken from a deep sleep. I tucked the key into my bodice and accepted a pouch from the footman. It jangled with coins. Balthazar thought of everything.

"Quentin, take Josie's bag and escort her home," Dane said. "Make sure Lord Barborough goes nowhere near her."

"You should rest now," I said. "Max, help him to the dormitory."

"I can rest here," Dane said.

I mouthed "Good luck" to Max over the top of Dane's head and left with Quentin.

* * *

I RESISTED the urge to find out how Dane fared all the following day. The day after that, I gave in and sent word to Balthazar. I knew I'd get an honest answer from him. He sent his cryptic response with Kitty and Miranda.

"He told us to tell you that all is well in the garrison," Miranda said as she accepted tea from me. Dora and Remy had gone out early that morning and not yet returned, leaving me alone with my thoughts and very little to do. The visit from my two friends was a welcome distraction.

"What does that mean?" Miranda asked.

Dane wouldn't want me telling anyone of his injury, and I didn't want to have to explain what had happened and where. I waved a hand in dismissal. "Two of the guards fought the other day."

"Over you?"

"No!"

Kitty sighed. "How romantic."

"They didn't fight over me," I assured her. "Kitty, are you all right?" She looked glum and not at all her perky, pretty self. Her eyes were slightly swollen too, as if she'd been crying.

"I'm well," she said with a smile. Kitty might not be all that bright, but she knew how to be a lady. It was second nature to her. And being a lady meant smiling when she was sad, laughing at jokes that weren't amusing, and dancing when her feet ached. This smile *looked* genuine, but I didn't believe it. "We have something to tell you, Josie. Some gossip."

I leaned forward. "Go on."

"The king is feeling better."

I waited but she didn't continue. "You came into the village just to tell me that?"

"No," Miranda said, glancing at Kitty. "There's another reason for our visit. Kitty?"

Kitty reached across the table and clasped my hand in both of hers. Her smile turned bright. "We wanted to see you, of course. And you're right, there is more. The king seems a little frosty toward Lady Morgrave lately."

"Really? The last time I saw him, he talked about her a lot. He seemed besotted with her."

"Not in the last day or two. It's nothing too noticeable, however, just a cooling between them. It's not on her part. She continues to flirt with him and push herself onto him at every opportunity. He still sits with her and talks to her, even kisses her sometimes, but something's changed."

"I heard he no longer takes her to his bed," Miranda added. "And he's flirting with other ladies."

"Including Miranda again."

I frowned at Miranda, worried that the king's renewed attention would encourage her parents to consider marrying her off to become queen.

"Don't look at me like that, Josie," Miranda said. "I know exactly how to manage the king and men like him. Now, Kitty has something to ask you. It's the real reason we came today."

Kitty stared into her teacup.

"Tell her," Miranda urged. "She's a midwife and your friend. You can trust her."

Midwife? Kitty was with child? Why did that make her unhappy?

It turned out I'd guessed wrong. Her announcement wasn't that she was with child.

"I'm barren," she said, blinking back tears.

Miranda gave Kitty her handkerchief and Kitty dabbed her eyes. "I thought you might have a remedy," Miranda said to me. "Not that I've ever heard of such a remedy, but I know you village apothecaries sometimes make up your own medicines and I just thought..." She trailed off and rubbed Kitty's shoulder.

"I'm afraid I don't," I said. "How long have you been trying?"

"Ever since we got married, two years ago. It never seemed to bother Gladstow until recently. Since we arrived at the palace, he's changed towards me. He used to be good to me, buying me whatever I wanted. Now, he ignores me. He doesn't come to my bed, and if he does talk to me, it's just to say something cruel." A tear slipped down her cheek. She wiped it away with the handkerchief. "He blames me for not giving him an heir. He says it's the only reason we married. He didn't want a wife, you see." She pressed the handkerchief to her mouth and sobbed into it. "He called me useless. As useless as a broken ornament, that's what he said."

Miranda put her arm around Kitty's shoulders. "Don't listen to him. He's a horrid man."

"He's my husband."

The Duke of Gladstow was more awful than they realized, but telling them I'd seen him torment Lady Claypool wouldn't achieve anything except further hurt.

"The problem could be him," I ventured.

"It's not," Kitty said. "He has an illegitimate daughter by a woman who used to work for him. It happened before he met me. I've seen the girl. She has the Gladstow nose and eyes. He's definitely the father."

"Sometimes these things take time. I know couples who had children after years of trying. My mother told me about a woman who bore a child after being married for eighteen years. There is hope."

"There might be, if he bothered to come to my bed."

"He will again," Miranda said.

I kept my mouth shut. I'd rather be accused of being barren than having that man in my bed. But I wasn't Kitty.

"What will I do if he keeps ignoring me?" Kitty wailed. "What if he decides he wants an heir more than he wants me as his wife?"

Was she suggesting murder? A man could only remarry after his first wife died. Barrenness wasn't an excuse to set her aside and marry another. Kitty needed to be diverted from such dark thoughts.

"Give it more time," I said gently. "And try not to worry. Eat healthy food and enjoy the things you've always enjoyed."

Kitty wiped her eyes with the handkerchief. "Thank you, Josie. Perhaps you're right and our time hasn't come yet. I'm sure he'll return to my bed soon."

"That's it, keep your spirits up," Miranda said, handing her the cup of tea. "You're the Duchess of Gladstow. Never forget that."

"No, Miranda. I am the Duke of Gladstow's wife."

C.J. ARCHER

WITH THE ELLS from Balthazar's payment, I was able to fill my basket the following morning at the market. It was wonderful to load it with fresh produce and the best fish. We'd dine well for a few days, and I might even do some baking.

I lingered in the market, enjoying conversation with people I saw less of these days. Many asked me about the palace, knowing I still went regularly. They listened intently to my report of the dazzling sights, the scale of the building and gardens, and the animals kept in the menagerie.

The mood of the marketplace was generally somber, however, with the usual complaints of high prices and rising rents on everyone's mind. Some spoke about the problems in The Row and the governor's now-abandoned plan to demolish it. Many thought as I did, that a dilapidated roof over one's head was better than no roof at all.

I returned home via The Row and waved at the two guards on duty at the entrance. Dane wouldn't appreciate me discussing his injury with his men, so I continued on without asking how their captain fared.

Once home, I gave Dora a loaf of bread and some apples to deliver to her friend in The Row. She and Remy set off, and I returned to the kitchen and searched for my mother's recipe for butter biscuits. It had been an age since I'd tasted them, and even longer since I'd baked a batch. My father would laugh if he saw me. Baking and the other domestic arts were not my strength.

The soft click of the front door opening had me looking up from the recipe book. I hadn't locked the door after Dora left. She might have forgotten something, but I'd had too many unwelcome visitors of late to assume it was her returning.

I grabbed the metal stirring spoon and tiptoed toward the dresser near the door where the knives were kept.

I didn't reach it.

Lord Barborough rushed into the kitchen, his black riding cape billowing behind him, his face twisted with wild rage. I barely had enough time to gasp before he kicked me in the stomach. I stumbled to the floor, breaking my fall with my hands, jarring my wrists.

He stood over me, a foot planted on either side of my hips. I scrambled back toward the table, but he pressed his boot against my thigh, hard enough for it to hurt but not hard enough to break the bone.

He withdrew a knife from his belt. "Don't move," he snarled. "I have no qualms about peeling the skin off your pretty face and serving it to the palace pigs."

CHAPTER 11

I tried to form words, to beg, but my heart pounded in my throat and nothing came out but unintelligible babble.

"You've been avoiding me," he snarled.

"No!"

His foot pressed harder. "I saw you at the palace in the company of a guard. Always in the company of a guard."

"I—I wasn't avoiding you."

"Stop lying! Have you told the captain about me? About our agreement?"

I nodded. He would have known it was a lie if I claimed I hadn't. "He forced me to. He wanted to know why I was asking him so many questions."

"You stupid fool!" He leaned forward, putting his weight on the foot, crushing my thigh, and thrust the knife under my chin. It stung as it bit into my flesh. "You've made me the captain's target."

"I don't understand."

He wiped his sweaty brow on his shoulder and adjusted his grip around the knife handle. The knuckles were white, the muscles taut. His hand would cramp soon or his palm might become too sweaty to grip properly. He couldn't swap the knife to his other.

"I was moved to a small, shit-hole of a room in the attic. No one would tell me why. And someone followed me one night and threatened me. It made no sense at the time, but the shadowy figure…it must have been that thug of a captain."

He pressed hard on my leg, and I cried out. Tears burned my eyes, blurring my vision, as he thrust his face into mine. He bared his teeth as he pressed the blade into my skin. "I'm going to cut you up so he doesn't recognize you."

"I learned something from him!" I blurted out. Desperation and fear loosened my tongue. I wished it hadn't. I wanted to be stronger, braver, but blood trickled down my neck and my leg ached from the pressure.

To my utter surprise and relief, he eased back. My words had intrigued him, given him hope. At that moment I realized I wasn't the only desperate and afraid person in the kitchen. He was facing execution in Vytill if he returned without information.

"Tell me," he snapped.

"It's about the gem. If I tell you, you have to let me go."

"That depends on how good your information is."

I swallowed. "I think the sorcerer's magic is contained within the gem Sergeant Brant told you about. The king used the gem's magic to create the palace."

"I know that already."

"No, my lord, you *suspect*. But I saw him use it to make a wish to improve his health."

He cocked his head to the side. "You saw him?"

I nodded.

"What words did he speak to it? How did he make the magic work?"

"I didn't see or hear, but I do know his health has improved." It was a risk to pretend that the king had used the real gem. If he started to feel ill again, Barborough would know I lied. But I had no other choice. "Has he been looking better?"

He eased right back, giving me my answer. "Where is the gem now?" he asked.

"The king has it." Lie upon lie upon lie. He looked like he believed me, thank the goddess.

"Where does he keep it?"

"I don't know. He doesn't confide in me. I'm nothing to him."

"As you are nothing to me. You're not even worth the bloodstains."

He removed his foot from my thigh, and I was able to scramble away toward the dresser. I used it for balance as I stood. Lord Barborough's gaze fell on the knives in the block, but he seemed unconcerned that they were within my reach.

"If you tell anyone that you've spoken to me about the gem, I will come back for you," he said. "And I won't be so gentle next time."

He tucked his knife into his belt and strode out of the kitchen. The sound of the front door opening and closing was the sweetest thing I'd ever heard. I sucked in a deep breath of pure relief and pressed a hand to my racing heart. My thigh would soon sport a bruise in the shape of his boot, and the cut beneath my chin still stung, but those had been worth it. Lord Barborough was finished with me. All I had to do was not tell anyone about this visit. Not even Dane.

One other positive had come out of Barborough's visit. I'd learned that he wasn't the one who'd followed us to the cottage. He hadn't known where the gem was located. If he had been the one watching us from the forest, my life might not have been spared when I lied about its whereabouts.

* * *

MY ENCOUNTER with Lord Barborough played on my mind overnight. So much so that I needed to see Dane. Not because I wanted to tell him, but because he made me feel safe and not weak. He lightened my heart and bolstered my spirit.

I had no excuse to go to the palace, so I went to The Row instead, and I was glad to see Quentin guarding the entrance with another guard. He hailed me with a beaming smile.

"Thank Merdu for sending me someone to talk to," Quentin said.

The other guard glowered at him. "Am I invisible?"

"You just want to talk about swords and fights."

"What else is there to talk about? The latest fashions?" He snorted. "Don't answer that. I know what you'd say."

"I'd rather talk about diseases and wounds."

"Come closer. I'll give you a wound to talk about."

Quentin edged his horse away.

"You're not wearing armor," I said, patting his horse's nose. "That's a good sign."

"There hasn't been any trouble in The Row for days," Quentin said. "Not since the governor abandoned his plans for clearing it out."

"The Vytill faction is no longer trying to take over from the Glancians?"

"Doesn't look like it. Captain says the injuries on both sides took their toll."

That was probably because Doctor Ashmole wouldn't see them. It wouldn't surprise me if some of the men now had festering wounds thanks to the poor conditions in The Row and lack of medical attention.

"I reckon the captain will withdraw all of us soon," Quentin went on. "There ain't no guards inside anymore, just us at the entrance."

"Speaking of the captain, how is he?" I asked, keeping my voice low.

"Annoying everyone, especially Max, Theodore and Balthazar. His list of orders is long, on account of he can't do most things himself. He rides into the village sometimes, though."

"So he's keeping off the foot?"

He chewed on his bottom lip. "I don't want to get him into trouble."

"So that's a no."

"He's on it less. Is that good enough?"

"He should be off it completely."

He leaned down and whispered, "Don't tell him I told you."

"I have no reason to go to the palace, so your secret is safe."

"He'll visit you, I'm sure of it."

I didn't tell him he was wrong, that Dane wouldn't make up an excuse to call on me.

"He's coming here soon, when the shift changes," he said. "Want me to tell him you asked after him?"

I hesitated then nodded. What Dane did with the information would be up to him.

I returned home, only to stop at the top of my street upon seeing a carriage outside my house. It must be Kitty and Miranda again.

It wasn't until I got close that I saw the distinctive crest depicting a stag, its sharp antlers reaching to the corners of the shield. A Deerhorn footman jumped down from the back and caught my arm before I could run into my house. He hustled me to the carriage door and knocked.

Lady Deerhorn peered at me through the window and gave a single nod. The footman opened the door and, before I knew what was happening, shoved me inside.

The carriage sped off.

I went to open the door, but Lady Deerhorn held it shut. She was a tall woman but no more solidly built that me. I might be able to force her to let go of the door handle, but then what? Jump out and risk an injury? Even if I managed to land on my feet, she'd send her footman to chase after me.

"So you are smart enough to realize you can't get away," she said, letting go of the handle.

"Where are you taking me?" I snapped.

"That isn't the right question. A better question is, what do I want to do to you?"

I swallowed.

"My son has need of you," she went on.

"Wh—what?"

Her lips curved into a smile. On anyone else, it would have been a nice smile, but with her ice-blue eyes, it was chilling. "Xavier doesn't know it yet, but he's about to get what he wants. For some odd reason that I can't fathom, he wants you." Her gaze dipped to my breasts. "So I'm giving him to you. Let's call it an early birthday present."

I stared at her.

Then I lunged at the door.

She grabbed me by the hair, jerking my head back hard.

I cried out and my hands flew to my head. She let go as she shoved me into the seat again.

166

I withdrew my hands even though my scalp felt as though it were on fire. "You're mad," I choked out.

"Not mad. Furious."

"Why? What have I done to you?"

"You filthy little liar. You *whore*. What did you get for the information?"

"I—I don't know what you're talking about."

A small crease appeared between her brows. For the first time, she seemed to be uncertain, as if she stood on shifting sands.

"Is this about The Row?" I asked. "Because I was *forced* into giving my opinion that night. I wasn't expecting anyone to agree with me, let alone for the governor to suddenly change his mind. I swear, that's not my doing."

"This has nothing to do with that stinking hole."

The carriage rolled over a dip, sending us both rocking violently. Lady Deerhorn grabbed at her hat before it slipped off. I glanced outside and my heart dove. We were on the road to the Deerhorn estate. Few village folk took this road. It led only to the Deerhorns' house. No one would pass us. Once we reached the family's stronghold, it would be easy to lock me up in a room where no one could find me.

I had to jump out and get away before we reached the estate's gate.

"The king heard a rumor," Lady Deerhorn went on. "One that *you* must have whispered in his ear."

"Me? But I don't have access to the king."

"You've been seen coming out of his rooms and riding off with him."

"I have no influence over the king. What rumor am I supposed to have told him?" I realized the answer as soon as the question was out of my mouth.

Merdu. No.

"He heard a rumor that Morgrave didn't die of a weak heart," she said. "He heard he was poisoned, not stabbed or strangled or suffocated. *Poisoned.* That's very specific. The only person who could have told him that is you."

"Doctor Clegg could have," I said weakly.

She scoffed. "I paid him too well."

"It wasn't me, my lady! Please, let me go."

"Ever since he found out, the king has changed toward Violette. He treats her warily, as if he's afraid she'll kill him next. The distance between them grows by the hour. Soon, he'll have a new favorite."

I understood her anger and frustration. She had been so close. She'd almost gained the throne through her daughter's marriage to the king. She didn't care about the situation in the village. The Row meant nothing to her compared to the power she could wield as the queen's mother. The magnitude of her daughter's fall matched the hatred she bore for the person she assumed orchestrated that fall.

Me.

I glanced out the window again. Hedgerows marking the edge of the Deerhorn estate followed alongside the road. Soon we would enter the gate.

"What did he offer you to tell the king?" she asked. "Money?"

"Who?" I muttered, trying to suppress my fear. If I was to get out, I had to watch her carefully, anticipate her moves, and choose my moment. I couldn't let fear freeze my mind or limbs.

"Don't play the innocent," she spat. "It might work on the captain of the guards, but it doesn't work on me. What did Barborough offer you? Or was it one of the dukes?"

I shook my head. "This is madness. My lady, please, I didn't say anything to the king." An idea gripped me, and wouldn't let go. It was a little mad, but it was better than jumping out of a moving carriage. "I can fix this problem for you. I can convince the king that Lord Morgrave *did* die of heart failure."

Her eyes gleamed as she regarded me. She was assessing me, and perhaps assessing whether I could accomplish what I promised.

"I'll say favorable things about Lady Morgrave to him," I added. "I'll tell him she's sweet and kind, that she'd make a wonderful wife and queen."

I searched her face for signs of it softening, that she was willing to let me try. But her eyes only hardened and her lips thinned.

"You've already told me you don't have his ear," she said. "How can you possibly turn the tide against Violette? It's too late. You've destroyed my family's chances of rising, so now I will destroy you."

She lifted her hand to strike me, but I deflected the blow. A ripple of shock passed over her as she realized she had no power over me. No *physical* power. No doubt she was used to maids cowering before her.

Then a slow smile stretched her lips, and her hard eyes turned cruel. She didn't have to be stronger than me. Her son was. And he would be waiting for me.

I shrank into the corner. From there I could see the gate ahead and the winding drive up to the Deerhorn castle, perched on the cliff overlooking Tovey Harbor. The antlers lining the top of the gate between the stone posts forked into the sky, a warning to the uninvited to venture no further.

When the carriage slowed on the approach to the gates, I would make my move. I steadied my breathing and readied myself.

But the carriage didn't slow. Up ahead, two men dressed in Deerhorn livery opened the gate. We would drive right through without stopping. Without slowing.

I would not escape before reaching the castle. Not unless I wanted broken bones.

CHAPTER 12

*L*ady Deerhorn studied me with a cold gleam in her eyes and a sneer on her lips. "My son will be pleased with his gift. He always did have simple taste. I have to say, I'm not happy with his choice this time, but I have no doubt he'll grow tired of you once he's had you. The real question is, what do we do with you once he's finished?" Her mouth stretched into a thin smile. "Not that it matters. You have no one waiting for you at home. No one to care if you go missing."

I didn't bother to respond. She was beyond listening to what I had to say.

"You've learned from your mistake, I see, and are keeping your mouth shut. It seems the lower orders can be taught after all."

Her smile suddenly vanished as the carriage slowed. Someone shouted as a rider rode past. I pressed my face to the window to get a better view, but the rider had disappeared. I reached for the door handle, but Lady Deerhorn caught my hand in a bruising grip.

She thumped the carriage ceiling. "Why have we stopped? Move on, driver!"

The carriage didn't move. The footman standing at the back strode past on his way to the front.

"What's going on here?" he demanded. "Move away, at the command of Lady Deerhorn!"

The footman suddenly stopped and the rider came into view. Dane! Thank Hailia and Merdu. He looked ferocious atop Lightning, his sword drawn, his features set hard.

His gaze connected with mine through the window and his chest expanded with his deep breath.

Lady Deerhorn's grasp loosened, and I pushed her off, only to be caught again. "I haven't given you permission to leave," she snapped.

"Let her go," Dane demanded.

"I don't take orders from you."

"But you do take orders from the king, and my sword acts on his behalf."

Her hesitation was all I needed to wrench free. I stumbled out of the carriage and ran to Dane. He let go of the reins to hoist me up, one handed, and settled me, side saddle, in front of him. I nestled against him, my shoulder to his chest. Safe.

"The king will hear about this," Dane said. "You can't kidnap his subjects and not expect consequences."

"I had just cause," Lady Deerhorn hissed. "Your whore is telling lies to His Majesty about my family, my daughter."

Dane's body tensed. "You're referring to Lord Morgrave's death? That wasn't Mistress Cully. I told the king. I was there when she saw the body in the sedan chair. I overheard her diagnosis."

Lady Deerhorn's lips parted with her gasp.

"Drive on," Dane ordered.

The carriage rolled forward. The footman jumped onto the back as it passed, and I got a final glimpse of Lady Deerhorn through the rear window, her face twisted with rage, before the gate closed behind the carriage.

Dane sheathed his sword and both arms circled me. I tucked my head beneath his chin and clung to him, my fingers curled into his doublet. His heart beat strongly, its rhythm as erratic as mine. I felt it through every part of me and pressed myself against it, wanting to be as close to that heart as possible, wanting his arms to hold me tighter.

I wanted to tell him how his presence was a comfort, but that might start something we couldn't stop, something he didn't want until he knew more about his past. Besides, I didn't trust my voice.

"Are you all right?" he asked, his voice rumbling through his chest.

I nodded.

"Did she hurt you?"

I shook my head.

His arms tightened, and we rode slowly back to the village. I closed my eyes and listened to his breathing and heartbeat as they steadied, and mine responded in kind. I relished every second, every breath and beat, but it was over all too quickly. The village came into sight and he loosened his hold.

"How did you know where to find me?" I asked.

"Meg and Dora both saw you pushed into the carriage. They were running to The Row to alert one of the guards on duty, but I happened to be on my way and intercepted them. They told me which way you'd gone. Other witnesses pointed out the route along the way. It wasn't difficult to work out she was taking you to the estate."

He spoke formally, the tenderness of earlier gone. I missed it.

"Did you tell the king about the poisoning?" I asked.

He suddenly looked at me. "No. Merdu, no. I said that so she wouldn't come after you again."

"Then who did?"

He shook his head, but I wondered if he had his suspicions. "She won't try that again," he said. "She knows it wasn't you who told the king, and she knows I'll come for her if anything happens to you."

I peered up at him, but he kept his gaze focused straight ahead. I touched his hand, resting on his thigh. "Thank you, Dane. For everything." I heaved a sigh. "Thank you isn't enough."

"It will have to do."

Remy was sitting on the stoop out the front of my house. He leapt up upon seeing us and banged on the door. "She's back! He found her!"

Dora and Meg rushed out, looking relieved. "What happened?" Meg asked. "Are you all right?"

"I'm fine," I said. "We just went for a drive. Don't worry."

Dane jumped down, landing on his uninjured foot. He reached

up and assisted me to dismount, quickly releasing me when I was on the ground.

"I must go," he said, watching Dora usher Remy back inside. "You have your friends to comfort you."

"Thank you again," I said.

"You don't need to thank me, Josie." He managed to leap onto Lightning without putting a foot in the stirrup. Between mounting and dismounting, he hadn't given any sign that he sported an injury. Only an extremely observant person would have noticed he didn't put weight on it.

"I forgot to ask, how is your leg?" I said.

"Fine."

"Keep the wounds clean. See a doctor if it becomes red and hot."

He gave a single nod then rode off. I tried not to let his cool manner affect me, but with the kidnapping fresh in my mind, and then the tenderness he showed after rescuing me, I felt raw. I watched him until he was out of sight, but he didn't look back.

Meg hooked her arm through mine. "Come inside and have some soothing tea. You look like you need it."

* * *

I DIDN'T WANT to leave the house for the rest of that day—or the next. Every time I considered it, my heart started to pound and I felt cold. Even though I knew Dane was right, and Lady Deerhorn wouldn't attempt to kidnap me again, I couldn't bring myself to go out. Fear was an insidious thing. It managed to seep through the smallest cracks and spread.

It was fortunate that neither of the expectant mothers called for me. Sooner or later I would have to leave, however, but not yet.

My house didn't provide the complete sanctuary I hoped for, however. Mistress Ashmole may not be as terrifying as Lady Deerhorn or Lord Barborough, but she was an unwelcome visitor nevertheless. I invited her inside for tea but was grateful when she refused. Polite conversation with her would be painful.

"Let's not pretend to be friends," she said, peering past my shoulder into the house.

I blinked, somewhat stunned by her bluntness. "We have to live in this village together," I said. "Let's be civil."

She plucked a coin purse from her basket. "How much for a bottle of Mother's Milk?"

"Oh. I'm glad you want to buy it. It really is a great pain reliever during surgery."

"How much, Mistress Cully?"

"Forty ells."

"Forty!"

"It's expensive to make and difficult to source ingredients. I only have one bottle left."

"You inflated the price just for me."

"You cannot increase the price if there was never a price to begin with," I said. "This is the first time it has ever been sold."

"So you simply made up an amount on the spot? This is unprofessional, Mistress Cully. You ought to be ashamed of yourself, charging the village's only doctor such a high amount for something that will bring comfort to his patients."

"That's the price, Mistress Ashmole." I stepped aside. "Do come in while I fetch the bottle."

She lifted her basket onto her hip and entered. "I'll buy one quarter of a bottle," she said, following me into the kitchen where Dora stood at the fire, stirring a pot. "For five ells."

"Ten is a quarter of forty," I said, heading into the larder. "I prefer not to sell it all anyway as I still need some for my patients."

"Patients?"

"Expectant mothers."

"You shouldn't call them patients if they're not ill."

I paused, bottle in hand, and frowned at her. "Why not?"

She sniffed. "People will confuse your service with that provided by a doctor."

I couldn't help the laugh that bubbled inside me.

"I wouldn't laugh if I were you, Mistress Cully. You wouldn't want that mistake to be made. The consequences will be severe."

"It's just a fine, Mistress Ashmole."

I measured out a quarter of the Mother's Milk into a smaller bottle, being very particular so she couldn't complain. She inspected the contents of the larder shelves as I worked, removing lids of jars and bottles, smelling contents, and reading labels.

"Is there something else I can help you with?" I asked, handing her the bottle.

She placed it in her basket and opened the purse. "One more thing," she said, handing me ten ells. "Does your maid have a friend looking for work?"

"Dora isn't my maid," I said. "I've never had a maid, but I'm sure you can find one if you ask around. There are many women in The Row who would be happy to—"

"I don't want one of those godless creatures in my house! A respectable woman can't associate with one of them, not even as an employer."

Dora tapped the spoon on the edge of the pot, hard. The clang reverberated around the kitchen. Mistress Ashmole hoisted her basket higher on her hip, and sniffed.

"I'm a respectable woman," I said. "And nothing terrible has come of me associating with anyone from The Row."

"But I am a doctor's wife."

"And I a doctor's daughter."

"But no man's wife."

She walked out of the kitchen. I picked up my skirts and marched after her, determined to slam the door behind her.

"A shame your father didn't find you a husband before he died," she tossed over her shoulder. "Now you're all alone with no hope of making a good marriage with neither family nor money to recommend you."

"Thank you for your advice, Mistress Ashmole," I said through a tight smile. "Let me reciprocate with some of my own. If you want to make friends in the village, be kind to your neighbors and patients. Otherwise they'll gossip about you in the market."

She matched my smile with a hard one of her own. "We already are making friends, Mistress Cully. We've been invited to dine with the governor, twice. But I see you are content with the sort of friends who are better acquainted with gutters than mansions."

"Gutters *and* palaces," I said, my smile turning genuine. "Paupers and kings. I like the variety."

Her face fell. I slammed the door on it and stormed back into the kitchen.

"That woman!" I said as I paced back and forth. "I've encountered snakes with less venom than her."

"It's not her tongue you should worry about," Dora said. "Why'd you sell her that medicine?"

I frowned. "I don't follow. Why wouldn't I sell it to her? She paid a fair price, and I still have some for my own use. I can't let Doctor Ashmole's patients suffer."

"She can use what you sold her to work out what's in it then make her own."

"She won't be able to work out all the ingredients, let alone the quantities. Not before she and her husband move on from Mull. And they will move on, Dora, I'm sure of it. That woman won't be satisfied with a seaside port, no matter how busy Mull gets. She'll have her sights set on Tilting, at the least, or preferably get her husband a position as private doctor to an important man. We'll be rid of them one day."

"Maybe," Dora said, turning back to the pot. "But what damage will she do to your business before she leaves?"

* * *

A VISIT from Quentin was a marked improvement on my last caller. I was so pleased to see him, I hugged him in the doorway.

"Everything all right, Josie?" he asked, blushing.

"Wonderful, now that you're here." I ushered him through to the kitchen and poured tea. Dora and Remy had gone for a morning stroll, enjoying the fresh air and freedom outside The Row.

Quentin removed his sword belt and groaned as he settled into the chair.

"Are you unwell?" I asked. "Injured? You haven't been fighting with Brant again, I hope."

"The captain doesn't let me near him. Brant's been on duty a lot anyway." He smirked. "He's working so hard he's too tired to bother anyone. He doesn't complain, though. It's like he wants it."

Perhaps he needed the hard work to take his mind off the hopeless situation he and the others found themselves in. I poured the tea into cups and handed one to Quentin.

"It's being on the horse all day at The Row," Quentin said, shifting his weight in the chair, trying to get comfortable. "My backside is sore and my thighs ache. One thing's for sure, I was no horseman before I came to the palace."

"Or guard."

"True. Wonder what I was."

It was impossible to guess. He was intelligent and could read and write, but his speech lacked the grammar of an educated man. Dane was educated, I was certain of it, yet he was a man of the outdoors too. He could ride, swim and use a sword and fists with ease, but he hadn't known about the spring in the rabbit trap. The king had, however.

"Josie," Quentin said carefully. "Do you think we'll ever remember?"

I placed my hand over his. "Yes, I do."

"How? We don't even know where to find the sorcerer. And if we do find him, will he even give us our memories back? We can't pay him..."

I squeezed his hand. "We'll worry about that later. For now, we wait. Balthazar has a plan. Trust him."

He slumped in the chair and leaned his cheek on his fist. He looked ready for bed. "Maybe not remembering is a good thing. Maybe our pasts were bad and we wouldn't want to remember. That's what Hammer said."

"He did?"

"Aye."

Dane may have said that, but he still wanted to know about his past. Without knowing it, he couldn't move forward. None of them could. It was like being frozen in time, paused mid-journey with no knowledge of either origin or destination.

"There's one thing I do know about your past," I said.

He sat forward. "What?"

"You were as likeable as you are now."

He sat back again. "I s'pose. Part of me hopes there's someone waiting for me, that I was loved. Then I think about how that person must feel, not knowing what became of me."

It was a sobering thought. It was awful for the servants to have no memory, yet if they'd been suddenly ripped from their lives by the sorcerer, their loved ones must be frantic. It was curious that we'd not heard reports of disappearances and searches.

Then again, many of the servants looked like Freedlanders, and very little news reached us from the republic. Tucked away at the bottom of the Fist Peninsula, with steep cliffs and treacherous ocean to the south and west, mountains in the east, and a deep river marking its northern border, it was an isolated nation. Even traders didn't venture there often. Freedland was mostly self-suffi-cient. Their mines exported stone for building, and a little gold and silver, but otherwise, it was a nation of desert sand and rebels. As the only republic on The Fist, it was treated as an unruly place by the neighboring kingdoms, where sedition festered.

My father, however, claimed Freedland and its people were full of surprises. He'd met free thinkers there, self-educated men who voiced their opinions and sometimes paid a high price for it. The revolution of forty years ago had been quite recent when he trav-eled, and the people and landscape still sported the scars.

I wondered if there were any ships from Freedland currently moored in Tovey Harbor.

"I asked the captain if I could see his foot injuries," Quentin said.

"Pardon?" I asked. "Sorry, I was miles away."

"The captain. I asked to inspect his injuries so I could learn, but he wouldn't let me."

"There's not much to see now that they're stitched up. Remind him that he must keep the wounds clean."

He brightened. "I could offer to clean them for him."

I was about to tell him not to be disheartened if the captain refused, when someone pounded on the front door.

"Must be urgent," Quentin said, rising. "Want me to get it?"

"It's probably one of my patients."

I opened the door to a woman dressed in little more than rags. Her hair fell from an untidy knot, down one side of a face marked by a curved scar, and an unpleasant smell wafted from her body.

"Are you the doctor?" she asked, eyeing me doubtfully.

"The midwife," I said.

"I need a doctor. I was told to come here. I was told you will help my sister."

"The doctor is named Ashmole. He lives on the edge of the village."

"Not him," she spat. "He won't come."

"Are you from The Row?"

She nodded. "My sister says you'll come. She says she saw you before. You helped Remy. My sister says not to bother the new doctor. He won't help the likes of us."

I chewed on my lip. I knew someone would come to me sooner or later, but I hadn't accounted for Doctor Ashmole refusing to enter The Row or even treat the slum residents if they visited him.

Quentin came up behind me. "She can't go," he said to the woman. "She's not allowed to do doctoring."

The woman's hands caught mine. They were as rough as some of the servants' but much dirtier. "Please," she said, tears filling her eyes. "She's cut up real bad and the bleeding won't stop. You have to come or she'll die!"

Merdu.

"I can pay." The woman fished out a coin from her pocket. She stared at it a moment before reluctantly offering it to me. "Please, miss."

"Keep your money," I said.

A tear spilled down her cheek. "But—"

"Let me fetch what I need."

The woman pressed a hand to her heart. "You'll come?"

"I'll come."

I grabbed bandages and suturing equipment as well as the bottle of Mother's Milk from the larder. I placed everything in my basket then added a loaf of bread. At the last moment, I filled another jar with fresh water from the pail by the back door and threw in a clean cloth. I covered it all with a second cloth then rejoined her and Quentin.

"Want an escort?" Quentin asked me.

"Thank you, but I don't think that's necessary," I said.

When Dane had entered The Row with me, the residents had looked at him as if they wanted to draw him into a fight. It was dangerous for the guards. Quentin wasn't equipped for fighting. The woman would be a better escort.

I left him and headed toward The Row, walking quickly. "My name is Josie Cully," I said. "What's yours?"

"Seely," she said. "And my sister's Lacey. She's in pain, Mistress Cully."

"Who cut her?"

"A man."

I didn't press her. She probably wouldn't know his name anyway, and he was most likely one of the dozens of dockers who ventured into The Row to pay for their pleasure.

"You know Dora and Remy?" I asked.

"Not well."

I greeted the two guards at the entrance and informed them I had a pregnant patient to see beyond. Thankfully Seely didn't correct me. The guards exchanged worried glances.

"It's not a good idea to go in, Josie," one said.

"It ain't bad in there no more," Seely told them. "There ain't no more fights."

"I'm not asking you," I said to the guards as I passed between them. "I'm simply informing you out of courtesy." I didn't look back as I strode off along the street.

Seely took me to a lane set back from The Row, the original thoroughfare that gave its name to the entire slum as it expanded. It was as quiet as she claimed, and I found it to be unchanged from the other times I'd visited. There was no unrest, no fights, only people staring at me as I passed. There seemed to be more in number. The Row was as busy as Mull's marketplace, but with residents congregating in narrower, grimier thoroughfares, and the only enterprise was that provided by the prostitutes. They were as conspicuous as any market stall holder, however, as they lounged in doorways, their shoulders bare and sometimes their breasts too.

"Through here," Seely said, holding back a curtain flap strung up in a doorway. No, not a doorway, but an entrance to the narrowest lane I'd ever seen. More curtains were strung up between stacked crates on one side of the lane for its entire length. The unmistakable sounds of sexual encounters came from behind some of the curtains.

Seely lifted one, revealing a cubicle that was little wider than the pallet of straw positioned in the middle of the room. A woman lay on the pallet, her arm cradled to her chest and eyes closed. The room smelled of sex and sweat, and it was as filthy as Seely's dress. Stains marred the crumbling walls and ceiling, and would have been visible on the floor if it had one. The pallet lay on uneven earth.

"Lacey?" I asked, kneeling beside the figure.

She stirred and tried to sit up but groaned.

"Stay still," I said. "Show me your arm."

Lacey hesitated. She looked a lot like Seely, with lank hair, small eyes and a wide mouth. Her face wasn't scarred like Seely's, but from the look of the cut on her arm, she'd forever have one there.

The skin was sticky with blood but at least it wasn't dripping. The cut was only two inches long but looked deep. Lacey cried out when I touched it.

"Why did the man cut you?" I asked as I cleaned the wound with the cloth and fresh water I'd brought from home.

"It don't matter," Lacey said. She screwed up her face but didn't cry out again as I gently wiped the blood away.

"It does matter," I said. "Men can't go about cutting up women."

"This is The Row. Men can do what they want."

The wound clean, I offered Lacey a few drops of Mother's Milk. "It'll sooth the pain while I stitch the wound." I showed her the needle and thread.

Seely made a small sound of protest in the back of her throat. "You going to stick that in her?"

"It's all right," Lacey told her sister with an encouraging smile. "You heard her. She's going to give me something for the pain."

"She'll barely feel it," I assured Seely.

Seely still frowned.

Lacey reached for her sister's hand. "You did good, Seel. Real good. Now go on outside while the doctor fixes me. Don't talk to no one, mind. Don't talk about this. It's our secret."

"Thank you," I said gratefully. "It can't be known that I'm doing this. I'm not allowed."

"Why not?" Seely asked.

"It's the rules," Lacey told her. "What will happen to you if they find out?" she asked me.

"I'll be fined and reprimanded."

Lacey relaxed into the pallet and opened her mouth to accept the drops of Mother's Milk from the spoon.

"I still got the coin," Seely said brightly, producing the ell. "Want me to put it with the others?"

Lacey nodded and Seeley slipped the ell beneath her sister's pallet before parting the curtain and leaving. It flapped back into place, but it was so thin it didn't stop the morning light coming through.

"My sister's simple." Lacey tapped her forehead. "But she won't blab. I can't say the same for the other folk around here, though. Understand?"

I gave her a reassuring smile. "In my experience, the people in The Row keep to themselves and don't talk to the authorities."

Lacey's eyes drooped and she yawned. I set to work and had the wound sutured in a few minutes.

My work done, I left her to sleep off the effects of the Mother's Milk. Seely wasn't outside, but I knew my way. Only one man approached me as I left, and he was clearly drunk.

"You're a pretty one," he said, stumbling. "How much?"

I bent my head and tried to move past him, but he stepped in my way.

"Leave her be," said another man, leaning against a wall. He had the crooked nose of a fighter and the brawn to match. "That's the midwife. Come in here, instead. I've got a girl for you."

With the drunkard distracted, I hurried on and breathed a deep breath as I rejoined the two guards at The Row's exit.

"Everything all right, Josie?" one asked.

"Everything's fine."

Despite my assurance, I was glad when I arrived home. I unpacked my things and returned the bottle of Mother's Milk and the loaf to the larder. I hadn't intended to give the bread to Lacey or Seely, merely use it to pretend I was providing help if my presence in The Row was questioned. But the visit had gone better than I'd expected, and I hadn't needed the ruse. The guards hadn't interrogated me and no one had accosted me. No one even knew I was there to perform a medical task except for the sisters. Even the thug in the doorway had called me the midwife, not the doctor.

All was well.

* * *

I VISITED the dock at Tovey Harbor before the workers finished their day and settled in for an evening of drinking at The Mermaid's Tail or The Anchor. I avoided the pier itself, where boats lined up to load and unload and porters and sailors jostled one another for position. Row boats and fishing vessels maneuvered around the larger ships anchored in the deep waters. In the harbor's center, the arduous process of removing sand from the floor, bucket by bucket, to deepen it had begun. I didn't envy the divers or laborers, but they were grateful for the work, so Dora told me.

I squinted to see the flags flying on the ships but could not make out Freedland's red star on a yellow background. I asked one of the porters I'd known my whole life but he said there'd been no Freedland ships for weeks, although some of the ships from other kingdoms had sailed there and traded with the locals. He couldn't point out any specifically, but told me to ask around at one of the taverns later.

It was a tempting idea. Perhaps I'd send Dane a message. By the time I reached home, I'd decided it was certainly worth pursuing. If folk in Freedland were searching for loved ones, surely the sailors from the trading vessels that passed through would know.

I was in the middle of writing the message when Dora answered a knock on the door. Her gasp sent my heart racing.

She entered the kitchen with Sheriff Neerim and one of his constables in tow. Thank goodness it wasn't Lady Deerhorn or Lord Barborough. The sheriff looked serious, however, and a sickening feeling settled in my stomach.

"Is something wrong, Sheriff?" I asked.

"Afternoon, Josie." He cleared his throat. "I'm sorry about this, but, er, you have to come with me."

"Where are we going?"

"Prison."

"You're arresting me! Why?"

Remy entered and Dora drew him to her. "You can't take her away!" Remy shouted. "Josie ain't done nothing wrong. She's a good person."

"Shhh," his mother said, hugging him.

"What's this about, Sheriff?" I asked, trying to sound calm for Remy's sake.

The sheriff shifted his weight. "You're under arrest for performing a medical task without a license."

"I don't know what you mean," I said weakly.

"It was reported that you sutured a wound of someone in The Row."

"Reported by whom?"

"A witness."

I cocked my head to the side and thrust a hand on my hip.

"I can't give you a name," he said, sounding exasperated. "I'm sorry, Josie. I have to do this. Come with me to the prison."

"But I merely have to pay a fine. You don't need to lock me up."

"I have to jail you until money for the fine is raised."

"How much is it? I'll pay now." I had the ells from the sale of the Mothers Milk plus a little left over from Balthazar's payment after I treated Dane's injury.

"A thousand ells."

Dora gasped.

I reached for the chair for balance as the floor seemed to shift beneath my feet. Sheriff Neerim took my arm, either to support me or to ensure I didn't flee.

"That's a ginormous amount," Remy muttered.

"I can't pay that," I murmured. "Why is it so much? The offence isn't that terrible."

He looked away and pressed his lips together. "I'm sorry, I don't decide the fines. The amount is determined by the magistrate. He set it before I came here."

I groaned. The magistrate was appointed by the governor, and the governor was the right hand of the Deerhorns. That's why the fine was high. They wanted to make sure I couldn't pay.

"What happens if I can't afford it?" I asked.

"You can." He gave me an encouraging nod. "You can, Josie. This house must be worth that, if not more. Until it's sold—"

"Sell my house!" My stomach rolled violently and tears stung my eyes. "B—but where will I live?"

"Worry about that later. For now, you have to come with me. We'll organize it from the prison." He tugged my arm but I resisted. "It'll be all right, Josie."

How could it be all right? It wasn't fair. The fine was out of proportion to the crime.

Yet there could be no appealing it. The Deerhorns would see to that. Lady Deerhorn had her revenge on me after all.

I blinked back tears as I stared at Dora and Remy. They would be homeless again too.

"Don't worry," Dora said, looking like she was holding back her own tears, but only just. "I'll speak to Meg's family and send word to the captain."

My first instinct was to tell her not to inform Dane, but I set my pride aside. I was going to need all the help I could get.

he prison cell reminded me of Lacey's cubicle. It was just as small, just as cramped and dirty. The only difference was the bars covering the entrance instead of a curtain. At least it didn't smell of sex, although the stink of urine was strong, overpowering the briny scent of the sea.

The prison's two cells were located in caves once used by smugglers, carved by waves into the cliffs just outside the village. At high tide, the water lashed at the entrance, prohibiting anyone from coming or going. In the past it hadn't been a problem, with so few arrests, but now the drunkards were more numerous and arrests happened all day and night. It meant the sheriff's men had to mind offenders in their office if the prison was inaccessible. Unfortunately, it was low tide when I was led into the cell.

I wasn't alone. Two women sat on the straw covered floor, both in their middle age and dressed in similar rags to Lacey and Seely. I recognized neither.

"You try to get some business at the dock too?" one asked, eyeing me up and down.

"'Course she didn't," said the other. "Look at her. She ain't a whore." She wiped her nose on her sleeve as she watched me search for somewhere to sit. "I've seen you before."

"I'm the midwife," I said.

I bunched up some dry straw with my foot and sat on the pile, wrapping my skirts around my legs. I wasn't taking any chances of something crawling up them.

The cell was damp and cool with iron bars built into the cave walls. If I wanted to use the bucket to relieve myself, I had to do so in front of not only the two other prisoners, but also anyone who happened to walk past. The bars afforded no privacy. Beyond our cell was another, occupied by male prisoners. A drunkard shouted abuse from time to time, followed by a second man growling, "Shut your hole."

I sighed and closed my eyes, only to open them again. While the two women might look harmless, I couldn't afford to take chances with my safety.

Thankfully they were in no mood to chat. I had to think of a way to get out of my predicament.

But as time slipped interminably by, I realized there was no way out. The Deerhorns had set a trap for me and made sure the fine was too high for me to pay. The magistrate and governor wouldn't go against them. Lacey and her sister had been part of the scheme too. I should have realized when they'd mentioned coins. No one in their predicament had enough money to offer me payment. Lacey had looked relieved when I'd told her I'd merely face a fine if someone found out what I was doing. Like me, she probably thought it would be an affordable amount.

I didn't blame them for taking the money offered by the Deerhorns. Lacey's cut had been very real, and their poverty was no lie. They had fewer options than me.

I blamed Lady Deerhorn. This scheme had her mark all over it. She'd probably ordered Lacey to be cut up to make it more authentic.

The light in the cell dimmed as the sun sank lower on the other side of the cliff. Soon it would be dark. I hadn't expected to spend a night in the prison, but it was looking likely. With the jailor guarding the cave entrance, out of sight from the cells, I couldn't see if anyone had come for me and been denied entry. I was entirely at the mercy of the jailor, an employee of the magistrate's office, not Sheriff Neerim, and not a man I knew. If he wanted to refuse someone entry, he could do so.

The rattle of the keys was a beautiful sound. I leapt up and clutched the bars as the jailor appeared. He scratched his beard as he regarded me through the bars.

"This ain't right," he said. "No one's s'posed to go free until the tide lowers. Ain't no visitors allowed and no one gets released at high tide, but my orders are to let you out." He shook his head as he inserted the key. "Ain't no one cares about the rules no more. It ain't right. Rules are rules. You got to enforce the rules or people get ideas—like them in Freedland. And then what? Revolution, blood gets spilled, and people lose everything." He continued to shake his head as he pulled the barred door open. "It ain't right. You shouldn't be going free until low tide, just like everyone else."

"Who is making you set me free?" I asked.

"Them's my orders."

He locked the cell door and hooked the keys onto his belt. I followed him into the office where the sheriff stood near the cave mouth, his hands behind him. He nodded at me.

"Glad to see persistence pays off," he said with a glare for the jailor.

"It ain't right," the jailor muttered as he wrote something in the ledger on the desk. "Go on, get out before the magistrate changes his mind."

The sheriff ushered me outside where small waves lapped at the sand and rocks. "You're lucky," he said. "Conditions are calm today."

I removed my shoes and lifted my skirt, but the hem still got wet. We climbed the steps built into the cliff to freedom above, where Meg waited. She scooped me into a hug.

"Thank Hailia and Merdu," she said. "I've been so worried. Are you all right?"

"Fine," I said.

"What was it like?"

"Filthy."

She checked me over, as if expecting me to have suffered physically in the short time of my incarceration. She looked grave and grim, and if I didn't know any better, I would have thought someone had died. "Come on, Josie. You have to come home."

"Just a moment." I hailed the sheriff before he mounted his horse. "The jailor says I shouldn't have been freed until tomorrow."

The sheriff cast a glance back down to the cave. "He's a fool who can't think for himself. I ordered him to set you free immediately, although it seems he had other orders to keep you as long as possible. But he can't argue with the official paperwork."

"The magistrate signed my release?"

"Seems the palace sent a stern letter, reminding him of the service your father once performed for the king. When a settlement was reached regarding the fine, the magistrate had no reason to keep you, and he didn't want to offend the king."

Dora must have got a message to Dane in time, and he had asked the king to help me. "The fine has been paid by the king?"

He shook his head. "Nobody paid it. The magistrate deemed you unable to afford the fine, so he ordered the confiscation of your house and possessions in lieu of payment."

"My house..." I muttered pathetically. It had happened so quickly, without even giving me time to find an alternative way to pay.

"I am sorry, Josie. It was out of my hands."

I folded my arms against the ice creeping into my bones. Where would I go? What would I do? I no longer had a roof over my head, and nowhere to make and sell my medicines. I'd spent my entire life in that house, it was impossible to imagine not living there.

In one day, my life had changed completely.

But I wouldn't be defeated yet. Surely I could appeal the verdict. Surely I could use my good name and that of my father to set it right again. Surely it wasn't too late.

Meg put her arm around my shoulders. "You can stay with us," she said gently. "My mother is already organizing it."

"What about Dora and Remy?"

"They're welcome to stay too."

We both knew the arrangement couldn't last long. The Divers couldn't afford to feed all of us and didn't have the space in their small house.

Meg steered me away, but the sheriff called after me. "A word of warning, Josie. Don't do any more doctoring. The first offence is a fine. The second is jail."

"For how long?"

"The length of the sentence is determined by—"

"The magistrate," I finished for him. I didn't think my heart could sink any lower, but it did.

I walked with Meg back to the village, glad that the streets were quieter than they had been earlier. I didn't want to face the stares and whispers from people I'd known all my life. I was too tired, too overwhelmed, and didn't want to cry in front of them.

The entire village must know what had happened by now, but I refused to feel humiliated. I'd done something to be proud of. It was Doctor Ashmole who should be ashamed for not treating the poor.

We were met crossing the village square by Dane, riding fast in our direction. He halted and jumped off his horse, landing lightly on one foot in front of me.

"You're free," was all he said. He didn't take my hand, didn't embrace me, but his worried look was enough to shred my last piece of strength.

I burst into tears.

Meg embraced me as I buried my face in my hands. "Let's go," she urged. "It's not far."

I allowed her to steer me the rest of the way home. No, not home. I had no home.

The thought left me feeling strangely hollow and light headed, as if my soul had vacated my body and only the shell remained.

I wiped my cheeks and glanced back at Dane. He had mounted and followed at a steady pace.

"Thank you for coming," I said, dully.

He frowned as he drew alongside us. "I would have come sooner but the king was being stubborn."

"I don't understand."

"Dora and Remy came to the palace. It was some time before I was informed, but when they told me what had happened, I appealed to the king to overturn the decision."

"And he refused?"

He peered over my head to a point in the distance. "He didn't want to interfere in a village matter. One of the ministers who was with him at the time assured the king it was best to look impartial since you were clearly guilty. Neither Theodore nor I could convince the king otherwise, despite reminding him of everything you've done for him." His grip tightened on the reins. "And Balthazar doesn't have access to that much money without a signature from the finance minister."

"Yet you sent a letter to the magistrate anyway, ordering my immediate release. That was your doing, wasn't it?"

"Mine and Balthazar's. The king's signature is easy to falsify." He finally lowered his stormy gaze to mine. "You shouldn't have spent a moment in that jail. You shouldn't have to pay the fine."

"I'm guilty of performing a medical task. There are witnesses. The arrest and fine are valid."

"Let me guess," he bit off. "Someone in The Row asked for you. A woman, probably. She was paid by the Deerhorns to trick you."

Meg gasped. "Is that true, Josie?"

"Most likely but how to prove it?" I said. "The woman's injury was real. The cut would have festered if I hadn't stitched it. Doctor Ashmole has already made it clear he won't offer his services to anyone in The Row, even if they can pay, which most can't."

"That's awful!" Meg cried. "It's wrong. How can he call himself a man of medicine if he'll stand by and let people suffer—even die? I loathe him. Him *and* his wife."

"I should have come sooner," Dane said heavily. "I'm sorry, Josie."

I patted Lightning's neck. "There's nothing you could have done. Appealing to the king was my best hope of avoiding the fine. You weren't to know he'd refuse."

He blew out a deep breath and his body lost some of the tension. It was as if he needed my forgiveness before he could forgive himself.

"You can stay at the cottage," he said.

"No, I can't."

"It's why I gave you the key. It's for an emergency. This is an emergency."

Meg looked from me to Dane and back again. "What cottage?"

"On the palace estate," I said. "Too far from here for my patients. Captain, I have to stay in the village. If I am to keep my position as midwife, I have to be accessible. And I must work, now more than ever. I have nothing else."

He once again focused his gaze over my head. I expected another argument about the cottage at a later date. At least for now, he let the matter go.

We turned into our street where a cart had pulled up outside my house. It was loaded with two chests and several crates, as well as a bed. Mistress Ashmole stood nearby, directing two men to unload the crates and take them inside, while Meg's parents watched from their side of the street.

I ran forward, but Dane was quicker on horseback.

"What's this?" he demanded.

Doctor Ashmole emerged from the house but backed away under Dane's glare. "We're not doing anything wrong," he said quickly. "It's all official. We have the paperwork to prove it." He disappeared inside.

Mistress Ashmole thrust out her chin. "This house is now ours."

"You can't have purchased it already," I said. "It was only confiscated this afternoon."

Her lips stretched into a thin smile. "It's leased to us, effective immediately." She glanced up at the sign of the cupped hands, swaying gently in the breeze. "I must say, it suits our needs perfectly. It's well located and will do nicely as my husband's medical practice. How fortunate that everyone already knows this as the doctor's house."

"Everyone?" Meg sneered. "Or just those who live outside The Row?"

I tightened my hold on her arm in case she lunged at Mistress Ashmole. "I'll raise the money to buy it back," I snapped.

She laughed, a brittle sound as dry as the summer air. "You are a foolish woman with no understanding of the world."

Her husband appeared behind her, waving a piece of paper. "The lease agreement."

Meg's parents joined us, both looking anxious. "He showed it to me," Mr. Diver said. "It's been signed by the magistrate and governor, Josie. The house has been leased to the Ashmoles." He patted my arm. "I'm sorry. There's nothing you can do."

"This is absurd!" Meg cried. "It's unfair!"

"The world isn't always fair, love." Mr. Diver tried to put his arm around her, but she shook him off and grabbed my hand.

"You'll stay with us, Josie," Mistress Diver said to me. "Your things have already been moved into Meg's room."

Meg shared a room with her sister. There was little space left for me.

"The magistrate's order says they can keep everything in the house except your clothing and a few items of a personal nature," Mr. Diver said.

Dane ordered Doctor Ashmole to hand him the lease papers. He read through them then handed it to me. Mr. Diver was right. All my belongings except for a few personal items had been confiscated to cover the fine.

I was utterly destitute.

"Thank you, Mistress Diver," I said numbly. "I accept your generous offer."

"You're our neighbor and your family have been great friends of ours for years," she said. "We won't abandon you now, when you need us most."

She was right. I needed every little bit of kindness now. The charity of people I'd known my entire life was my only hope.

Tears welled again. Accepting charity was more humiliating than my arrest.

Mistress Ashmole barked orders to the men carrying her things inside. I turned away, no longer able to watch the only home I'd ever known being taken over by a pair of vipers.

Dora and Remy hurried toward us down the street. Remy immediately turned his attention to Dane's horse, but Dora took my hands in both of hers.

"You're free," she said on a breath. "Thank the goddess."

"Thank you for fetching the captain. But what will you two do now?"

She gave me a wobbly smile and cast a sad look at her son. "Don't worry about us. You have enough problems of your own."

How could I not worry about her? Her only option was to return to The Row. Her old room in the run-down building was most likely taken now, and she'd have to fight for a small patch of floor beneath a leaking roof. Or she'd have to work in one of the brothels.

There was only one way to keep her and Remy safe, yet it wasn't in my power to give it to her.

"Come to the palace," Dane told Dora. "I can find you a position in the kitchen. You'll be paid the same as the other servants."

I gawped at him. He was willing to take the chance of placing Dora among the servants? He'd do that for her? For me?

"That's kind of you," Dora said. "But my son will get in the way."

"Remy can spend the day in the commons courtyard," Dane said. "One of the maids teaches some of the other servants to read and write when they're not working. She seems to enjoy it. She can teach Remy, too."

Dora touched her lips, tears pooling in her eyes. She blinked at Remy, who'd turned his full attention onto the conversation when he heard his name.

"I'd like to read," he said. "Josie's been teaching me the letters."

"Are you sure it will be all right?" Dora asked Dane.

"I wouldn't offer if it wasn't," he said. "There will be rules."

"I'll follow them," she said quickly. She stood behind Remy and placed her hands on his shoulders. "We both will."

"Collect your things from the Divers' residence and come with me. You can start in the morning."

Mistress Diver took them inside. I approached Dane and lowered my voice. "I thought you'd offer her the cottage."

"There's only one key. If she has it, you can't open the gate or the door." His gaze turned warm. "The cottage is for your use, Josie."

I touched the key hanging around my neck, nestled against my skin. "Balthazar won't like this."

"Balthazar owes you."

"Why?"

His gaze shifted to the activity at my house, where Mistress Ashmole snapped at one of the movers. "Be careful," he said to me. "The Deerhorns won't like that you're out of prison already."

"What more can they do to me? They've taken my home, rendered me destitute, and restricted my ability to sell medicines." All those tonics, salves and ointments in the larder, gone. They were Mistress Ashmole's to sell now. She'd got her full bottle of

Mother's Milk after all, and paid a mere quarter of its worth. A fire of anger lit inside me, replacing the hollowness.

"Before you go, will you wait while I fetch something? Something I suspect wasn't included in my personal belongings."

He nodded and informed the Ashmoles that I had an item to collect. Mistress Ashmole crossed her arms but didn't bar my entry. If she knew I was fetching the recipe book for medicines, she probably would have tried.

I found the book in the larder and tucked it under my arm, then rejoined Dane outside. I knew all the recipes inside by heart, but I wouldn't let Mistress Ashmole have it. "My private journal," I told her.

She didn't look like she believed me, but with Dane watching on, she didn't dare challenge me.

Dora and Remy returned too, their meager belongings fitting into one pack. Dane attached it to his saddle and they set off, Remy chatting excitedly about seeing the palace. Just before they left the street, Dane turned around. He lifted a hand in a wave before settling it on his thigh.

Meg sighed. "How romantic."

"It was just a wave, Meg."

"I mean giving Dora and Remy a home. He did that for you, Josie."

One of the movers dropped the end of a large dresser he was carrying and Mistress Ashmole informed him she would pay him less because of it. They would have an abundance of furniture now, between theirs and mine. They could profit from selling pieces off.

"I hope the council is charging them a fortune in rent," Meg said as we walked to her house together.

"I'm not sure it will stay in council hands for long. I suspect they'll sell it to the Deerhorns to add to their tally of properties in the village."

"Speaking of the Deerhorns, they must be held accountable for what they did to you."

"How? We can't even prove they're behind it, let alone do anything about it if they are."

I paused on the threshold and looked across the road to the

house I'd been born and raised in. The house where my parents had died, where I'd learned to be as good a doctor as my father, and where Dane and I shared our first kiss. So many memories had been created there, and now two heartless wretches had taken it over.

But those memories weren't in the house, they were within me. And I would hold them close.

* * *

WITH ONLY MY midwifery duties to occupy me now, I visited my two patients early the following morning to reassure them nothing would change except where to find me. I then went into the village square and spoke to as many people as I could at the market, informing them I was living with the Divers.

"I'm still the midwife," I told the women.

"And your medicines?" more than one asked. "Will you still sell them?"

"Not at the moment."

I couldn't take over Mistress Diver's kitchen and larder for the purpose. She'd done so much for me already and continued to reassure me that I could stay with them until I married. I wasn't quite sure whom she expected me to marry, but I didn't ask.

I made sure I was seen by as many as possible at the market before heading to the dock. I answered more questions there from concerned villagers about my arrest. All commented on the injustice and the steepness of the fine. If nothing else, the morning proved to me that I had many friends and well-wishers in the village. It was heartening.

That wasn't my only reason for visiting the dock, however. I stopped some of the sailors and asked them if they'd been to Freedland in recent weeks but none had.

I started heading back to the village square only to be hailed by Ivor Morgrain. I groaned and considered not stopping, but I hesitated too long. He dumped the sack he was carrying and cut off my path.

"What's going on?" he asked.

"Nothing I feel like discussing with you, Ivor."

"I hear you've been asking around about Freedland. Why?"

"None of your business."

"You should be careful. Talking about Freedland might make people think you're interested in revolution."

I rolled my eyes. "Don't be ridiculous. Step aside, please. I'd like to go."

"Go where? I hear you ain't got a home no more."

"My home is with the Divers now." I didn't know why I was explaining anything to him. I owed him nothing. "Good day, Ivor."

He caught my hand and stroked his thumb along mine. "Josie," he murmured, stepping closer. "You've lost your house, and you have no folk."

"I have friends."

"It ain't the same."

I withdrew my hand "What do you want, Ivor?"

He rubbed his shirt front over his heart. He reminded me of the youth he'd been before he'd fallen in with Ned Perkin and his friends. Those innocent days seemed so distant now. "I know I ain't the man you want, but I can be better. With you beside me, I *know* I can be better. You can guide me, help me become the sort of man you like."

This couldn't be happening. Not now, when my emotions were raw and my world was in turmoil. "Don't, Ivor. We've been through this."

"Things are different. I've got money saved. I can't buy a house, but I can rent one. For you and me, Josie. A nice home here in the village for you to call your own again. You can make it look real nice, just the way you want. Let me help you."

"In exchange for marrying you?"

He swallowed heavily. "Marry me, and I'll give you a house and let you continue with your apothecary and midwife work. You'll be happy again, and as my wife, you won't have to worry no more about going to prison. I'll protect you."

"Ivor..." I sighed. "I'm not going to marry you."

He pressed his lips together. "You don't have to answer now. Think about it. You *have* to get married, Josie, and I'm offering you a good life. A safe life." He pecked my forehead. I was too stunned to pull away in time. "I'll call on you."

"My answer will be the same," I said. "I won't marry you. You can't make me happy, and I can't make you happy."

"That ain't true."

There was no arguing with him. He saw himself as my rescuer, and nothing I could say would convince him otherwise. Not yet. In time, it would sink in. I just had to avoid further encounters with him until then.

* * *

NEWS OF A BRAWL in The Row spread quickly the following morning. The two factions were at war again, and it had taken more palace guards than last time to stop them. It was Lyle who alerted us to the trouble. He'd seen four guards leave my old house sporting bandages and had made inquiries.

"One of them asked after you," he said to his sister.

"Me?" Meg sucked on the inside of her cheek and frowned. "Oh no."

We raced outside but the guards had left.

"Was he a square-set fellow?" I asked Lyle.

He nodded.

"I told you Max liked you," I whispered to Meg.

"There's more," Lyle said. "The guard told me one of the sheriff's men, Uther Lessing, was stabbed. He lost a lot of blood and Doctor Ashmole couldn't save him. He died in there early this morning." He nodded at my old house.

"How awful," Meg murmured.

When would it end? How many more lives would be lost before the two factions stopped their senseless war?

We decided to head to the market even though we had no intention of purchasing anything. Gossip was free in Mull and plentiful today.

The strange looks began immediately. Sometimes they were furtive, embarrassed almost, but others scowled at me.

"Don't listen to them," said Sara Cotter, her baby wrapped in a sling tucked against her chest. "They're just malicious tattlers with nothing better to do."

She went to walk off, but Meg called her back. "What's everyone saying? Why are they looking at Josie like that?"

Sara frowned. "You don't know?"

"Would we be asking if we did?"

Sara glanced around. Two women I knew, a mother and her adult daughter, pretended not to see me, but I noticed their sly looks, their mutterings to one another out of the corners of their mouths. This was different to yesterday's reaction after my release from prison. Something had happened.

"They say the trouble in The Row is your fault, Josie," Sara said.

"Me?" I cried.

"They say Uther Lessing would still be alive if you hadn't interfered."

"Why do they say that?"

"Because you patched up the thugs in there so they could fight again."

"I did not! I attended a woman, not men. No one else, just her."

"Honestly!" Meg said, hands on hips. "Everyone believes whatever absurd stories are passed around without checking the facts first. For Hailia's sake! How can they believe such nonsense when they've known Josie her whole life?"

"That's the problem," Sara said. "We know Josie would help anyone, no matter who they were, no matter what their circumstances. Some don't think she ought to help the whore masters and gang members. Some say she should just let them die."

It was a heartless view, but it was impossible to argue against it after the death of one of Mull's own. I'd grown up with Uther Lessing's daughters. He'd been a good man. "Who is spreading these rumors?" I asked.

"Everyone. I don't believe them." Sara raised her chin and her voice. "If you tell me you didn't help the gangs then I believe you, Josie."

"Thank you," I said, pressing my fingers to my aching forehead. "I would appreciate it if you continued to tell those who think otherwise."

She gave me a pitying smile and went on her way.

Meg sidled closer to me and lowered her voice. "We should go. I don't like the way some are looking at you."

We edged away from the market, but we didn't get far before Arrabette Fydler intercepted us. "You should be ashamed of yourself," she said, loudly enough for those nearby to hear. "If it weren't for your meddling, Josie Cully, Uther would still be alive."

"His death has nothing to do with me," I said. "You're believing stories that aren't true."

Arrabette clicked her tongue. "Lower your voice. You're making a scene."

"I have a right to defend myself," I said, not lowering my voice one bit. "Listen. All of you!" I scanned the faces, gratified that I had the attention of most. "I stitched up the wound of a woman, not a man. She was destitute, dressed in rags, and living in a filthy room no bigger than a larder. If I didn't suture her wound, she would have died, leaving her simpleton sister to fend for herself. I am not ashamed that I helped her when the village doctor would not, and I am certainly not responsible for last night's riot or Uther's death."

It was a relief to see some nods of agreement and to receive smiles of encouragement. But not everyone nodded or smiled. Some walked past, their faces averted.

Arrabette sniffed. "You've changed since you've been going to the palace, Josie. You used to be full of youthful innocence and sweetness. Now you're…different."

"I grew up," I said.

"She lost her father!" Meg spat. "She's had to fend for herself since his death."

"And whose fault is that? You should have been married, Josie. None of this would have happened if you had a husband to advise you."

I couldn't stand listening to any more of her drivel. I marched off, Meg by my side, and tried to look as composed as possible. But inside, my blood boiled and my heart raged.

CHAPTER 14

a message from Dane was a welcome distraction from my aggravating morning. It was just a single line, asking me to meet him late in the afternoon at Half Moon Cove.

I told Meg where I was going but asked her not to inform her mother. Mistress Diver wouldn't approve, and I'd become used to doing as I pleased without censure.

I passed some older children with damp hair on my way to the cove. They must have gone for a swim in the shallows. I also passed a man bent under the weight of a large pack he carried on his back. He looked like he'd been walking all day and was grateful when I informed him the village wasn't far. I hoped Mull didn't disappoint, but I suspected he'd not find it the sanctuary he was expecting.

Dane's horse wasn't at the top of the cliff above the cove so I was surprised to see him on the beach. He couldn't have walked with his injury. Indeed, he shouldn't have even descended the steep steps.

"How did you get here?" I asked, striding up to him. He stood in the shallows, his pants legs rolled up to his knees, the water lapping at his bare ankles. His doublet, boots and the bandage were nowhere in sight. He'd stroked his wet hair back from his face, and his shirt clung to his frame in a way that made me hot all over.

"Good afternoon to you too," he said.

"If I find out you've walked all the way from the village, I'll unstitch every one of your sutures myself. You don't deserve medical attention if you're going to be so careless after all the work I put in."

He pressed his lips together, suppressing a smile. A smile! The man was infuriating. I was in no mood for this today. "Before you yell at me again," he said, "I'd like to point out that I didn't walk here. I swam."

My mouth dropped open. I looked out to sea as the waves rolled through the cove's narrow mouth to lap at his ankles, completely covering his wounds. "From where?"

"From the prison. It's only one beach over. The cliffs surrounding it aren't as high as these. I left Lightning there and swam around the heads."

"You could have been smashed against the rocks!"

"It's calm today."

"It's a foolish thing to do. Don't do it again."

"Midwife's orders?"

"Don't test me, Dane. I've had a trying day."

His face turned grim. "I heard. But it sounds like your friends believed your explanation."

"Not everyone did."

"They don't matter." He lifted a hand, hesitated, and rubbed my shoulder. "They don't matter, Josie."

I blew out a breath and relaxed into the soothing touch. Just as I was beginning to enjoy it, however, he withdrew. He looked out to sea, his gaze distant, as if he were searching for his past in the horizon. Unless he was from Zemaya, he wouldn't find it in that direction.

It was difficult for me to see that look in his eyes. He was a strong, proud man, yet in unguarded moments like this, he was immeasurably sad. I couldn't begin to fathom what it must be like for him.

I lowered my gaze, but that didn't help me set aside my feelings for him. The damp shirt only made the ridges of muscle, flat stomach, and broad shoulders more obvious and more enticing. My throat felt dry, and swallowing didn't help. As a medically minded woman, I shouldn't be distracted by the human body, but I suddenly found him the most fascinating subject in my lifelong studies.

"It stings," he said.

"Pardon?" I shook my head and focused on his eyes again, now watching me. Their color matched the deeper waters, and were no less distracting than the rest of him.

He lifted his injured leg out of the water. The stitches looked as they should, and the skin surrounding them wasn't red or inflamed. "It stings but Quentin told me the salt water would be good for it."

"Quentin said that?"

"He read it in your book." He nodded at my feet. "Your dress is wet."

I stepped back onto the beach and shook the droplets off my dress. "See what you did?" I teased. "You distracted me."

"Sorry." He joined me on the sand. "I have no other clothes to put over my shirt. I left my doublet with the jailor for safekeeping."

I laughed. "I meant news of your swim around the heads distracted me. Don't worry about your lack of clothes. I'll try not to swoon."

"You? Swoon? You're the most pragmatic and resilient woman I know." He indicated I should sit on a rock with as much formality as if he were offering me a seat at his dining table.

"I'm not always resilient," I said, looking at the wounds on his lower leg. "If I were, this morning's rumor mongering wouldn't have bothered me."

"How are you?" he asked.

"Fine."

He touched my chin, forcing me to look up at him. "How are you really?"

His gentle voice, insistent touch and earnest eyes all conspired to undo me. My lower lip wobbled and a tear slipped down my cheek.

He let my chin go and wiped the tear away with his thumb. He didn't speak, and that made my heart ache even more. I wanted him to fill the silence, to say something silly to break the tension, to tease me or scold me or *something*.

This tender gravity shredded me. Fresh tears spilled down my cheeks. He joined me on my rock and scooped me into his arms, tucking my head beneath his chin. His strength and the steady throb of his pulse surrounded me, making my problems seems smaller. I felt like I could overcome any obstacle with him by my side.

My tears dried, but I did not move away. Why would I want to? The sun warmed my back, and Dane warmed everything else. I could stay with him forever like that, or leave Mull altogether if he promised to hold me every day of our lives.

I pushed aside the voice of reason telling me it couldn't happen. I didn't want to hear reason, right now. I just wanted this moment to last a little longer.

But he withdrew all too soon, putting inches of distance between us. He settled his elbows on his knees and stared down at the sand at his feet. His hair had dried at the ends and hung over his forehead, obscuring his eyes. His whole body moved with his deep breath.

"I made your shirt damper," I said pathetically. "Sorry."

He straightened and swept the hair off his face. "You don't have to pretend to be brave for me, Josie."

My lip wobbled again, but I managed to keep my emotions in check. I blinked up at the sky to ensure his beautiful, caring eyes didn't undo me again. "It's been an overwhelming few days," I said. "But this has helped."

"Send a message to the palace if you need me. I'll come as soon as I can."

"Thank you."

He returned to the other rock, putting all his weight on his good leg.

"You should be off that foot entirely," I said.

"That's not possible."

"You don't have to patrol The Row personally. Your men can do it."

"And they will. I have to be present at the palace. The situation there requires my full attention."

"Are you referring to the king knowing that Lord Morgrave was murdered?"

"That's part of it. Knowing Morgrave was poisoned doesn't seem to concern him as much as his own health. His chest pains have returned, making him irritable. He won't listen to advice because, as he put it, he shouldn't have to change his diet. He should feel fine."

"'Should,'" I echoed.

"He suspects the gem's magic didn't work, but I don't think he suspects it's a fake. Theodore overheard him grumbling to himself that it must have weakened; we assume he meant the magic. We can only hope he continues to think that way."

"He will work it out, Dane. You know he will."

He leaned his elbows on his knees again and lowered his head. "Hopefully Balthazar's plan will come together before then and we can confront the king while he still trusts us."

"What is Balthazar's plan?"

"He hasn't been forthcoming with details, but it involves black-mailing the king. Part of the plan involves needing the king to continue to trust us."

"Something he won't do if he realizes you swapped the real gem for a fake one."

It seemed too precarious and unreliable. Surely Balthazar could have worked out a safer plan than that—one that couldn't go wrong in so many ways.

We both sat on our rocks and stared out to sea, watching the waves break gently against the shore and the gulls soar through the air. A ship sat on the horizon, a mere speck in the vast landscape spread before us.

It was quiet, uncomplicated perfection.

"I wish I could stay," Dane said heavily. "But I have to get back."

"May I come to the palace tomorrow?" I asked on a whim. "I'd like to see how Remy and Dora are fitting in."

"Of course. The men are always happy to see you."

I wanted to ask if he was always happy to see me too, but I bit my tongue. "Don't get sand in your wounds," I said, watching him hobble to the water.

He waded in until he was waist deep then plunged into the waves and swam. I watched until he was level with the heads, where he stopped and looked back. He waved and set off again.

Once he was out of sight, I trudged back up the stairs and returned to Meg's house.

* * *

REMY JUMPED UP, when he saw me enter the commons courtyard, and threw his arms around me.

"Good morning, Remy," I said, laughing. "Have you settled into life in the palace?"

"It's ginormous!" he said, taking my hand. "I've been lost three times already."

"That's because you keep wandering off," said one of the maids, rising from a chair positioned in the corner of the courtyard. She was of middling age, with soft brown eyes and wide hips. She smiled, revealing two rows of perfect teeth. "You're Mistress Cully, aren't you?"

I smiled back. "Yes. How did you know?"

"I've seen you here before, and your name has come up numerous times. My name is Olive."

"You're tutoring Remy?"

"And some of the servants who wish to learn too. Remy is my only student at the moment. The others are busy." She ruffled his hair as he passed her. "It's different, teaching a child, but enjoyable."

"You're doing a wonderful thing. If all the children could be tutored, Mull would be the smartest village in Glancia."

She leaned closer and whispered, "I might have been a governess before."

"Perhaps you were, although I'd wager your schoolroom was nothing like this one." I indicated the vast courtyard and the dozens of servants crossing back and forth, some stopping at the fountain to wash or enjoy a chat, others hurrying to the kitchens, laundries, or workrooms housed within the square building.

Remy trotted back to me, holding a slate. "Look what Olive gave me. It's for writing on. When I'm finished, I just wipe it off. See?" He rubbed the writing out with his hand.

"You're supposed to use the rag," Olive chided.

"Sorry, Olive."

She smiled wistfully, and I suspect she was wondering if she had children and if they missed her.

"Is your mother working?" I asked Remy.

He nodded. "In the kitchen. She chops and stirs. She's real good at it."

"I saw how good she was when you lived with me."

"I liked your house," Remy said, quite seriously. "But I like the palace more. It's ginormous! Did you see it?"

"It's rather hard to miss," I said, trying to contain my smile.

"There's gold all over it, and that pink stuff is marble. Olive says it's expendive."

"Expensive," Olive corrected.

"The fountain is ginormous too! My ma says I'm not allowed to swim in the fountains. It's against Captain Hammer's rules."

"I suspect there are a lot of rules to remember."

He tucked the slate under his arm and counted items on his fingers. "Don't swim in fountains or lakes, don't leave the service parts of the palace, don't ask anyone where they came from, don't steal, don't talk to lords and ladies or the king. He held up his hand, all five fingers extended. "See, I remembered them. There are five, one for each finger."

"So few."

"Five's a lot!"

"Josie!" cried a familiar accented voice.

I turned around, only to be scooped up by a big guard with long ropey blond hair. Erik's hug lifted me off my feet.

"Are you here to learn too?" he asked, setting me down again.

"Josie can already read and write real well," Remy said. "Come on, Erik, you're late." Remy took Erik's hand and tugged him toward the chairs in the corner.

"You're learning too?" I asked, following them and Olive. "I didn't know you couldn't read and write."

"Not in this language," Erik said. "Except for Erik. E.R.I.K. The captain showed me the letters on the roster. Quentin tried to teach me more but he makes me yawn." He made a grand show yawning and stretching his arms over his head.

Remy giggled, and Erik ruffled the boy's hair and grinned.

"Olive is a good teacher," he went on. "She does not make me yawn. And she is a beautiful woman, so I want to be here."

"Stop it," Olive said, laughing. "He's such a flirt, and not just with me. All the young maids are half in love with him."

"I can well believe it," I said.

Erik crossed his arms, puffing out his chest and making his muscles bulge. "Not Josie. She is a friend, not lover. Hammer would not like it if I kissed her. Sorry, Josie, I know this will make you sad, but I like my face looking this good." He laughed, so I wasn't quite sure if he was serious or not.

"What's a flirt?" Remy asked, blinking up at Erik.

"A handsome man with a big co—"

"Erik!" both Olive and I cried.

"A big opinion of himself," I said quickly. "Olive, I think Erik needs some vocabulary lessons too."

Olive pointed at one of the chairs. "Sit down, Erik, and listen. There are certain words you cannot say to children. Perhaps I'll give you a private lesson later and we can go through what some of those words are."

Erik winked at her. "I would like a private lesson with you, Olive."

Poor Olive flushed to the roots of her hair. "That's not what I meant. Truly," she added for my benefit. "It's not."

Remy resumed his seat and leaned toward Erik. Erik leaned down so the boy could whisper in his ear, albeit loudly. "I already know the word you were going to say. You better not say it in front of my ma. She'll yell at you too." No doubt he'd heard that word and worse in The Row.

"Some ladies do not like to hear it," Erik said on a sigh. "But some do. I am still learning which do and which do not. Maybe Olive can teach me the difference in our private lesson." He beamed at her.

She blushed again and fought back a smile.

I left them to their education and was about to leave the commons to head to the garrison when Dora hailed me. She crossed the courtyard with another kitchen maid, a basket over her arm. "What a nice surprise," she said, smiling. "Have you come to see Remy?"

"And you, but I didn't want to interrupt while you were working," I said. "Have you settled in?"

She nodded. "Morna is going to show me where to pick fresh herbs in the garden. It's my first time there, and this place is so big. I don't want to get lost."

"I know where the kitchen garden is. I can take you if Morna has other duties to attend to."

"I'd be grateful, miss," Morna said, bobbing a curtsy.

Dora cast a glance toward Remy, sitting on a chair too large for him, writing something on his slate. "He's very enthusiastic about learning."

"I'm pleased," I said, heading out of the commons with her. "I worried about him being here with only adults for company."

"I'm worried too. I'm also worried what the king will say when he finds out. None of the other servants have children at the palace. I'm not even sure if any of them have children at all, or are even married. None wear wedding rings."

I remained silent as we left the commons behind and headed south.

"They might not have been able to afford rings, I suppose," she went on. "But I can't ask. The captain forbade it. He said if they want me to know anything about themselves, they'll offer me the information."

We continued on, leaving the palace behind. "There are trees in that building," she said, looking to our right.

"That's the greenhouse. It's where they grow fruit trees."

"Those trees live better than me and Remy used to," she muttered. "You know, I always thought magic had something to do with creating this place, like everyone says. It's amazing and beautiful and grand, like nothing I could have imagined. It is magical. But the staff are ordinary folk. They don't talk fancy, they don't look different or act different to us. They have secrets, but don't we all?"

We veered left and entered the walled kitchen garden. We both took a moment to take in the scale of it, but I shouldn't have been surprised. It took a lot of vegetables to feed hundreds of nobles and almost a thousand servants. Dora's basket suddenly looked too small, even for herbs.

One of the gardeners escorted us to the herb section and helped us pick several bunches. He asked us a lot of questions about ourselves. Dora and I asked none.

At one point I looked up and saw Lord Barborough pass by outside the garden entrance, heading away from the palace. It was an odd part of the estate for him to use. Few nobles were interested in the functional greenhouse and kitchen garden, although they were attractive in their own right. Thankfully he didn't see me. I didn't want a confrontation.

We were about to leave the walled garden when Sergeant Brant strode past too. He glanced through the entrance but didn't see me, and continued on his way. He'd been heading in the same direction as Lord Barborough, toward the lake where I'd secretly met with Dane, and Kitty and Miranda. It was a secluded spot behind the dense line of trees separating the avenue from the lawn surrounding the lake.

Dora hoisted her basket higher and we headed back to the commons, but I stopped after only a few paces. "Do you know your way?" I asked.

"It's straightforward. Where are you going?"

"To the lake down there." I pointed. "If I haven't returned by lunchtime, tell the captain."

"Is everything all right?"

"It's just a precaution."

We parted and I hurried along the avenue. Brant was far ahead. Too far to make out his face, or for him to identify me. Even so, I remained well back until he disappeared into the trees.

I followed until I reached the same spot. The two men were visible through the trees, but I couldn't hear what they were saying. I crouched low and headed toward them, careful not to step on any dry leaves or twigs. I huddled into a dense bush that shielded me from them, and listened.

"I've seen it," Brant was saying. "With my own two eyes."

Lord Barborough made a scoffing sound.

"I have!" Brant clutched Barborough's shoulder, the one attached to his useless arm.

"Unhand me," his lordship demanded.

Brant let go, but not before giving him a violent shake. "Listen," he hissed. "I know where to find it. I ain't lying. Why would I?"

"For money," Barborough said.

"I don't want money. I want answers."

"To what questions?"

"I can't say," Brant said, scrubbing a hand over his unshaved jaw.

"Then I'm not interested." Lord Barborough tugged on the hem of his doublet. "Good day."

So Brant hadn't told him about the memory loss. I was relieved but surprised. Had he not told Barborough because he didn't trust him? Or because he understood the dangers of discussing it with outsiders, particularly a lord from Vytill?

"Isn't this what you wanted?" Brant asked. "The sorcerer's magic? It's in the gem. I know it is."

"I told you, I'm not interested right now."

"I saw the king use it."

Barborough tilted his head to the side. "What do you mean?"

"He held it and spoke some words to it."

"You didn't hear the words?"

Brant shook his head. "I couldn't get close enough."

"Do you have an inkling what he asked of it?"

Brant merely shrugged.

Barborough muttered something I couldn't hear then asked, "Where is the gem now?"

"North west of the palace. It's too hard to give directions. I have to show you. Today. Now."

Barborough rubbed his forefinger over his top lip and glanced across the lake, toward the palace. "I can't. I have an important meeting with the king and his advisors which I can't put off."

"A meeting," Brant scoffed. "I'm prepared to show you the sorcerer's gem and you want to go to a *meeting*!"

"I'm about to secure an alliance between Glancia and Vytill. This meeting is of the utmost importance, and until it's over, it requires my full attention. I expect it to take all day. There are a lot of details to discuss."

Brant took a step away then suddenly rounded on Barborough.

He stabbed his finger in his lordship's face, a mere inch from his nose. "Isn't it what you want? The gem? The source of the magic?"

"What I want is to not have my head on a spike," Barborough snarled through gritted teeth.

"I don't understand."

"Of course you don't.

Brant might not understand, but I did. Lord Barborough had to get results for the king of Vytill or be executed for murder. The results the king desired most was his daughter's hand in marriage to King Leon. Failing that, he wanted a Glancian civil war. Now that Lady Morgrave was no longer the king's favorite, it would seem he was seriously considering marrying Princess Illiriya. So much so that he needed to discuss terms with the Vytill representative. Events were moving in the direction Vytill—and Lord Barborough in particular—wanted. No wonder he looked so pleased. Not only had he almost secured the marriage, but the gem was within his grasp too. He'd almost achieved everything, but the marriage alliance came first.

Brant threw his hands in the air. "I'm going to talk to the dukes. They'll be interested in what I have to say."

Barborough raced after him and caught his arm. Brant shook him off, unbalancing Barborough. His lordship tumbled backward and fell to the ground.

Brant sneered down at him.

Lord Barborough lurched to his feet and thrust out his chin. "Don't speak to them. Wait until I'm free. Tomorrow, at the latest."

Brant's sneer vanished. He met Barborough's glare, matching it with his own fierce one. Neither seemed willing to look away first. "Will you be able to use the gem to find the answers to my questions?" Brant asked.

"Considering I don't know your questions, I cannot say."

"But you can use the gem's magic, can't you? You know how?"

"I can't use the magic, only the king can. He's the one who found the gem and freed the sorcerer. Until all three wishes are spoken, that gem is for the king's use only. So don't expect me, or anyone else, to steal one of the wishes. It can't be done."

Brant cocked his head to the side and rested a hand on his sword hilt at his hip. "That better not be a lie."

Barborough's gaze momentarily fluttered in the direction of Brant's sword before rising again. "So you'll show me where it is tomorrow?"

Brant hesitated. "I'll meet you back here in the morning." He turned and strode off, passing a short distance from me.

I remained utterly still, hardly breathing, and watched Lord Barborough. After several moments of staring across the lake, he turned and left too.

I waited some time before leaving my hiding place and returning to the commons. I found Dora chopping herbs in the kitchen, along with four other women all wearing white aprons over palace uniforms. She greeted me with a smile but it was the conversation of the others that interested me.

"I heard he's real sick," one said.

"His heart," said another with all the authority of a doctor.

"Just like Lord Morgrave," said the first with a shake of her head.

"He died of poisoning, not a heart problem. Haven't you heard?"

A finger stabbed into my shoulder, and I turned around. The head cook crossed his arms, resting them on his stomach. "You're disturbing my staff," he barked.

I backed away. "I was just—"

"Get out."

"But—"

"Out!"

All activity ceased. Kitchen hands looked up from their chopping boards and pots, and stopped rushing between tables and fireplaces. The hiss of fat dripping onto coals from the roasting pork seemed unnaturally loud in the cavernous space.

"I'm going," I assured the cook.

I felt his glare on my back until I'd left the kitchen behind.

I crossed the courtyard but stopped suddenly. Brant stood talking to a palace footman, his hand on the footman's arm. The footman shrugged but Brant didn't seem pleased with the response. The footman pointed to another fellow dressed in the Duke of Gladstow's livery as he headed out of the commons.

The first footman departed, heading towards me, while Brant

had a brief exchange Gladstow's man. The duke's footman nodded and they left together.

"What did Sergeant Brant want?" I asked the palace footman as he reached down to scoop water from the fountain pool. Perhaps I should have been more discreet, but I needed a fast answer and indirect questions would take too long.

He splashed water on his face, blinking the drops off his lashes. "He's looking for the Duke of Gladstow. I don't know where he is, but Gladstow's footman will."

I thanked him and headed out of the commons, intending to go to the garrison to inform Dane. But what could Dane do? If he confronted Brant, the sergeant would only lie and delay finding the duke until another time, when Dane wasn't watching. Then we'd never know the duke's response or his intentions.

I had a better idea.

I headed back to the commons and asked maids and footmen until I found one who'd seen Kitty recently.

"She was returning to her rooms to change out of her riding outfit," said a palace maid.

I thanked her and headed into the palace via the service stairs opposite the commons. I knew my way to the Duke and Duchess of Gladstow's apartments. They were afforded the best rooms due to their rank, with several chambers for their personal use.

I cracked open the door between the service corridor and the formal one, and checked that I was alone before entering. This corridor was familiar to me from when I'd attended to Miranda after she'd been poisoned. As the king's favorite, she'd been briefly elevated to the ducal corridor. I wondered if those rooms were now empty or if Lady Morgrave lived in them.

I knocked lightly on the door to the Duke of Gladstow's apartments and the duchess's maid answered. She took one look at me and frowned.

"Who're you?" she asked.

"Josie Cully, a friend to the duchess. Is she here? I need to see her."

"On what business?"

"It's private," I said, trying to peer past her.

214

She regarded me down her nose. "Unless you can tell me what this is about, you may go."

For Hailia's sake. "Kitty!" I called out. "It's me! Josie."

I heard Kitty's voice from the depths beyond, telling her maid to let me in. The maid didn't look pleased but stepped aside nevertheless.

Kitty swanned into the sitting room from an adjoining room. "Josie, how lovely." She extended her hands to me and I took them. "Josie is a dear friend from the village," she told her maid.

"That can't be," the maid said with a wrinkle of her nose.

"Why not?"

"She'll want something from you, Madam, mark my words. I know how her type are."

Kitty stiffened. Somehow her features settled into a more regal bearing, taking her from silly girl to duchess in an instant. "I find your attitude increasingly rude, Prudence. Please leave."

"But—"

"Leave now or you'll be searching for new employment without a reference."

"The duke employs me, Madam." Prudence left, a defiant shine in her eyes.

Kitty shut the door. "I loathe her."

"Is she correct, and you can't replace her?" I asked.

"Unfortunately, my husband employs all the staff, even the housekeeper and maids. He doesn't think me capable of running a household, and he'd been doing it all alone before we married anyway, so he saw no reason to change. I think I'll have a word with him about Prudence, though. She's been quite horrid to me, ever since—" She pressed both hands to her stomach and drew in a fortifying breath. "Ever since the duke has started to show his frustration toward me."

I touched her arm, knowing it wasn't the protocol when addressing a duchess yet not caring. She gave me a rallying smile and took my hand.

"What a pleasure to see you here," she said. "But why are you here?"

"I need your help."

"Does this have something to do with my husband's secret meetings with the Duke of Buxton and the king's magic?"

"I suspect so."

"How thrilling." She clapped her hands lightly and grinned. "I do need a distraction."

"This is very serious, Kitty. It could also be dangerous. I wouldn't have involved you, but I couldn't think of another way."

"What do you want me to do?"

"I want you to help me spy on your husband. He's about to have a meeting with a sergeant of the palace guards, and I need to hear what is said between them. Can you help me get close? Could I pretend to be your maid and we can approach? Your presence wouldn't be considered unusual."

"An excellent idea." She looked like she would bounce out of her skin, she was so excited. Perhaps I ought to mention the gravity of what I was asking her to do again. "I have a better way, though. Let's dress you in one of my gowns. Passing as a lady will make it easier to walk around the gardens."

"I'm not sure we have the time for me to change. The sergeant is already looking for your husband."

She took my hand and led me into the adjoining bedchamber. Just as we were about to go through to the wardrobe and dressing room, the door to the corridor opened and low male voices drifted to us. I recognized the Duke of Gladstow and Sergeant Brant—and one other.

Lord Xavier Deerhorn.

CHAPTER 15

"This is the most private place," the Duke of Gladstow said to Brant and Lord Xavier. "We might be overheard in the gardens."

I pressed my finger to my lips and Kitty nodded, wide-eyed.

"Your wife?" Sergeant Brant asked.

"Out riding."

"I have to check she's not resting."

I grabbed Kitty's hand and dragged her into the adjoining dressing room. Behind us, Brant's footsteps thudded on the thick rug. Kitty and I just managed to slip into the wardrobe, among the hanging gowns, before Brant appeared in the doorway. He took in the chairs, velvet stools, dressing table and drawers then sniffed the air. He licked his lips.

I willed Kitty not to move and give away our location in the shadows among the gowns. I willed Brant not to follow the scent that had caught his attention. Kitty's perfume was strong, even after a ride.

The Duke of Gladstow appeared behind Brant. "I told you, she's not here. Now, what's this about? I haven't got all day."

The men left and must have returned to the sitting room. I removed my boots and crept out of the wardrobe and into the bedchamber. Kitty followed, barefoot and silent.

"Why's he here?" Brant asked. "I just wanted to speak to you two, not some lordling."

"The Deerhorns want what we want," the Duke of Buxton said. So it was the four of them, the two dukes, Lord Xavier and Brant. An unexpected but dangerous combination.

"To overthrow the king?" Brant asked. "I thought your sister was going to marry him, my lord."

"Not anymore," Lord Xavier growled. "I can assure you, my family does not want the king to wed the Vytill slut."

"Or anyone else," the Duke of Gladstow sneered. "Your delightful mother knows she'll have to side with one of us after this is over, doesn't she?"

"One step at a time. The king can't be overthrown. You haven't got anything against him."

"We do now," Brant cut in. "You wanted evidence he used magic, I can give it to you."

Lord Xavier barked a disbelieving laugh. "You're wasting my time."

"Wait," Buxton said. "Listen to what he has to say."

"You believe him?" Xavier asked. "You think the king used magic to obtain the throne? You're all mad."

"Not necessarily."

"You *know* there's something strange about this place, about the king and how he came to power," Gladstow added. "This guard claims he can prove Leon used magic."

"There's an entire country that believes in sorcery," Brant pointed out.

"The Zemayans are simple and gullible," Xavier said. "Your Graces, this fellow is having a joke at our expense."

"Be quiet," Brant growled. "I didn't want you here, so shut your hole or I'll shut it for you."

Xavier didn't respond. It wasn't like him to let someone in an inferior position speak to him in such a manner. Brant must have given him one of his threatening glares or settled his hand on the hilt of his sword. The sergeant had a way of instilling fear in most people with just a look.

"The Zemayans believe the magic is contained in a gem," Brant went on. "I found that gem. It was in the king's possession but was removed at his order for safekeeping. I saw him speak a spell into it."

"Did it work?" Xavier asked.

"I don't know what he wished for."

"Did anything happen?" Gladstow asked. "Did the gem react in any way?"

"No, but the gem *must* contain the magic. It *must* be important or the king wouldn't have hidden it so well."

Silence, before Xavier said, "Why do *you* believe in magic, Sergeant?"

"I just do," Brant mumbled.

"Who do you work for?" Buxton snapped. "It can't be Vytill or you wouldn't be telling us this information. Freedland?"

"I'm just a guard," Brant said.

"Why are you so interested in proving King Leon used magic to gain the throne? Out with it, man, who do you work for?"

"I work for no one," Brant growled. "I have my own reasons for wanting you to confront the king."

Brant knew he couldn't confront the king himself about the gem and the use of magic. He couldn't even get near the king on his own. His Majesty was always surrounded by one of his advisors or staff. Even if Brant dug up the gem himself, and was able to confront the king, he must know that he wouldn't get straight answers. It was the same reason Dane, Theodore and Balthazar hadn't confronted him. They had no leverage. *They* couldn't overthrow the king.

Brant had expected Barborough to do it, but now Barborough was hoping for a marriage alliance instead. The dukes, however, were more interested in a rebellion.

"I'll show you where it is now," Brant said. "It's on the estate, a short ride away."

"How do we know we can trust you?" Gladstow asked. "You might be leading us into a trap."

"How can I lead you into a trap?" Brant said. "Does anyone have evidence you're plotting against the king?" After a silence, he added, "I didn't think so. If we're caught, you three will say you were doing some gardening. You'll be believed over me. Are you willing to do this or do I give the gem to Lord Barborough instead?"

Someone muttered under his breath.

"I'm willing," Buxton said.

"As am I," Gladstow said. "Deerhorn?"

Xavier hesitated.

"With the king ranting a lot lately, many nobles won't be too sorry to see him go," Gladstow added. "You might as well join us."

"Ranting?" Xavier asked.

"About Morgrave's murder, among other things."

"The murder hasn't been proved." Xavier sighed. "Very well. I'll come too and see what this gem is all about. Sergeant, take us to it."

"You have to agree to one thing first," Brant said. "I have to be there when you confront the king about magic."

"Why?" Gladstow hedged.

"Because I want to ask him something."

"We can ask for you."

"No. I have to be there. I have to see his eyes, because that's the only way I'll know he's lying."

"Agreed," Xavier said darkly.

Their footsteps receded then the door opened and closed. I sank to the floor beside Kitty and drew up my knees.

She peered around the door into the sitting room. "They're gone." She lowered herself onto the bed. "What does it mean, Josie?"

"It means your husband and the Duke of Buxton are very close to overthrowing the king. They need evidence to prove that he's not the real king, that he used magic to gain the throne. And Brant is going to hand them that proof. It means I have to warn some people." I got to my feet. "Kitty, don't speak a word of this to anyone. Not even Miranda. Understand?"

She nodded, all wide eyes and earnest brow. "Be careful, Josie."

I went straight to the garrison, but it was empty, so I headed to Balthazar's office. A voice drifted to me, growing louder and clearer as I drew closer. It was the king, and he was furious.

"I'm dying, Balthazar!" he shouted. "Do you understand? Do you even care?"

I didn't hear Balthazar's response so crept forward until I was just around the corner.

"Where is it?" the king demanded. Shouldn't he be in a meeting with Lord Barborough and his advisors?

"We took you to it, sire," Balthazar said. He sounded like a parent impatient with a pestering child. The modular tones of deference that I'd heard him employ in discussions with the king had vanished.

"That wasn't the real one!" The king's screech bounced off the stone walls and traveled past me into the depths of the corridor.

"It was, sire."

"Liar!"

Something crashed, a chair against the floor perhaps, and smaller items clattered.

"Sire, please, let him go!" Theodore cried. "He's an old man." It must be just the three of them inside, not Dane.

"An old man who's lying to me," the king said. "You both are. That gem wasn't real, and don't pretend it is."

Balthazar coughed. "Why..." Another cough. "Why don't you think it was real?"

"Because I still feel ill."

"I don't understand, sire. Why should seeing the gem make you feel better? It's just a stone, nothing more."

The profound silence was broken only by the king clearing his throat. "Where's Hammer?"

"I don't know," Balthazar said.

"Why don't you know? Are you not in charge of all the staff?"

"Not the guards. I'll tell him you wish to see him when he returns."

"I wish to see him *now!*" A short silence followed, and I picked up my skirts, preparing to run off in the other direction the moment I heard footsteps. But then the king spoke again. "I want my gem. The real one."

"Sire," Theodore said, nervously, "the meeting. You must attend. Allow me to walk with you—"

"He knows where it is!" the king snapped.

"Pardon?"

"The real gem. Hammer knows where it is. I can't believe he betrayed me!"

"Betray?" Balthazar prompted. "He is your humble servant, Your Majesty. The captain—"

"Shut up, Balthazar! Shut up, shut up, shut up! Hammer is hiding the real gem from me, I know it. The question is why. How does he—?" He cut himself off. "Tell Hammer I want to see him immediately. And be warned, if I find any of you are in his confidence, you will be punished and dismissed."

"You can't dismiss us," Balthazar said, low and threatening. "Those without memories must remain together at the palace. All of us. Including you."

I strained to hear, but there was nothing but silence that stretched on and on.

"Everything must change eventually," the king said with more composure. "I will *not* be lied to by my own staff."

"Nobody likes to be lied to," Balthazar said darkly. "Especially over something so important."

Footsteps approached so I ran off until I came to an intersection of corridors. I headed down the dimly lit one and pretended to inspect my shoe. The king marched past without a glance my way.

I returned to Balthazar's office and knocked. Theodore let me in.

"It's just Josie," he said, sounding relieved. To me, he added, "Hammer isn't here."

"I know." I stepped into the office and shut the door. "But I have something to report, and you two *are* here."

The conversation with the king seemed to have taken its toll on both men. Balthazar rubbed his forehead and looked even older, while Theodore's hand shook as he offered me a chair.

"I overheard your discussion with the king," I said. "I didn't mean to, but his voice carried."

Balthazar grunted. "Not surprising, at that volume."

"I hope no one else heard," Theodore said.

"I didn't come across any other servants as I retreated," I told them. "And the king didn't see me."

"Good," Balthazar said. "He no longer trusts us, but at least you're not tangled up in this mess."

Theodore poured himself a cup of wine and drank the lot. He filled two other cups and offered them to Balthazar and me. I refused but Balthazar accepted a cup and sipped.

"So you heard everything." He cradled the cup between his knotty fingers and nodded at the door.

"I heard him say he believes he wasn't shown the real gem," I said. "And that the captain knows where the real one is. Did the captain tell you where he hid it?"

Balthazar and Theodore both shook their heads.

"Did he tell you?" Theodore asked.

"No. He claimed it was safer if only he knew."

"Safer for us," Balthazar said. "Not for him."

"We must warn him. Where is he now?"

"The village, meeting with the sheriff." So Balthazar had lied to the king about not knowing Dane's whereabouts. I was glad of it and glad to put to bed any lingering doubts I had about him. I could trust him now. "He should be back shortly. Why did you need to speak to us, Josie?"

"I have been doing a lot of listening in to conversations I shouldn't be privy to today." I told them about Brant's conversation with Lord Barborough near the lake, and his meeting with the two dukes and Lord Xavier afterward.

"Deerhorn?" Balthazar frowned. "Why was he there?"

"As his mother's representative," I said. "The Deerhorns are ambitious. I suspect they'll try to take advantage of the chaos that ensues after the king is dethroned."

"They can't take the throne for themselves, can they?" Theodore asked. "The Deerhorn title is a minor one. They have no right."

I shrugged. "Nor do the dukes. Not really. They have no royal blood."

Balthazar regarded us both over the top of his steepled fingers. "Anything can happen in times of unrest. People like the Deerhorns shouldn't be underestimated."

"What shall we do?" Theodore asked. "Is it too late to stop them digging up the gem?"

I shook my head. "They will be at the cottage, by now."

"It doesn't matter," Balthazar said. "It seems Brant isn't aware that we substituted the real one for a fake. Let them take it. It has outlived its use to us anyway. The king suspects it's not real."

"Do we just let them confront the king once they have it?" I asked.

"We can't stop them. But we can speak with the king first and try to get answers. I wish Hammer were here. I need him for this." He rubbed his throat and winced. "The king could become violent if he's backed into a corner."

"Let's go to the garrison," Theodore said. "If Hammer hasn't returned, we'll have to speak to the king on our own."

"So your plan is ready?" I asked Balthazar.

He pushed himself up from the chair and grabbed his walking stick from where it leaned against his desk. "My plan has now come to fruition, such that it was."

I frowned. "I don't understand."

"My plan is hardly strong enough to be called such." He leaned heavily on the walking stick as he rounded the desk. "I wanted to diminish the number of friends the king could depend upon. I wanted to weaken him, and that meant undermining his trust in the Deerhorns—and by extension the other lords too. That was achieved." He stopped and folded both hands over the head of the walking stick. "I believe I owe you an apology, Josie."

"Why?"

"It was me who made sure the king heard about the poisoning of Lord Morgrave, and suggested the party most likely to benefit from it would be Lady Morgrave and her manipulative family. I knew it would trouble him and that he would distance himself from her. It worked better than I expected. He set her aside very quickly, and Lady Deerhorn panicked."

"By kidnapping me," I said on a rush of breath.

"I should have realized she'd get her revenge upon you," he bit off. "I should have anticipated her next move."

"Don't blame yourself, Balthazar. She's unpredictable and cruel. Be happy you don't think like her." I offered him a smile, but he merely grunted and continued toward the door.

Theodore and I followed him out.

"In Hammer's absence, I feel I should warn you to be careful,

Josie," Theodore said gently. "You shouldn't have listened in to the sergeant's conversations. You could have been caught."

I took his hand and squeezed. "Thank you for your concern." I appreciated it more than I cared to admit. He reminded me of my father more than Dane. Of all the things I missed about my father, I hadn't expected his repeated warnings to be careful to be one of them.

Dane wasn't in the garrison, but two guards who'd just arrived assured us he was on his way, so we waited. Dane entered a short time later, not limping. It must have cost him considerable effort to not show his pain.

He paused inside the door upon seeing us. "This must be important."

Balthazar glanced toward the two guards helping themselves to the jug of ale, paying us no mind. "We came to warn you," he said. "The king is displeased."

Dane stilled. He gave a single nod of understanding.

Balthazar's fingers tightened around the head of his walking stick. "It's time."

"Yes," was all Dane said.

"The only question is, do we do it now or wait until after the king's meeting with Barborough?"

The internal door to the garrison suddenly burst open, and the king stormed in. His dark hair clung to his damp forehead and beads of sweat edged his top lip. His sharp gaze speared into Dane.

"You!" He pointed a finger at Dane. "Liar! Thief! *Traitor!*"

Theodore quickly stepped forward, hands clasped in front of him. "Sire, your meeting with—"

"Forget the fucking meeting!"

"Yen, Ray," Dane said to his two shocked men. "Leave us."

"No!" The king shoved one of the guards in the shoulder, pushing him in Dane's direction. "Arrest him! Arrest Hammer and throw him in the palace prison."

Neither guard moved. They stared at their king then at their captain. Dane gave them no instruction; he merely stood there, waiting.

The guard named Ray gulped. The other shifted his feet.

"Go on!" the king shouted. "The captain is a traitor, and I want him arrested. Do your duty or you will be punished."

Both guards looked to Dane again.

"Who will punish them?" Dane asked. "You? Ray, Yen, step outside and make sure the others don't enter. I'll be with you in a moment when I've sorted out the king's problem. I'm sure it's just a misunderstanding."

"Misunderstanding!" the king spluttered. "You stole from me!" When Dane didn't try to defend himself, the king turned to the two guards as they collected their sword belts from the hooks by the external door. "Wait!" He stepped forward but stopped when Dane rested a hand on his sword hilt.

The two guards left quickly.

"Cowards," the king spat. "Your men are scared of you, Hammer."

"My men respect me, *Leon*."

A muscle pulsed in the king's neck. His spine stiffened. "You will use the proper title when speaking to me."

"I *am* using your proper title." Dane pulled out a chair and turned it toward the king. "Sit down and let's discuss this civilly."

The king stamped a hand on his hip and barked a laugh. "This is absurd. Give me the gem, the real one, and I won't have you arrested."

"His men won't arrest him," Balthazar said, lowering himself onto a chair. "They respect him and trust him, whereas none of the staff trust you anymore. Including us. So sit down and answer our questions."

"I answer to no one!"

"Today you do," Dane said in that calmly threatening tone of his. He tapped the chair back. "Sit."

The king turned and walked away.

With a few giant strides, Dane reached him. He grabbed the back of the king's doublet and forced him to sit. The king's face paled but he did not try to get up.

"What happened to us?" Dane demanded. "Who are we? Where did we come from?"

"I—I don't know," the king said. "Like you, I have no memory."

"Don't," Dane growled, low in his chest. "We've had enough of your lies. We want the truth. Why can't we remember? Why can you?"

The king lifted his chin and crossed his arms over his chest. "I won't answer anything until I hold the gem in my hand."

"No," Balthazar said.

The king gave a high pitched maniacal laugh. "It's just a stone."

"We know what it is," Balthazar went on. "We know it's the sorcerer's gem, that you found it and had three wishes bestowed upon you. If you possess that gem again, you can wish this situation away, so forgive us for not obliging you."

The king blinked hard at him, then turned to Dane, to Theodore then finally to me. "Mistress Cully, you must get help! They've gone mad. As your king, I'm begging you to do the right thing. I have no idea what they're talking about...gems, magic... It makes no sense."

Balthazar hit his walking stick against the table, making the king, Theodore and me jump. "She can't help," Balthazar said. It was an ambiguous response; it could mean I refused to help or that I was also being held hostage and unable to.

Theodore took my hand and steered me toward the other end of the table. Both our hands shook as we sat.

"You too, Theo?" the king whined.

Theodore's grip tightened. "I—I'm sorry. You have to answer them, sire. We have to know. I can forgive you for stealing our lives for your own purposes. The temptation to make yourself king must have been strong, and it would take a unique man not to submit to that temptation. But I cannot forgive you for continuing with the lies anymore. It's cruel."

The king studied the faces of his three servants as they regarded him in turn. In the thick silence, every facet of this man's character passed over his face, from youthful insecurity to arrogant king.

"So," he said darkly. "You think I should not be king. You think I was given this position through sorcery."

"We know it," Dane said.

"Just saying so is treason."

Dane stared back at the king until the king shifted his weight on the chair and looked away.

"You have no proof," the king said with a sniff.

"We have the gem."

"A pretty stone, nothing more. Do you think anyone will believe otherwise?" He snorted. "The lords will laugh at you if you tell them the gem is magical."

"You misunderstand," Dane said. "We have no intention of telling the world what we know. You can continue to be king. We don't care. In fact, Glancia will be a more peaceful kingdom if you remain on the throne. We only care about getting our memories back. We do not need proof of magic, and I don't intend on showing the gem to anyone. I intend to keep the gem hidden until you tell us what we want to know."

The king's gaze darted between his three servants then settled on me. "Where is it? Mistress Cully? Do you know?"

"No," I said.

"But you must! As his mistress, he must have told—"

Dane grabbed the front of the king's doublet and lifted him off the chair until their faces were level. "She is no man's mistress."

The king swallowed and nodded quickly. Dane released him, and the king fell back onto the chair so heavily it rocked.

"You'll address her respectfully," Balthazar added. "As you will address all of us, from now on. For all we know, you could be the servant and we the lords. Besides, Josie doesn't know where the gem is. It was given to someone for safekeeping. Someone you would least expect, who is not in this room."

Did Balthazar really know where the gem was hidden? Or did he say it to add another layer of secrecy out of caution?

Dane's gaze narrowed as he continued to stare at the king. "If you want the real gem back, you will tell us the truth."

"I… I will tell you all I can," the king said. "I remember pieces of my past and what happened. The greater part of my memory is lost, however, just like yours."

"Liar," Dane said.

The king scrutinized him just as closely as Dane studied him in return. Perhaps he was trying to decide if Dane would draw his weapon or whether he could be trusted to give up the gem if the king told them everything.

Balthazar smacked his walking stick against the table again, and the king fidgeted in the chair. "You have no one to turn to," Balthazar said. "The servants no longer trust you, the guards certainly don't, the nobles have turned their backs on you too. The dukes want to overthrow you, and the lords can't be trusted. The Deerhorns proved that, didn't they? They even killed Lord Morgrave so his widow could trap you into marriage. People who can kill a lord and get away with it are very dangerous, wouldn't you agree?"

The king nodded quickly.

"Almost everyone under this roof wants you either dead or deposed," Balthazar went on. "We only want answers. That makes us your closest allies."

"Allies?" the king blurted out. "You're forcing me!"

"We are your best chance of keeping the throne. We are your closest confidants, and the only ones with an interest in helping you remain as king. If you give us our memories back, we will see that you do."

The king sucked in his lower lip and chewed on it. His gaze connected with Balthazar's before shifting to Dane's. He made a non-committal grunt in the back of his throat and opened his mouth to speak. A commotion outside cut him off.

The external door opened and the Duke of Gladstow marched in, followed by the Duke of Buxton, Lady Deerhorn, Lord Xavier and finally Brant. Yen and Ray protested, but Brant shut the door in their faces and bolted it.

Dane stood in front of the king, his hand on his sword hilt. "No further," he warned.

"It has come to our attention that you may not be the rightful king," the Duke of Gladstow declared.

The king shot to his feet. "This is outrageous! You dare accuse me of being an imposter?"

Gladstow grunted. "I haven't accused you. I have merely stated a fact, that it has come to our attention that you may not be the rightful king."

"Hammer, arrest him for treason."

Dane didn't move. His gaze shifted to Brant, and Brant stared back, defiant.

"Stand back, Your Grace," Dane said. "Or I will be forced to follow my orders."

Gladstow looked uncertain. The Duke of Buxton and Lord Xavier both glanced at Brant, as if waiting for him to offer up the gem as proof. It seemed they were all still uncertain of Brant's claim, and not willing to accuse the king directly. In the presence of witnesses of their own station, it could be a fatal move. The claim had to be proved first, and they weren't sure how to do so.

Only Lady Deerhorn had an air of confidence about her. Her calculating gaze and small smile settled on me. I gripped Theodore's hand tighter.

"Some evidence has come to light," Gladstow declared. "It would suggest you obtained the throne through..." He licked his lips. "Through trickery."

The king spluttered but no words came out.

"What evidence?" Dane asked levelly.

"I don't answer to you," Gladstow sneered.

Balthazar tapped his walking stick on the floor for attention. "If real evidence had been presented, you wouldn't be here, Your Grace. You would be presenting that evidence to the ministers and other noblemen. Sergeant Brant, is this your doing? What tales have you been telling these gentlemen?"

"It ain't a tale, Bal, and you know it." Brant dug his hand into his doublet pocket and pulled out the gem. It nestled on his palm, the deep red facets drawing in the light. It didn't pulse.

If Brant realized the gem in his hand wasn't real, because it didn't respond to him, he didn't show it. Nor did the king.

The king's eyes lit up. "*You* have it." He wiped the sweat from his top lip with his sleeve. "Someone I least expect, eh? Clever, Hammer."

Had Balthazar said that deliberately, knowing Brant would come, and he wanted the king to believe Brant held the real gem? What else had Balthazar anticipated? The deep wrinkles and watchful eyes gave nothing away.

The king stepped around Dane and reached for the gem.

Brant snatched his hand back. "Not until you answer my questions."

The king stiffened. "Get it, Hammer."

Dane didn't move. "Brant, leave this discussion for a later time."

"I ain't waiting no more," Brant snapped. To the king, he said, "What happened to our memories?"

The king's high laugh wasn't convincing. "I don't know what you're talking about."

"Who are we?" Brant growled. "What happened to us? Why are we here?"

The king glanced at each of the dukes. "He's mad. Hammer, arrest him for insolence. I won't stand for this kind of behavior."

The dukes frowned at one another. Lord Xavier looked as if he wanted to burst out laughing but wasn't quite sure if he dared. Lady Deerhorn had gone very still, only her eyes moving as her gaze shifted between the king and Brant.

Brant bared his teeth. "Answer me!"

The king put out his hand. "Give me the gem, and I'll spare your life."

Brant's lips stretched into either a grimace or a grin, I couldn't tell. "You want it, don't you? You want it desperately."

The king stiffened.

The sergeant held up the gem between his thumb and forefinger. "Come and get it."

"Brant!" Dane barked. "Trust us. Don't do this here."

Brant held the gem within the king's reach. The king only had to be faster than Brant and he'd have it in his possession. But not a single person in that room would expect him to be faster than Brant, including the king himself.

"Give it to me," the king growled.

Brant sneered. "You need this to keep your throne, to wish all your problems away." He indicated the dukes with a jerk of his head.

Gladstow and Buxton looked nervous, a look that didn't sit well on either man.

"Abdicate then disappear," Gladstow said quickly, as if he wanted to say his piece before he changed his mind. I wasn't sure if he was brave or foolish. Perhaps his greed for power drove him to speak such a rash statement. "Or we will be forced to tell the world that you used magic to gain the throne. Do I need to tell you what the consequences will be?"

The king blinked rapidly, although he didn't take his focus off Brant.

"The sentence for the crime of impersonating a monarch is death," Buxton told him. "Come now...Leon. Do as Gladstow says and abdicate. Your life will be spared."

The king swallowed heavily. "The gem, Sergeant."

Brant's smile thinned. "Answers first."

A drop of sweat dripped down the side of the king's face. "Hammer!" he screeched. "Arrest this man for theft!"

Dane's hands curled into fists at his sides. "This can be resolved if we talk privately. Sergeant, come to Balthazar's office."

The king moved forward until he was within reach of Brant's palm and the gem. Brant remained still, his hand outstretched, the gem like a beacon, beckoning the king, or taunting him.

"Answer me!" Brant shouted.

"Hammer!" the king shouted back. "Get me the gem!"

"Answer the fucking questions!"

The king's chest rose and fell with his deep, ragged breaths. "You always were the rebel. I should have known you'd be the one to cause problems."

Brant's breath hitched. A ripple of shock washed over his face before it settled into the hard, unforgiving planes again. "Who am I? Where am I from?"

The king snatched at the gem.

Brant simultaneously pulled back the gem, drew the knife from the belt at his hip with his other hand, and stabbed the king in the stomach.

CHAPTER 16

$\mathcal{T}$he king fell to his knees, clutching his stomach. His eyes bulged, full of tears of fear and pain as he silently appealed to Brant. A hush fell over the small party in the garrison, as if no one could quite believe what had happened. We all froze, unable to move, to speak, to breathe.

All except Dane. He caught the king and lowered him to the floor. Stirring into action, I crouched beside him and applied pressure to the wound.

Dane pulled my hands away and shook his head. A flick of his gaze toward Lady Deerhorn was all I needed to know why.

"Fetch Doctor Clegg," Balthazar ordered.

Theodore ran from the garrison and Dane took over from me, pressing against the wound. I cradled the king's head in my lap. There was little else I could do anyway, even if I'd been allowed to use my medical knowledge. The bleeding had to be stopped before a doctor could inspect the injury. Dane seemed to understand and didn't ease back, despite the king's cries.

"Merdu," one of the dukes muttered. None of the nobles came closer, but nor did they leave.

Brant stood over the king. "This is the only way I can insure you will answer my questions. I know about the wishes. Barborough told me." He held the gem in front of the king's face. "If you want to live, you need to use a wish while holding this, and I won't give it to you until you give me answers. Understand?"

The king nodded quickly.

Brant placed the gem in the king's hand but didn't let it go entirely. "Wish for our memories to be returned first or I take it back."

"The gem is fake!" Dane snapped. "It won't work."

Brant's face went as pale as the king's. "Wh—what do you mean?"

"Didn't you notice it doesn't pulse?"

"Pulse?" the king muttered.

Brant stared at the gem, all the fire gone out of him. He looked like a man who'd just lost everything. "The pulse," he muttered. "I forgot…"

The king pressed the gem to his lips. "Sorcerer, grant me my wish. I wish to be made healthy again."

Nothing happened.

"I wish to be made healthy again!" he cried, only to wince in pain.

"I hid the gem," Dane told him gently. "And had this one made in its likeness."

The king clutched Dane's arm. "The real one…get it, Hammer. Please, hurry."

Dane looked to me. "How long?"

Blood saturated the king's clothes, Dane's hands, and pooled on the floor. Too much blood, and it hadn't stopped. Even if Doctor Clegg arrived before the king passed, there was nothing he could do after this amount of blood loss.

"Long enough if you need to go somewhere within the palace," I said, wanting to give him some hope.

But I knew from Dane's face that the gem wasn't in the palace. It mustn't even be within the estate, because I had no doubt he would have tried to get it.

Tears slipped down the king's cheeks. He knew it too.

Brant collapsed onto a chair and rubbed his jaw with a shaking hand.

Dane eased back and gently brushed the king's hair from his forehead. "Tell us, sire. Do the right thing now."

Balthazar joined Dane and Dane helped him to settle on the floor beside the king.

The king started to cry. "Forgive me."

Balthazar took the king's hand and smiled softly. "We forgive you. Now tell us."

"My first wish was to be a rich king." The king laughed but it made an ominous bubbling sound in his chest. "See what I did? I combined rich and king into one wish instead of two."

Brant joined us on the floor. "Who are we?"

"I am an actor, and this was my grandest performance. My stage was the most spectacular ever seen. And you, Hammer, Bal...you were my friends for a short time. Theo too." He tried to lift his head. "Where's Theo?"

"He'll be here soon," Dane said.

"Go on," Brant urged. "We were your friends..."

"Not you," the king said, his voice so weak we had to lean in to hear him better. "But I saved you, too. I saved you all. The magic... it was the only way to save your lives."

"Saved us from what?"

"A slow and painful death." The king's eyes turned glassy. He didn't have much time.

"Keep talking," Brant prompted.

The door opened and footsteps approached. Doctor Clegg knelt by the king and inspected the wound. It took him a mere moment to come to the same conclusion as me. He shook his head at the two dukes then stepped away.

Theodore took his place and clasped the king's hand. The gemstone lay on the floor now, forgotten.

"Sire," Theodore said, tears slipping down his face. "Sire, can you hear me?"

But the king didn't respond. I felt the last flutter of life leave his body. His chest sank and didn't rise again.

"He's gone," Doctor Clegg announced.

Brant sat back on his haunches, as if he hadn't quite believed that death would come. He didn't take his wide gaze off the king.

Theodore closed the king's eyes and kissed his forehead. When he drew away, the king's face was wet from his valet's tears. I took Theo's hand and we assisted one another to stand.

Dane helped Balthazar, leaving only Brant kneeling beside the body.

He shook his head over and over and pushed to his feet too. With a roar of frustration, he kicked over a chair, but that wasn't enough for him. He picked it up and threw it against the wall, shattering it into pieces.

"Sergeant!" Dane gripped his shoulder and whispered something in his ear.

Brant's gaze slid to the dukes. Then he ran off, out of the garrison, passing Lord Barborough and the king's advisors as they entered. No one stopped him, not even the witnesses to the murder. The sergeant had done the dukes a favor by killing the king. Their reward was to let him go free. He was no threat to them.

The advisors gasped upon seeing the king's body and started talking all at once. Barborough stood very still, his face ashen, his throat moving with his swallows.

"What happened?" one of the ministers asked.

"A guard went mad," the Duke of Gladstow said. "He killed the king and escaped. Everyone here witnessed it."

Buxton and Lord Xavier confirmed the claim, and the advisors seemed satisfied with the explanation.

"You will find him and arrest him, Captain," said one.

"Of course," Dane said but didn't leave.

The advisors murmured among themselves again.

"There is no magical gem, is there?" the Duke of Buxton asked Balthazar. "I have no doubt that sergeant and the king both believed in its existence though."

Balthazar sat on a chair and passed a hand down his face. He didn't answer, and I doubted the duke expected one.

"The king is dead because he believed old Zemayan stories of magic," Gladstow announced to the room. "His foolishness cost him his life."

Both dukes departed, but Lady Deerhorn and her son remained. They had moved away from the others, out of earshot. Lord Xavier whispered in his mother's ear. She listened and watched, her shrewd gaze taking in the reactions of not only the advisors, dukes and Barborough, but of us as well. If she believed as the dukes did, that magic didn't exist and played no part in the king's rise and fall, she gave no indication.

Lord Barborough picked up the gem beside the king's body and glanced toward the door again. His frown deepened.

Dane put out his hand. "I'll take that."

"No," Barborough said.

Dane clasped Barborough's wrist. "Give it to me."

"Unhand me!"

No one came to his aid. Some of the advisors even left. Barborough winced as Dane's grip tightened, and he opened his fingers. The stone dropped onto Dane's palm.

Dane let him go, and Barborough rubbed his wrist down the sleeve of his limp arm. "It's not real, is it?" he asked with a smirk. "*You* kept the real gem from him, didn't you? You killed him."

Dane pocketed the gem. "Will you be staying much longer in Glancia, my lord? I suspect you will want to return home now there's nothing for you here."

"I may stay a while, to get the lay of the land. I'm sure the three of you will keep the palace running smoothly until a new king is appointed, and that foreign dignitaries will continue to enjoy Glancian hospitality."

"Of course," Dane said. "We servants will continue to perform our duties. It's the noblemen who might not like having a Vytill spy in their midst."

Barborough's jaw hardened. He must realize the peril of his situation now, but his desire to learn more about magic, and perhaps even the whereabouts of the real gem, might be worth the risk to stay longer. Any news of a pending battle between the two dukes would also greatly help King Phillip. As a distant cousin to King Alain, the Vytill king was in a strong position to take the Glancian throne for himself. He would want as much information about his rivals as possible.

"We'll prepare the body for a suitable burial," Balthazar said to the remaining advisors and the Deerhorns. "If you don't mind, the king should rest in peace now." It was purposely said to dismiss Lady Deerhorn, I was sure of it.

She hesitated but left with her son. Only Lord Barborough remained, and it wasn't until the door had closed that I realized it was because Dane held him by the elbow.

Dane forced Barborough to face him. "We want answers."

"I don't have answers," Barborough said.

"You know more than we do—more than you've let on so far."

Barborough's gaze settled on me. "Is that Mistress Cully's opinion?"

Dane forced him to sit on a chair. "Tell us everything you know about magic. Everything you haven't told Mistress Cully."

"Or?"

"Or I'll tell the lords and ministers that Brant admitted you paid him to assassinate the king."

Barborough sucked air between his teeth then released it with a hiss. "You are ruthless, aren't you? You give me no choice, but first, tell me how you are involved in the magic and why it interests you so much."

Dane's hand curled into a fist and the muscles in his jaw bunched.

"No, Hammer," Theodore said quickly. "Enough violence. The king is gone, and it's time for some truths to be spoken." To Barborough, he said, "We have no memories of our pasts. The magic erased it somehow."

Barborough slumped back in the chair, his lips parted in a silent gasp. "No memory? None of you?"

"None of the servants can remember their pasts. The king told us he didn't either, but we came to realize that wasn't true."

"The king admitted making a wish on the gem," Balthazar said. "That's all we know. So now you tell us what you know."

Barborough picked up his limp arm and settled it across his lap. "I don't know anything for certain. Everything I know I learned in Zemaya, but there is nothing to say that their beliefs have more truth to them than any other story." He glanced at me. "I didn't lie to you about that, Mistress Cully."

"Tell us the stories," Dane said.

"The sorcerer's powers are limited to three wishes. Those wishes are bestowed upon the person who finds the device, no one else. The wishes cannot be used to grant more wishes, nor can they be used to destroy the sorcerer. Once freed, the sorcerer is beholden to the one who found the device. It seems the gem is the device."

"It would seem so," Balthazar said.

"The sorcerer cannot perform magic of its own free will, only what is asked of it through one of the wishes. So it cannot perform magic to benefit itself unless that magic fulfills a wish."

"What do you mean?" I asked.

"For example, if the gem's finder asks for his enemy to fall in love then be jilted, the sorcerer can turn itself into a rich, beautiful woman and beguile the enemy, but it can't take that form simply because it wants to."

"So it cannot use the magic to destroy its own enemies," Dane said.

"Precisely."

"What happens to the unused wishes now that the king—now that Leon—is dead?" Balthazar asked.

"I don't know."

Dane removed his sword and touched the tip to Barborough's throat. "You lie."

Barborough leaned back, raising his good hand in surrender. "No! I swear to you, I don't know. It's possible no one does. This situation may never have arisen before."

Dane hesitated then sheathed his sword.

Barborough swallowed heavily. "May I ask a question?"

"Go ahead," Dane said.

"Did anything happen to you when the king died?"

Dane shook his head and looked to Theodore and Balthazar. They both shook their heads.

"I thought perhaps you might have felt something," Barborough said. "Or remembered something."

"Nothing," Dane said.

Balthazar stood over the body and stared down at the lifeless face of the king. "We're still here," he murmured. "That's something, at least."

Dane's gaze connected with mine. "It means we're real," he said. "We have real lives."

"I never doubted it." I offered a faint smile. It was all I could muster.

"Do you know where the real gem is?" Barborough asked.

"I do," Dane said.

I tried to glare at him, to tell him not to give too much away to this man, but he wasn't looking at me. He held Barborough's gaze.

"I am the only one who knows," he went on. "Understand?"

Barborough nodded. "Thank you for your honesty." He stood slowly and, when Dane didn't stop him, left.

Theodore released a heavy sigh and slumped into a chair. He bent over the table, head in his hands. Dane grasped his friend's shoulder, and I suspected Theodore wept silently.

I joined Balthazar and stared down at the face of the man I'd known as the king. He looked so young in death; so innocent and not at all like a monarch. Yet if it hadn't been for Dane and the others, throwing suspicion over him, I would never have thought of him as anything other than the king of Glancia. Had that been because his performance had been so good or because I had merely believed what I'd been told?

"He was so proud of his...performance," Balthazar said, a measure of strain in his voice. "It was just a game to him, a piece of theater." He nudged the body with his walking stick. "I feel no sympathy for him. What he did is unforgiveable. I won't mourn him."

Dane and Theodore joined us. Theodore sniffed, and his eyes were red but he no longer cried.

"He was as naive as a child," he said. "He trusted us, in the beginning. He *needed* us."

"But he changed." Balthazar leaned heavily on his stick. "He grew fat on the power and wealth and all the benefits both provide. He forgot about us, about where he came from."

"Wherever that is," Dane muttered.

"What do you think he meant by saving you?" I asked. "Saving you from a terrible death, he said."

"Perhaps we all had a disease," Theodore suggested. "Many of us were very thin when we first came here, and some were terribly pale."

Balthazar shrugged. "We'll never know now."

"We will," Dane said. "This isn't over. Someone, somewhere, is missing us."

"Or they already think we're dead so aren't even looking."

It seemed like the most logical explanation, but even that gave hope. We had to find places where plague ravaged the population.

"I'm not giving up," Dane said as he strode toward the door. "Not yet."

He invited the guards in. There were twenty, at least. He gave orders for the head gardener, grand equerry, grand huntsman, grand forester, menagerie keeper, and head cook to be fetched. "Inform any servants you meet on the way that the king is dead, and there will be a staff meeting in the commons tonight. All will be given an opportunity to voice their questions and concerns."

Several guards peeled away while the others filed inside. Dane asked Zeke to fetch sheets to cover the king's body.

Quentin crouched beside it and parted the fabric of the king's clothing over the wound to inspect it.

"Quentin," Theodore snapped.

Quentin stepped back to stand with me. "It looked deep."

"We can discuss the medical aspects later," I told him. "Now is not the appropriate time."

I wasn't needed anymore, but I didn't leave. I wanted to remain, not for them but for me. While I hadn't been close to the king, nor had I particularly liked him, there was something missing now that he was gone. Perhaps I was merely a Glancian without a monarch, or perhaps the king had signified something else to me that I couldn't quite explain yet.

An eerie hush fell over the staff gathered in the garrison and continued until the heads of each department arrived. It was Dane who addressed them, not Balthazar. The master of the palace had more seniority, and perhaps more authority, but he probably knew that Dane held their respect. Dane also had a stronger voice, which carried. Balthazar seemed terribly frail as he sat, leaning heavily on his walking stick.

Dane told the staff everything that had transpired, including Brant's involvement, the fake gem, and the king's final words. He answered questions but had few answers. The only question he could answer with any certainty was that he knew where the real gem was hidden, and he did not plan on telling anyone.

"Powerful people will want to get their hands on it now," he said. "I won't risk anyone else's life."

Several of the men muttered but no one outright objected to him keeping the information from them.

Zeke returned with sheets, and the king's body was wrapped in them and taken away to be stored in the cellar until burial. The heads of all the departments left to speak with the staff under them, leaving only the guards, Balthazar and Theodore.

"Those of you on duty, continue to perform it," Dane told his men. "For now, nothing changes. I meant what I said. If we want to keep a roof over our heads, we must continue to work." Some of the men filed out, but he called Max back. "Not you. I need you to remain here while I escort Josie home."

"I don't need an escort," I said. "Besides, I don't think I'm ready to go home. I want to be here for a little longer."

"Then I have some questions to ask you."

"About the death?"

"No. On the likely reaction of the people. What can we expect from Glancians, as a whole, and the villagers in particular?"

I blinked. "Shouldn't you be worried about what the dukes will do next? Or what you ought to do to find out more about your pasts?"

"I will think about that too, but Mull has been restless lately, and I want to know if we should worry about further unrest in light of the king's death."

"Ordinary folk won't care too much," I said. "The comings and goings of kings doesn't alter their lives. Some of the troublemakers might think to take advantage of the confusion, but I don't see how they can. I don't think you'll need a stronger presence in the village because of this."

He looked relieved.

Max asked for a quiet word with Dane about sergeant duties now that Brant wasn't available, and the two of them sat in the corner to talk. Erik set down a cup in front of me.

"Thank you," I said. "I need an ale."

"It is not ale."

I sniffed the contents and sipped. It was something stronger than ale and I gratefully took another sip in the hope it would unwind my knotted nerves. The liquid burned as it went down and I pulled a face. He laughed softly.

"You're in a good mood considering the uncertainty that surrounds you now," I said.

"I am still Erik, you are still Josie. We have food, drink, shelter, friends. We will serve the next king here in the palace. It is a good life."

"I suppose."

He crossed his arms and rested them on the table. The twists of his hair fell forward, obscuring his face. "If the king says he saved us, then maybe this is better life than we had. Yes?"

"Perhaps," I said on a sigh. "But what of your past?"

"I do not like thinking of the past. Only future."

"What of your loved ones?"

He picked up his cup and flicked his hair back over his shoulder. "I do not wish to think of them if I can never know them."

"Don't give up, Erik."

"The king is gone. Nobody else knows where we came from."

There was no point to the discussion. He would continue to put on a brave face, yet I knew underneath he was as anxious as the rest of them. It was written in their somber faces, their sad eyes. They weren't sad for the loss of their king but for the opportunity he represented—the opportunity to find out about their pasts. He'd been their only connection to it.

Quentin joined me and asked quiet questions about the position of the stab wound, the damage it might have caused to internal organs, and subsequent blood loss. I answered him by rote, hardly thinking. My gaze wandered to Dane frequently. He spoke to Max for a time, then to each of his men, one by one, offering them reassuring words or gestures. Finally, he told Theodore to take Balthazar to his room. The master of the palace looked exhausted. The day had taken its toll on him.

"Do you want me to check on him?" I asked Dane when he rejoined me.

"He's fine. He's tired and blames himself for not confronting Leon earlier."

"Poor, Bal. Theo looks lost too."

He watched them leave and asked me if I was ready to return to the village.

We walked together to the stables. The forecourts were eerily quiet, with no nobles wandering about. They were probably all meeting in small groups, discussing the future of the kingdom and their role in shaping it. The dukes would be shoring up their supporters, now no longer allies but rivals for the vacant throne. The nobles would most likely leave the palace within days to go home and plot. I only hoped I would get to see Kitty and Miranda before they left.

"Do you want me to saddle Sky?" the stable boy asked.

Dane hesitated then said, "Let Sky rest. Josie can ride with me."

I settled on Lightning with Dane at my back. His solid, familiar presence was a reassurance, but it wasn't until I felt his body sigh when we left the estate behind that I realized he might need reassuring too.

"Are you all right?" I asked.

"I'm frustrated the one person who could give us answers is gone."

I turned in the saddle to see him better. "It's more than that, though. You lost someone today, Dane. The king may not have been your friend, but he was a constant in your life. He had a big impact on it. Indeed, your entire life revolved around him, from the moment you woke to the moment you went to bed."

His gaze lowered to mine, his eyes two oceans of the deepest blue. "Not my entire life. There are other influences too," he said, his voice smoky. "They might not take up as much time, but they were more important."

I reached up and stroked his cheek and jaw. He turned into my hand and kissed my wrist before focusing forward again. His arms tightened ever so slightly around me.

"Thank you," he said quietly. "I needed this."

We rode in silence until the village came into view. The sight of it offered me no comfort. I no longer had a home to go to in Mull, no sanctuary to call my own, where I could be myself. Losing a set of walls and some furniture shouldn't have mattered, but it did, and my heart weighed heavy in my chest.

As if he knew, Dane's arms tightened again. "I don't know what happens next," he said, a note of vulnerability threading his voice.

I leaned into him and folded my arm over his. "Nor do I, but we'll find out together."

CHAPTER 17

"*J*osie, wake up." Meg's voice hardly registered in my sleepy state, but her violent shake of my shoulder certainly did. "Wake up, Josie."

"I'm awake," I mumbled. "Is it one of my patients?"

"No. Something happened at your house, last night."

Weak dawn light filtered through the window, but Meg was fully dressed. She looked worried, and that made me sit up straight. "What's wrong?" I asked. "Is someone hurt?"

"The sheriff is here. He wants to speak to you about a commotion at your house."

"It's not my house anymore."

She helped me dress quickly, and we joined Sheriff Neerim in the kitchen, where he was eating oat cakes covered in honey. Mistress Diver poured tea into his cup and offered me one.

"I'm sorry to wake you, Josie," the sheriff said, indicating I should sit.

"Are the Ashmoles all right?" I asked, accepting the cup from Mistress Diver. "Meg said something happened to them."

"They're fine. They were tied up in their beds."

Mistress Diver and Meg gasped.

"Merdu, that's awful," I muttered. "Who would do such a thing?"

The sheriff concentrated on his oat cakes. "These are delicious.

Better than my wife makes, but don't tell her." He avoided looking at me—and answering.

"You think *I* did it?" I cried. "Sheriff, I had nothing to do with it."

"Josie never left the house," Meg said hotly. "Honestly, Sheriff, how could you think she would do something like that?"

The sheriff licked honey off his fingers. "I don't think Josie did it, but the Ashmoles wanted me to question her, so here I am."

Mistress Diver had been about to slide another oat cake onto the sheriff's plate, but she withdrew the pan. "The Ashmoles are new to the village, so I'll forgive them for jumping to conclusions about Josie, but you, Sheriff, you know her well. She wouldn't tie people up in their own beds during the night. That's utter madness."

"I know she wouldn't," he said again.

"Then why come here at all?"

"Because I need to be seen doing my duty." His gaze connected with mine. "Particularly now."

"You're right," I conceded. "You have a job to do."

"You're not strong enough to overpower both of them anyway. You're also not the type," he added when both Meg and Mistress Diver protested again. "I've told the Ashmoles as much, but they still insisted I question you. Meg, you sleep in the same room as Josie, don't you?"

"Yes," she said.

"The same bed too, and I'm sure you're a very light sleeper."

"Actually— Ow." Meg rubbed the back of her neck where her mother pinched her. "Yes, same bed, light sleeper. I would have noticed her get up."

"Thought as much." Sheriff Neerim offered Mistress Diver his plate, but she didn't take it. She slid the extra oat cake onto it and dribbled honey over the top.

"Don't go yet," she said. "You haven't finished. Tell us, why were the Ashmoles tied up in their beds?"

"Someone rifled through their things. Well, not so much through their things but through the house. They emptied drawers, moved furniture around, pulled up loose stones and boards, and generally left the place in a real mess."

"It seems like they were looking for something," Meg said. "I wonder what."

My stomach dropped. I felt sick. The Ashmoles were partly right; it was my fault their house was searched. It was searched because it used to belong to me, and someone suspected Dane hid the gem there on one of his visits.

"Did the Ashmoles notice anything in particular about the intruder?" I asked.

The sheriff shook his head. "It was one person, they said, but they didn't see his or her face."

"What did he say to them?" Meg asked.

"The intruder didn't speak. It seems he or she tied them up to keep them out of the way while he conducted his search. Whoever did it didn't seem to think they could assist him."

"How strange," Mistress Diver said.

Sheriff Neerim finished his oat cake and licked all of his fingers. "I'd best be off."

I followed him to the door, Meg at my heels. "What was the village like last night?" I asked. "Aside from the Ashmoles' situation, I mean. Was there more unrest?"

"It was quiet," he said. "Everyone was too busy gossiping about the king's death and speculating about what will happen next. The people are worried. No one knows what to expect. This has never happened before."

"It's sudden and shocking," Meg agreed. "I can't imagine how the servants must feel."

"Captain Hammer tells me you witnessed the assassination, Josie," the sheriff said.

I nodded. "It was awful."

"And you didn't see which way the assassin went?"

"No."

"Nor did the captain, so he tells me. He says the sergeant fled." He plucked his hat from the table by the door and settled it on his head. "I can't think why the captain didn't chase him."

I swallowed and nodded along.

"I never liked or trusted Sergeant Brant," the sheriff said. "He reminds me of too many thugs I've arrested. If you see him, Josie, stay out of his way. Stay out of the Ashmoles' way, too. They don't like you."

I watched him go, and then my gaze fell on the door of my old house opposite. Had Dane hidden the gem there on one of his visits? If so, where? And did he intend to retrieve it?

* * *

MEG and I decided to venture into the village later in the morning to hear the gossip for ourselves. It was just as the sheriff said, and everyone seemed anxious about the future of Glancia, and Mull in particular. The dukes' names were mentioned frequently.

"They haven't left the palace yet," one woman said.

"They'll probably stay for the king's burial," said another.

"My husband says they're staying to shore up support from the other lords. It's convenient, having most under the one roof."

"Except for the Deerhorns. They left last night."

The same sentiments were repeated over and over. Brant's name came up too, always with a shudder of fear and a heavy dose of loathing for throwing the kingdom into turmoil.

Magic was never mentioned, and nor was the gemstone.

"Why do you think Brant did it?" Meg asked as we returned to her house.

I merely shrugged, not willing to add to the lies I'd already told her.

"He must have been working for someone, but who? That Vytill lord? One of the dukes?"

I felt guilty for not offering answers, but she didn't seem to be asking for any, merely speculating.

We parted outside her house, and I went on to the graveyard. I laid wildflowers on the graves of my parents and watered the riverwart plant Dane had planted after my father's death. Its leaves wouldn't be ready for harvesting for another year but it looked healthy.

I sat under a tree and closed my eyes, grateful for the peace and quiet to think. I was so tired, after a poor night's sleep, however, that I nodded off.

The sound of my name startled me awake. "Josie."

"Dane," I said on a gasp.

He crouched beside me, his sword pushed back out of the way, his gloves clutched in his hand. "Sorry. I scared you."

"Not at all. What are you doing here?"

"Looking for you." He removed his sword belt and sat beside me, tossing the gloves on the ground. "Meg said you were here."

"Is everything all right?"

He heaved a sigh. "As much as it can be, considering yesterday's events. The servants are anxious. We've tried to allay their fears, but they know the king was the only one who could answer our questions. With him gone, some have lost all hope."

"And you?" I asked quietly.

"Not me." He stretched his fingers on the ground where his hand lay and touched the edge of my skirt. "I have more to be hopeful about than most."

I rested my hand over his, lightly trapping it.

We stayed like that for a long moment, each of us content with the silence, neither prepared to break it or end the contact. It did more to comfort me than any words could have.

Dane eventually withdrew his hand, however. "Brant is still at the palace."

"I thought he fled."

"He came back early this morning. We talked. He was contrite."

"That's something, I suppose. I thought he'd be angry you kept the location of the real gem from him."

"He asked about it, and I repeated what I said yesterday. No one else knows where it is, and no one will. He understood my reasoning." He stared into the distance. "He asked me if he could stay at the palace, in hiding. He wants to remain with us, near the other servants. He's not ready to face the world alone without his memories."

"And did you agree or did you throw him in prison?"

"I agreed." He smirked. "It's still a punishment, of sorts. The servants know it was he who killed the king and are angry with him. So far he has borne their anger, but his temper may get the better of him again. His real concern is the nobles. If any who witnessed him assassinating the king see Brant, they might demand I arrest him."

"So he's remaining well hidden?"

"He is."

"Do you think he will try to find the gem?"

He nodded. "I spoke with the sheriff this morning. He told me he spoke to you in relation to an incident at the Ashmoles'."

"Do you think it was Brant looking for the gem?"

"It's possible. I'll speak to him when I get back to the palace."

I wondered if he would merely speak to Brant or if he intended to use brute strength and violence—the language the sergeant understood, according to Dane. I didn't ask. I didn't want to know. It could ruin these moments of shared peace.

"How long are the dukes and other nobles expected to remain at the palace?" I asked.

"It's unclear. Certainly until after the burial, perhaps longer. Each duke is trying to convince the noblemen to follow him instead of the other." He huffed out a breath. "Once allies, now enemies."

"I heard the Deerhorns have returned home."

"They have. The Duke of Buxton left the palace to speak to them just before I came to the village."

"Has magic been mentioned by any nobles?"

He shook his head. "It seems the dukes don't believe anything Brant told them."

"I don't blame them. He sounded mad and his claims were fanciful. They were willing to believe when it suited them, however."

"It no longer matters how the king gained the throne. Not to them."

I sighed and rested my head back against the tree trunk. "I feel as though the world has moved back through time. This is how everyone felt when we heard King Alain was dying, before Leon came forward. There was so much uncertainty about the future, so much anxiety. It's happening all over again. I hate the dukes for putting us through this." I lifted my head again. "Don't tell Kitty I said that. If you see her and Miranda, can you pass on a message for me?"

"Of course."

"Tell them I'd like to see them before they return home if they're able to spare the time."

"I'm sure they will make the time for you, Josie, unless they have to leave in a hurry. Gladstow is unlikely to tell his wife anything until the last possible moment."

"He doesn't trust her?"

"Nothing like that. He simply doesn't like or respect her, so I'm told. My own observations support that theory."

"Poor Kitty," I said on a sigh. "I can't imagine being married to such a horrid man."

We fell into silence again, and my thoughts wandered back to magic and the two unused wishes. "I wonder what will happen to them."

"Perhaps nothing," he said. "Perhaps three full wishes have been restored for the gem's next finder to use."

"*You* know where it is. You could find it and claim the wishes."

"It might have moved. The sorcerer could have hidden it somewhere it won't be discovered for hundreds of years."

"So you haven't checked if it's still there?"

He gave me a sly smile. "Is this your way of attempting to find out where I hid it?"

"I know you well enough to know you won't tell me, and I can't trick you into telling me. You're stubborn and a man of your word."

"I'm going to take that as a compliment."

I laughed softly. "I can list a lot of good things about you, but being stubborn isn't one of them."

"I'm going to disagree about that. Stubbornly." He smiled and nudged me with his elbow.

I smiled and nudged him back, then I blushed. I looked away so he couldn't see and we fell into silence again, but this time it felt awkward, as if something hung between us, something I couldn't quite grasp.

"I should go," Dane said. He didn't get up, and I finally looked at him. "But I don't want to," he added. "I'm tired of trying to keep the peace at the palace and in Mull. The graveyard is the quietest place I know. I can think here, or not think at all."

"You should come every day to clear your head. I often do." Too late I realized he wouldn't want to risk running into me every day. My presence might not help clear his head.

He still made no attempt to get up. "I've been thinking about something."

"Yes?" I asked, breathily.

"It might be significant. Or it might not be." He shook his head. "That didn't make sense."

It didn't sound like a personal matter, nor did he seem troubled by it, but rather confused. "Out with it," I said.

He turned to me. "The Rift was a series of earthquakes, wasn't it?"

I nodded. "They happened close together, within a matter of weeks. They were so strong, they caused The Thumb to break away from the mainland peninsula."

"And shortly afterward, Leon was declared the heir to the Glancian throne by King Alain."

"You think the two things are linked? You think the sorcerer caused The Rift to fulfill the king's—Leon's—wish?"

"I don't know, but ever since the idea struck me, I haven't been able to shake it. I found some documents in the library about The Rift, but they said little more than you did, that it was a series of earthquakes. Do you remember what Leon said as he lay dying? That he combined two wishes into one?"

"To be a *rich* king." I was beginning to put the pieces together too. "The sorcerer chose Glancia because the succession was in doubt, and King Alain's son's visit to Freedland, years ago, provided the perfect means for a secret love child to exist."

"All the sorcerer needed to do was create a document declaring Leon the legitimate grandson of King Alain and hide the document somewhere no one would question its authority when found."

"The High Temple," I said, recalling the story of Leon's ascension to the throne. "But Glancia was poor, so to fulfill the *wealth* part of Leon's wish, the sorcerer had to turn the kingdom's fortunes around. With The Thumb removed, almost all trade to and from the Peninsula now goes through Mull. Merdu and Hailia," I said on a whisper. "You're right. I'm sure of it. Such a cataclysmic series of earthquakes was unheard of before." I met his gaze, and there was no surprise in it, only wonder. "The Rift was caused by the sorcerer."

"I think so too," he said.

"To change the landscape like that forever..." I murmured. "It is truly powerful."

I stared into the distance, barely seeing the gravestones any more. My thoughts tumbled together, and I tried to tease them apart to consider each separately.

"You're overwhelmed," Dane said gently. "I'm sorry. I shouldn't have mentioned it."

"I'm glad you did. I feel foolish for not realizing it before."

"As do I."

"Do you think Leon knew the extent the sorcerer went to, to fulfill his wish?" I asked.

"He must have. He was naive in many ways, and often foolish, but he was clever enough to keep up the ruse for as long as he did. Clever enough to know that a poor kingdom suddenly becoming strategically important due to a major earthquake event after he wished to be rich was too much of a coincidence. It might not have occurred to him that his wish would displace people from The Thumb."

"Or it might have," I said. "He was selfish and uncaring. Look what he did to all of you."

His eyes focused forward, staring into the distance as I had done. "I liked him in the beginning, before I suspected he was lying about his memory loss. He was how I suspect a younger brother to be, sometimes annoying and immature, but someone I needed to protect." He sighed. "How could I have been so wrong about him?"

I took his hand between both of mine, aware that it was more intimacy than he wanted but doing it anyway. He glanced down at our hands and then up at me. His eyes were full of emotions he couldn't express.

"He was an actor," I said. "He played the part of naive young king well. It was only later that his true character came out. Besides, you didn't have any knowledge of yourselves, but he did. He used that knowledge to manipulate you all into helping him."

He gave me a flat smile. "I knew you'd make me feel better about my foolishness."

"Not foolishness, Dane. You were trusting and caring, just like an older brother should be." I pressed his hand to my lips, not quite aware of what I was doing until it was too late.

I let him go, but his hand lingered. He flattened his palm to my cheek. His fingers reached into my hair, and his thumb stroked.

My heart thudded so loudly I felt sure he could hear it. I willed him to kiss me, to touch me, to tell me he wanted me. But he said nothing and did nothing, just continuing to lightly stroke my cheek and stare into my eyes with shattering intensity.

When he suddenly pulled away and stood, I felt disoriented, unbalanced, as if he'd been propping me up.

"I have to go," he said, retrieving his sword and gloves. "I enjoyed our conversation. Thank you."

He sounded so formal. I wanted to say something to strip it away and return to the friendliness, but my head felt woolly and I couldn't think of anything.

I watched him go, his broad shoulders squared and his head high. Even the slight limp, favoring his injured leg, added to his masculinity. There was so much physical perfection in him that sometimes I wondered if he were indeed real after all.

Then I shoved the thought to the back of my mind. The sorcerer might be powerful enough to cause earthquakes, but it couldn't possibly be powerful enough to create multi-faceted beings with the range of characteristics the servants exhibited, complete with emotions, strengths and weaknesses.

Dane was very real, and my response to his presence was very real. So real that my heart bruised watching him walk away.

AUTHOR'S NOTE:

By now you might have realized where the idea for the AFTER THE RIFT series came from. I was watching the stage production of Aladdin and being a logical person, I kept thinking how foolish the people around Prince Ali were for not realizing he was an imposter. How can a prince suddenly appear from nowhere and no one question his background? Didn't they want to know which kingdom he came from and who his family were? Why didn't Princess Jasmine's father make inquiries?

While I love a good fantasy story, I still want it to be grounded in reality, even if it's essentially a story for children.

I set my speculations aside, however, and thought no more about them. It wasn't until much later, when I decided to set a story in a fantasy world as opposed to my Victorian-era novels, that I remembered my musings about Aladdin. It coincided with seeing a documentary on the Palace of Versailles, the gloriously extravagant French palace near Paris. It seemed like the perfect setting for a story about a monarch gaining the throne through magic.

I hope you're enjoying my reimagining of the Aladdin tale, and will continue the journey with me as Dane, Theodore, Balthazar, and the other servants try to regain their lost memories with Josie's help.

Look out for:
THE TEMPLE OF FORGOTTEN SECRETS
The 4th After The Rift novel by C.J. Archer.

To be notified when THE TEMPLE OF FORGOTTEN SECRETS is available, subscribe to C.J's newsletter.

A MESSAGE FROM THE AUTHOR

I hope you enjoyed reading THE WHISPER OF SILENCED VOICES as much as I enjoyed writing it. As an independent author, getting the word out about my book is vital to its success, so if you liked this book please consider telling your friends and writing a review at the store where you purchased it. If you would like to be contacted when I release a new book, subscribe to my newsletter at http://cjarcher.com/contact-cj/newsletter/.

ALSO BY C.J. ARCHER

SERIES WITH 2 OR MORE BOOKS

After The Rift

Glass and Steele

The Ministry of Curiosities Series

The Emily Chambers Spirit Medium Trilogy

The 1st Freak House Trilogy

The 2nd Freak House Trilogy

The 3rd Freak House Trilogy

The Assassins Guild Series

Lord Hawkesbury's Players Series

The Witchblade Chronicles

SINGLE TITLES NOT IN A SERIES

Courting His Countess

Surrender

Redemption

The Mercenary's Price

ABOUT THE AUTHOR

C.J. Archer has loved history and books for as long as she can remember and feels fortunate that she found a way to combine the two. She spent her early childhood in the dramatic beauty of outback Queensland, Australia, but now lives in suburban Melbourne with her husband, two children and a mischievous black & white cat named Coco.

Subscribe to C.J.'s newsletter through her website to be notified when she releases a new book, as well as get access to exclusive content and subscriber-only giveaways. Her website also contains up to date details on all her books: http://cjarcher.com She loves to hear from readers. You can contact her through email cj@cjarcher.com or follow her on social media to get the latest updates on her books:

51279275R00163

Made in the USA
Lexington, KY
01 September 2019